T0279743

BEYOND

THE GATES

BEYOND
THE GATES

A Novel

Cynthia Bardes

Octobre Press

Editor / Editorial Development Devon O'Brien
Book Design Virginia Best

ISBN 979-8-218-36437-3

Published by Octobre Press
Vero Beach, Florida

PRINTED IN CANADA

This book is dedicaated to Aubrey, Avery, and Cindy

CHAPTER 1

GINGER STEPPED OUT of the town car and walked up the steps of the red brick Georgian mansion. Berdetta, in her gray uniform with its crisp white collar and turned up cuffs, was at the door ready to meet her. Only this was no surprise. Berdetta always anticipated Ginger's movements and needs.

"I can't believe he's really gone," Ginger said.

"He's finally at peace, Mrs. Johnson."

"It's been so difficult for him for so many years. That awful disease."

"And for you, too. You've been awfully stressed. Now Mr. Johnson has gone home to the Lord. You go home now, too, back to Florida. No use staying here in Atlanta with just his kids here. Now, take off the funeral clothes, have a soothing bath and ring when you're finished. I'll make you a tray and bring it upstairs."

Berdetta's warm, brown eyes conveyed kindness, something Ginger needed, especially now.

"Thank you, Berdetta. You always know what's best. Mr. Johnson depended on you, just like he depended on your mother. First it was Hattie, and then you grew up and started helping. Now, here you are, running the house all on your own and Mr. Johnson's gone. We've both been part of this house for so many years. Why, my first day here seems like yesterday."

"I remember when you came. There had been so much sadness here. Then

Mr. Johnson brought you home, a young bride."

"I guess there's no use keeping it now that he's gone. You're probably ready to retire, relax and spend all your time with your family."

"Don't you start making plans now, Mrs. J. Go and rest, I got lots to do," Berdetta said and bustled off in the direction of the kitchen.

In the foyer, Ginger paused before the floor-length gilt mirror. She removed the black straw hat and veil that covered her eyes to the tip of her nose and studied herself. Her red hair was pulled back into a bun and pinned at the nape of her neck with a modest clasp. Her black suit was Chloé, and her low pumps were Chanel. The clothing looked like a costume designed for her new role as widow. She sighed. Virginia Bennet Johnson was now alone. She knew the very feeling when she was in her early 20s. Alone in the world with no one to take care of her — until, that is, she met her husband. Now, everything was terribly different. Ted had been "gone" for the past three years; that dreaded disease had been true to its reputation. First, you lose your mind — then slowly but inevitably, your life. Ted wasn't here anymore to take care of her, although she knew he had left her well set up. He and Jim Donnelly, their lawyer, had seen to everything.

His children had planned most of the funeral, save for a couple of hymns she had suggested. They'd only used one, but that was fine. She was grateful how they'd taken control of their father's funeral. They hadn't been around all that much in the last three years though, had they? Then the club had handled the reception perfectly. They'd had lots of practice, of course. Of Ted's peers, almost all were gone now, only a few were left lingering in nursing homes.

Ginger ascended the stairs and walked the long hall to their bedroom. Recently, they had spent very little time in Atlanta, but for their first 15 years together, they had lived here. Ted had kept the house with Hattie, then Berdetta, running it. His children would feel he had abandoned them if he sold the house they'd grown up in. It was hard on them when he'd married her. Not only had they lost their mother to cancer, but they had to accept a stepmother who was closer to their age than their dad's. For years, Ted travelled back and forth. He kept an office in Atlanta, too. But Ginger preferred Florida. Atlanta weather was not Florida weather. Ginger walked into their master bedroom, and the phone rang.

"Hello?"

"Ginger! The service!"

"Oh, Dottie! Do you think everything went alright?"

"It was wonderful. Too bad Ted couldn't hear it."

Dottie Morris knew just how to make Ginger smile. Like Dottie, Ted's first wife, Catherine, was from an old Atlanta family. When she died, she'd left Ted with the three children. Dottie had been Catherine's friend and then she became Ginger's. Dottie had helped her navigate Atlanta society.

"That hymn! *Old Rugged Cross.*"

"I picked *Old Rugged Cross.*"

"Well, of course you did. The Johnson children didn't pick a hymn of that vintage. Or grandeur! I got goosebumps!" Dottie never missed a thing.

"Ted loved it, that's why I suggested it. But the children handled most everything else."

"Were they in charge of the luncheon?"

"Yes. Not that I ate. But the whole menu, the sirloin, the salmon, the asparagus — "

"The banana cream pie?"

"Yes, well. I guess Emily forgot."

"How could she?"

"That was a long time ago, Dottie."

"We had to rush you to the hospital!"

"Her one misstep."

"Well, everything was exquisite, I have to give them that. The white cap peonies!"

"I told her the red and white peonies were Ted's favorite."

"I've never seen such lovely peonies."

This was a real compliment. Dottie had been president of the Atlanta Garden Club. Flowers were her life.

"I should have had a vase delivered to you! I sent half to the hospital and half to the club. What was I thinking?"

"Goodness, Ginger. You know my house. There's not an empty vase or tabletop. I practically live at my own funeral. But my peonies never look like that. Such lovely blooms! They reminded me of the first day I met you. You and Ted had just married, and he brought you to the club. All heads turned and I said to Bert, 'That delicate flower needs someone to fend-off the vultures.'"

"You got me through everything."

"And now, well Bert is probably up there talking to Ted right now. And we're just two widows."

"Oh, Dottie! I'm glad you phoned. The house is so empty."

"I walked in, removed my hat and called."

"I was remembering my first day at International Lumber. Ted walked by my desk and introduced himself. I had no idea that he was CEO. I was a lowly girl at reception; his name didn't even register. He always walked each floor just to let people know he cared. No matter how low or high level you were. Two weeks later, I heard that my father died just as he walked by, and I was hanging up the phone. Tears were rolling down my cheeks. He said, 'Anything I can do, Red?' And I started to cry and told him my father died."

"I remember how he called you 'Red.'"

"'Take as much time as you need, Red,' he said. 'You'll always have a place here if you want it.' I was gone ten days. The day I returned, he asked me if I needed anything and would I like to talk over a drink. That's how we started."

"He was always there for others, even though he'd lost Catherine. She'd been dead for two years and he had those children. The boys were already at college. Emily was just a teen. Of course, Hattie and Berdetta were taking care of things, and he had friends. But he wasn't the sort to go out during the week. You were the best thing that happened to him!"

"Thanks, Dottie. The house never felt so empty. Even though Berdetta's here. Thank God for Berdetta."

"She's a jewel. How long will you be in town?"

"Not sure. Jim Donnelly wants to meet tomorrow morning to go over some things."

"Probably just papers to sign. How're the children doing?"

"I don't know, they were quite distant at the reception. Probably just sad. They'll have to handle their own affairs now. All three have always asked for Ted's help. Money-wise, I mean. I'm so glad we've got Peter Palmer at International Lumber."

"Ted always took such good care of everything."

"Peter shared the helm with Ted, and then he was right there, already in place, when it was too much for him. Peter flew over to visit Ted more than the children did, actually."

"You were a wonderful wife. He adored the ground you walked on. And despite your age difference, he always considered you an equal. He knew how hard it was to have someone else's kids, particularly when they were practically your age! That young Emily, she was always a pistol. The boys were sweet, but not exactly ambitious. Ted spoiled them, I guess. And it's true, they didn't give their father enough attention. Oh, I'm rambling. You must be exhausted, dear."

"I'm going to take a bath. Berdetta is bringing me a tray and then I'm into the arms of Morpheus."

"Dinner tomorrow?"

"Dinner tomorrow. Thank you, Dottie. For everything."

Ginger hung up the phone, walked into the bathroom and drew her bath. In the dressing room, she opened the closet. Ted's tweeds, his golf shirts and hunting clothes. She had hesitated before, getting rid of his things. But now, she'd have to. Ted was truly gone.

She switched off the water and slipped down in the tub. She had loved Ted. They had a good marriage, a good life. She had been attracted to him but never head-over-heels in love with Ted . . . No butterflies, no desperate passion, and no pain. It wasn't that sort of love, and that was a relief. She had respected, admired, and loved her husband. She had visited him every day for the last three years at The Palms. She was lucky that Treasure Beach, where she and Ted lived in Florida, had such an excellent elder facility which included a state-of-the-art Memory Care Unit.

CHAPTER 2

T HE NEXT MORNING, after a good sleep, Ginger dressed and left for Jim Donnelly's office. When she arrived, she noticed that the children's cars were already there. Doris Barrett was standing when Ginger walked into the reception.

"Good morning, Mrs. Johnson."

"Good morning, Doris. I see the Johnson clan is already here."

"Yes, they've been here since nine," Miss Barrett said as she opened the door to Jim Donnelly's office.

Jim crossed the carpeted office to greet her. He had the clean, energetic, and virtuous aura of a man who'd already been to the gym. He was tall, formidable, and almost always pleasant.

"Hello, Ginger. How are you feeling today?" He asked, kissing her on the cheek.

"I thought you said 10 — "

"I did, I did. Emily, Jack, and David just got here a little early."

Ginger turned, and there was Jack and his brother David. When she entered, they had stood up from their chairs at the conference table. Emily was there too, but she had stayed seated. Ginger moved towards them.

"I don't think yesterday could have gone any better. You all did such a wonderful job. Your father would have been very proud."

"Em did most of it," Jack said. He had his father's commanding height but was more laid back. His hair was blonde and, in a cowlick, giving him a boyish charm.

"The peonies were perfection," Ginger said.

"Thank you," Emily said. Emily was petite and impeccably dressed. Her features were an interesting combination of delicate and determined. She did not smile easily.

"The hymns sounded mighty fine," David said.

"But *The Old Rugged Cross?*" Jack said. Smart and assertive, Jack was the most like his father.

"Yeah," David chimed in. "What were you thinking, Em?"

"Actually, Ginger chose that one," she said. The kids eyed one another.

Jim changed the subject.

"Well, let's get started, shall we?" He pulled out a chair across from the three Johnson children and Ginger sat down.

"I was just telling the kids that their father was very generous, no surprise there. He left them well-fixed. He did the same for you, Ginger. There is a glitch, however, and it has to do with Ted's new trust, the marital trust."

"Yes? What about it?"

"Ted made a new marital trust. It grants you all the income during your lifetime then redirects the principal and income to the children and grandchildren upon your death."

"That's right."

"The thing is . . ."

Ginger's eyes went from Jim to Jack, David, and Emily questioningly. Was it her imagination, or did each one avoid her glance?

"The problem is . . . Ted's signature is not on it."

"What do mean?"

"He never signed the new trust."

"He created that years ago."

"That's right. Years ago. Only he never signed it."

"He created that with you, didn't you have him sign it?"

"I reminded him a few times and he finally said, 'Jim my affairs are my affairs. I have always handled my affairs, haven't I? I'm not going to die tomorrow. Don't hurry me, Old Man.'"

The kids did not protest. The more impassive they seemed the more alarmed Ginger became.

"Ted made that second trust years ago. More than four years."

"That's right."

"*Before* he went to The Palms. To the Memory Unit."

"Yes."

"So, how could he have forgotten?"

"I've explained this to Emily, Jack, and David, and they understand that the income is the same income that you and Ted had from the trust. However, the principal is much, much larger now than when Ted set up the original trust. Ted put a lot of money and stock from International Lumber into it — "

"Yes he did. That was his strategy."

"He wanted to increase the value of the trust to provide more income for the two of you while he was alive. Ted left you 25% of his International Lumber stock, and a hefty life insurance policy."

"That sounds right. Is there an issue with that, too?"

"No, not at all. But the major income was from the second marital trust."

"Jim, you worked with him on the second trust, and he discussed it with me. We know his intentions."

"It's unsigned."

Ginger glanced again at the Johnson kids, seeking an understanding look or a reassuring word. But Jack looked down at the conference table, David stared blankly ahead, Emily looked away.

She was stunned. Ted had gone over everything: the income she could expect from the trust was two million a year. *And that was a decade ago!* It had to be worth more now. How could they question their father's intentions?

"Emily, Jack, and David want to think things over. Everyone needs to take a breath and recover from yesterday. I've scheduled a meeting for the day after tomorrow."

"Wednesday?" said Ginger.

"I'll meet first with the kids. Just the kids."

"What a good idea," Ginger said, hoping she was masking her surprise.

"Let's the five of us meet on Friday and see if we can get all this resolved."

"Are you anxious to go back home? To Florida?" This was the first thing Emily had said to her.

"Friday's fine," Ginger said. There was another awkward silence.

"Well then, how about lunch? Jack? David? Em . . . ? The club? It's cheeseburger day."

"Sure," said Jack.

"I love cheeseburger day at the club," David said.

Emily glanced at Ginger. "Thank you, but we can't," she said. "Goodbye, Jim. We'll see you Wednesday." She stood, and Jack and David followed suit.

"See you Friday, Ginger."

"See you soon."

"Thanks for making it in, Ginger."

One by one Emily, Jack and David kissed Ginger. Each kiss felt like a blow. The three Johnson children moved to the door and filed out silently. Ginger started to say something to Jim. She wanted time alone with him, to talk things through. They both knew what Ted had intended, and Jim would let her know that this mattered, meant more than a signature.

"Friday, Ginger? 9:00 o'clock?"

Taking her cue from him, Ginger reached for her pocketbook.

"Perfect. Thank you for everything Jim. I'm glad you're in charge. Ted always liked you. That's why he had you as trustee and executor — "

"Doris?"

Doris appeared at once.

"Walk Mrs. Johnson out, please."

"Yes, Mr. Donnelly."

Doris offered to walk Ginger to her car, but she declined. Shaken, she walked alone to her car, and drove away. She was so confused. Why had Ted not signed the new trust? Jim would work it out with the children. He understood Ted's intention. *He had written the new trust!* Everyone needed to take a breath. Still, she wished Jim had had a minute to talk with her. Did I misread something, she wondered. Was I blind to how Ted really thought? Did he actually put them first? Did he just forget? Why did he put off signing it? Yes, he was always busy. He was very private about some things. Ginger knew not to ask about money and investments. It was 20 years before he told Ginger anything. Did he have a secret that he kept from her?

Thank goodness she was having dinner with Dottie.

Chapter 3

DOTTIE PICKED GINGER up and they went to The Grill at the club. It was a Monday night.

"It's only half full," Ginger said. "Good. I just can't talk to a lot of people."

"Oh Ginger. Maybe we should have gone somewhere else — "

"No, no. This is fine. We'll just hide in the corner."

Ginger and Dottie claimed a corner table. Immediately, Sam appeared.

"Mrs. Johnson, Mrs. Morris. May I get you cocktails?"

"Yes, please, Sam!" Ginger and Dottie said in perfect unison, and they all laughed. Sam had been at the club for as long as Ginger could remember. Tall and thin, his jacket was always immaculate, and now his hair was as white as his jacket.

"A vodka gimlet, please, three onions. And Ginger, wine, or bourbon?"

"Oh, I think bourbon. On the rocks. With a twist, Sam."

Sam gave a slight bow and left.

"Dottie, I'm glad you suggested this. The last ten days have been a blur."

"Let's hope now you can start to recover."

It was clear to Dottie that Ginger was stressed. Her hair was severe, pulled back away from her face. Her face was drawn, and she hadn't bothered with make-up.

"Ever since Ted went into The Palms, I knew the day would come. The dreaded day. Sometimes I was afraid it would come too soon. Then, sometimes

— well, you know, he was there for three long years."

"You never missed a day."

"It felt like the end would never come. Then, suddenly, I was in a black dress at the church. Like, I was in a dream. Everyone was there — "

"Except Ted."

"That's right. You went through it when you lost Bert."

"Yes, been there, done that," Dottie said with a sigh. "It gets better, I promise."

Ginger smiled. There was no doubt that Dottie was thriving. But Dottie had the social scaffolding of generations of Atlanta society, four children, a pack of grandchildren and certainly more to come. Ginger had none of that. All she had was three stepchildren who suddenly seemed like enemies. Would she tell Dottie?

Sam appeared with their drinks, and he set them down on the white tablecloth. Glancing up, Ginger noticed the centerpiece at the round table by the entrance. A vase of peonies, white peonies, with a pale red center. It was the first time Ginger noticed the flowers from Ted's service. They were lovely. But they, too, would die.

"I suppose the day went as well as could be expected. The people at The Palms handled everything. The cremation at Scott's Funeral Home, and they even chose the urn!"

"It was gorgeous. So tasteful."

"The children handled the service with Reverend Miller. St. Francis was Ted's favorite church. He loved the Episcopalian service."

"You're not Episcopalian."

"No. All that formality. The sitting and standing. I thought the smoke would kill me — "

"The incense — "

"That's right, I never could get used to it. I was raised Presbyterian. But Reverend Miller is such a caring person."

"It's always better when the minister knows the deceased."

Dottie and Ginger sipped their drinks. The bourbon was helping. And it was comforting to be at the club. The hustle and bustle of the waiters back and forth across the large, carpeted room. The sound of the silverware and plates, the rhythm of conversations and laughter. All of it was familiar and soothing.

"Speaking of the children . . . how did it go at Jim Donnelly's?"

She decided the last thing she wanted to do was to voice her fears, even to Dottie.

"We're meeting again Friday."

"Is there a problem?"

"Everyone just needs to take a breath."

"I'm sure Ted left everything in good order. Bert always said there should be a saying, 'The Theodore Touch.' Like the 'Midas Touch.'"

Ted had been outstanding in the world of finance and philanthropy. The Johnson Foundation gave money to organizations all over the world. The bulk of Ted's fortune was in his foundation, and she would help continue what he had started. Peter Palmer would run the foundation, along with the company, and Ginger was co-trustee. She and Ted had gone over this. Everything would be just as he'd intended, her place in the world without him was secure. Everything was going to be okay.

Ginger exhaled. "Dottie. Thanks so much. This is just what the doctor ordered. A good drink, a good dinner, and a good friend."

Chapter 4

RIDAY CAME QUICKLY. Waiting alone in Jim Donnelly's office, Ginger looked out the window at Atlanta. She had loved the city when she was with Ted. Its tree-lined streets, made up of oaks, dogwoods, and magnolias and each blooming at a different time during the year. Was it her imagination, or did Atlanta seem less friendly now that Ted was gone? She looked around the office. The walls were covered in serene grass cloth on which hung faded sailing prints, numbered by the original printer. The mahogany partners desk was topped with a burgundy leather and brass circular knobs or handles on the many drawers. How many times had Ted sat in this chair and at this desk, discussing his estate and hammering out the details with Jim?

The door opened.

"Ginger," Jim began, pulling her from her thoughts. "The Johnson children are not coming in. We met Wednesday and talked things through. They called yesterday to say they wished to abide by the old trust. They believe their father wanted the old trust to hold."

"Jim, how can they?"

"There is no signature on the new trust, Ginger. I'm sorry."

"But you and I know that Ted wanted the new trust! He just forgot! Ted was busy, he had a lot of responsibilities, but we knew how he felt. Why would he have bothered to prepare it? He wanted me to be taken care of the way the new trust specified. The two of you spent time on this! You've got to talk to them."

Jim said nothing.

"You have to tell them to abide by his wishes."

"I can't do that, Ginger. I'm their representative, lawyer, and executor, also the trustee of the estate. I can't represent you and the kids at the same time. That's a conflict of interest, you know that."

Ginger lowered herself into a chair. She felt blindsided.

"How could you let this happen? Ted always told me, 'If something happens to me, ask Jim for anything, at any time. He will help you.'"

"Ginger, I'm sorry. But if you want to pursue this — "

"Pursue this?"

"Yes. If you want to pursue this, you'll have to get yourself a lawyer. I've had a set of papers made up for you."

Jim pushed a button on the intercom.

"Doris? Bring in the papers for Mrs. Johnson, please."

"Yes, Mr. Donnelly."

Doris entered and handed him a large envelope. He passed this to Ginger.

"Now, here are duplicates of everything in Ted's estate pertaining to you and the children."

Ginger realized the meeting was over, and maybe a portion of her life, too. She stood and looked at Jim straight in the eye. What she saw there was steely. This wasn't the Jim she had known, and Ted had known, or was it?

She extended her hand but offered no kiss.

"If you need to be in touch," she said. "You can find me in Florida."

She walked out the door.

In a daze, Ginger drove home slowly. Meanwhile, her mind raced. Ted had meant for her to have the income for life. *He himself had told her so. So many times!*

Those kids! They were greedy and lazy. "Greedy and lazy!" she said aloud to herself. *She needed her own lawyer.* But who? She had never talked with anyone about finances before. She had never had to! Ted and Jim had always handled everything.

Ginger passed through the gates. The guard waved her through with a nod. When she turned into the gravel drive, she saw Berdetta on the front step.

Berdetta anticipated Ginger's movements and read them as clearly as she read her facial expressions. She didn't need to be told how Ginger felt; Berdetta understood Ginger, almost like a mother knows her child. Now, Ginger seemed lost and confused. Like a child.

"You don't look yourself. I think Mr. J's passing is finally taking its toll. You know that Mr. J is up there looking out for you. He isn't going to let nothing happen to you, you know that. And he sure doesn't want to see you like this. Now go on up and sit yourself down. I'll bring a nice coffee, with cream and brown sugar, pep you up. Like my mama always did for me."

"I will. Bring me the coffee, Berdetta. It sounds wonderful."

Mechanically, Ginger set her things down on the table by the entry and climbed the stairs. She entered her bedroom, closed the door, picked up the phone and dialed.

"Dottie? I need to talk."

"What happened? What's wrong?"

"I had the appointment today. It was supposed to be me and the kids."

"And?"

"The kids didn't come."

"Why not?"

"Where to begin! The new marital trust. Jim Donnelly. The kids. Ted. Oh, Dottie — everything I counted on — !"

"What?"

"Has vanished!"

"Come this evening. Pearl is making chicken crepes and salad, and her blueberry pie. We can have a nice quiet talk. Come early. Like 5:30, for a cocktail. We can talk as long as you want."

"Thank you. I can always count on you!"

A few moments later, there was a knock at Ginger's door.

"Come in, Berdetta."

"Here's your coffee." She set down the tray. "And I made you cinnamon soldiers. That's what Mama always called them when we cut them in a row like that with the crusts off."

Ginger looked down at the beautiful Flora Danica bone china. Tiny green leaves and lavender-colored flowers peeked out from under the three delicious little rectangles arranged side by side. Berdetta had served the coffee and toast using Ginger's favorite pattern.

"Thank you, Berdetta."

The women exchanged a look of tenderness. Ginger fought off tears.

"Will you take all phone calls? I'm going to rest, like you said. And don't bother about dinner. I'm dining with Mrs. Morris tonight."

CHAPTER 5

PEARL LED GINGER into Dottie's sitting room. The room was French-paneled and decorated with antiques Dottie had purchased at auction locally or found on her wanderings through France. She was watching TV seated on the blue silk, Louis XVI sofa.

"Ginger, dear, you're here, at last. Now I can turn off the news."

Dottie clicked the TV off and set the remote down on a Louis XIV end table.

"Come, sit. Pearl will get us cocktails. I'll have my usual Pearl, and, Mrs. Johnson will have . . ."

"A Manhattan, please."

"A Manhattan. Two cherries — ?"

Ginger nodded. Dottie always remembered.

"Two cherries. And Pearl, bring in those pecans you made. Wait till you try them, Ginger! They're out of this world!"

"Thank you, ma'am."

As soon as Pearl left, Dottie turned to her friend.

"Ginger, what's wrong?"

"Oh, Dottie! Everything!"

"Now start at the beginning. We have all night."

"I went to Jim Donnelly's office on Monday and, Emily, Jack and David were already there. I thought I was late, but later I realized they had planned to arrive earlier and meet without me. It never dawned on me that they were up to something! Jim told us, but clearly they had all known earlier — maybe even last week!"

"Known what — ?"

Before Ginger could answer Pearl re-entered the room with a lacquered tray. She carefully set down each drink and then passed a cut glass dish of pecans.

"Delicious," said Ginger. "Thank you, Pearl."

Pleased, Pearl left the room. Ginger sipped her drink.

"Ted loved Manhattans. Oh, Ted, I wish you were here now!"

"Ginger, what had they all known?"

"Ted had set up a trust for the children, it had many investments and lots of International Lumber stock — you know, and it gave him a sizable income. Then, after we were married, Ted wrote a new trust directing the income from this trust to me and then, after my death, to the children, then to their children, and so on — "

"Ted took such good care of things."

"That's what we thought!"

"What's the problem?"

"He never signed the new trust!"

"What? Why not?"

"I have no idea, but it's unsigned!"

"How could that be? Ted was so detailed."

"I know. And he worked on it with Jim. He told me about it. But it isn't signed. Jim said he reminded him many times."

"Do you think he was struggling, I mean, before he went into the Palms?"

"Maybe, but you know Ted, he never liked being told what to do. He told Jim he'd get around to it. But then, I guess he just forgot!"

Dottie was speechless. Ginger finished her drink and Dottie rang the silver bell on the table. Pearl appeared.

"Another Manhattan for Mrs. Johnson, and I'll have another also."

Pearl left, and Dottie stared ahead, in shock.

"This is so unlike Ted . . ."

Ginger nervously munched a cherry. When she continued, her voice quivered.

"I suppose he meant to sign it years ago. And Jim told the kids their father's intentions. But they looked over the new unsigned trust, and said they wanted to think about it and talk things over among themselves. Today we were all supposed to meet, but they didn't come. Jim said they called to say they'd decided to honor the original trust, the one Ted had signed before we were married."

"How could they do that? This is awful."

"Then Jim said that since he's representing the kids he could no longer represent me. A conflict of interest."

Pearl entered again with her tray, and briskly gathered the empty glasses and replaced them with fresh ones. The friends were too mired in silence to notice, and Pearl left swiftly. Dottie was preparing to ask the crucial question.

"Ginger. What did Ted leave you?"

"International Lumber stock, a nice-sized life insurance policy, and the houses. That's it. The major portion of my income was supposed to come from the second trust. Ted's foundation has the bulk of the estate; we both decided that was best. That's about 120 million, public knowledge. Jim said I ought to get my own lawyer if I want to pursue anything. Dottie, I have to do what's right and fair. I know in my heart what Ted wanted."

"You and Ted are Florida residents, correct?"

"Yes."

"Doesn't the law say you are entitled to a certain amount of Ted's estate regardless of the will?"

"Dottie, I don't know!"

"Well, then we get a good Florida lawyer. I know just the person. Carl Phillips was Bert's lawyer. He heads a major law firm in Palm Beach and he's very tough. He's semi-retired, but his son, Carl Jr., runs the firm and CJ is a true chip off the old block. In the morning, I'll phone Carl, and we'll get things moving. Carl will be formidable in dealing with Jim Donnelly, I can assure you of that! Jim's estate fee will diminish greatly; you wait and see. Now let's eat before Pearl has got to carry us into dinner!"

Dottie reached for the silver bell and rang.

"Pearl is making us crepes, and this afternoon she made her famous blueberry pie. Pearl's pie and one more Manhattan! — and we'll forget all about this mess!"

Pearl appeared.

"Mrs. Johnson and I will have dinner now, Pearl."

LATER AT HOME and in bed, Ginger's troubles came back to her. How had this happened? Ted had always taken such good care of her. Hadn't he? The idea of fighting the children unnerved her. Once, she had been a fighter. But that was a long time ago . . . She had never talked with anyone about money — she'd never had to! Now, she needed a lawyer and prayed that Carl was the right lawyer. She thanked God for Dottie. Dottie had always been there for her, from her very first days as a bride in Atlanta to now, as a new widow. She wished that Dottie lived closer to her. But Dottie was 4th generation Atlanta, and not about to leave her home. Now that everything else she had relied on was uncertain, Ginger was starting to feel that her friend was the only good thing about Atlanta. At last, Ginger fell into the arms of Morpheus.

CHAPTER 6

IN THE MORNING, Ginger decided to return to Florida. Ginger summoned Berdetta and told her that as soon as she'd had her usual breakfast, she wanted to begin to pack up and leave. The two worked liked dervishes for three days and then said a tearful farewell on the steps.

Airport Way, the road leading to the private airport, was off the main road. The small, one-story building with a *porte cochere* stood alone. Half a dozen planes were parked, most all privately owned. A few years ago — or was it more like eight, or ten years ago? — the runway had been lengthened to accommodate a 30-seater for the Northeast flights, a great convenience for the residents of the gated communities on the Treasure Coast.

Ginger settled into her window seat, relieved to be leaving Atlanta. She looked at the empty seat beside her, Ted had always preferred the aisle. Ginger cracked open a new magazine, *Town & Country*. The plane taxied down the short runway and soon was airborne. The flurry of the last few days and the high emotions of saying goodbye conspired with the lull of the engine; Ginger quickly fell asleep. Her future was a blank canvas and, when light turbulence woke her, she knew she had not dreamed.

She checked her watch. The flight would last one more hour, and there would be some bumps caused by late afternoon storms in the Southeast. She looked out at the clouds, and her thoughts lingered over the many times she and Ted took short flights to the Bahamas for days in the sun and balmy nights dancing under the stars. I've had more than my share of fabulous times, she thought. Now, a hiccup.

The pilot announced their descent and Ginger looked out, searching for the first sight of home. Soon, she saw the ocean, then the plane circled back over 3-Oaks. The pattern of homes, some oceanside and others set around the golf course, and the man-made lakes, all signaled home.

3-Oaks was their enclave in Treasure Beach. About 30 families lived there, including their closest friends, Diane and Bill Butler. She would call Diane as soon as she walked in the door, they'd make plans to ride together and have lunch.

AFTER 14 YEARS in Atlanta, Ginger and Ted were looking for a place in Florida and they fell in love with the small town of Treasure Beach, bordered by the Atlantic Ocean on the east and the Indian River on the west. There were no high rises in the town and the beaches were glorious. There was a Yacht Club and four golf courses. Treasure Beach just crossed the line into Central Florida, so it had many old oaks, and a wide variety of palms. 3-Oaks was brand-new then, a gated community. The architecture of the homes behind the gates was reminiscent of the islands, colored stucco houses with porches. Having spent so much time in the Bahamas, they fell in love and bought a spec house on the golf course.

This is home, Ginger thought, descending the steps of the small plane; the familiar, warm Florida air brushed her cheeks.

Paul, the driver from 3-Oaks, was waiting for her on the tarmac. He was tall, with blond hair, and fair skin. Ginger always wondered how Paul, being so fair, could withstand the year-round sun. He ushered her through the airport, which was just a single room. The attendants knew almost everyone who arrived, the regulars who flew in and out all the time. Treasure Beach had a few in-house pilots, they lived close by in a motel-like building. The pilots loved Treasure Beach, some even had families there. Air Safety, the flight training school was on the grounds, in a small building to the west.

It was a short drive through flat fields to the entrance of 3-Oaks. There was a guardhouse, only it was an unassuming structure with a white tile roof matching most of the houses of 3-Oaks. The gate itself was slats of wood in a vertical pattern and painted bright white. A uniformed guard stood sentinel there around the clock. The guard stopped visitors, taking down their names and license numbers, and admitted the members and staff with a nod, a wave, or a bit of friendly chatter.

Paul was waved through and, after following the loop, he pulled up in front of a pink stucco Bermuda-style house. She stepped out onto the gravel drive and up a couple of small front steps, lined by a pair of Ionic columns.

The door opened. Margale was expecting her. Margale never changed. She was small and thin. Her hair was cut short and pushed back behind her ears. She wore powder, blush, and mascara, always looking her best. Her uniform was a blue and white striped shirt dress. An apron-skirt was tied around her waist.

Margale looked calm and serene, a comfort to Ginger especially now.

Ginger hugged Margale and Paul took her suitcases upstairs.

"Oh Margale, I'm so glad to be home! It seems so much longer than two weeks since I left."

"I'm glad you're home Mrs. Johnson. You need to get settled and back to normal life."

"I will, Margale. Let's unpack right away, and it will be like I never left."

Ginger went to the phone.

"Hi Diane?"

"You're back?!"

"I just got back! You're my first call. I need to get out and I'd love to see you."

"Are you hungry?"

"Starving!"

"Great. 12 o'clock at the golf club? Lunch on the terrace?"

"See you then."

The phone rang. Ginger picked it up and heard a man's voice.

"Is this Virginia Johnson?"

"Yes, to whom am I speaking?"

"Virginia. This is Carl Phillips. Dottie Morris phoned this morning and asked me to get in touch with you."

"Oh, Mr. Phillips — "

"Call me Carl. We met in Atlanta years ago when Bert was alive. Dottie said you're her best friend. What can I do for you?"

"I'd like to make an appointment. It's about my late husband's . . . about Ted's estate."

"Dottie told me a little. Do you have the will and all the trust papers?"

"Yes. Jim Donnelly, my lawyer — that is, my former lawyer — he had copies made up for me."

"Well, send them to me registered mail and give me a couple days to look them over. I'll also want to show my son Carl, Jr. Did Dottie mention CJ?"

"Yes, she did."

"Then, let's see . . . Can you come down to Palm Beach?"

"Palm Beach is easy. An hour and a half drive."

"Good. I'd like to handle this personally to start, since Dottie referred you. Then CJ can take over. Is that all right with you?"

"Of course."

"Good. How about we talk a week from Friday? That's about ten days."

"Great, Carl. Thank you."

"And Virginia — ?"

"Ginger."

"Ginger don't worry. The Phillips team will take care of everything."

CHAPTER 7

"I JUST LOVE this light stone terrace," said Ginger. They sat overlooking the 9th hole. "Such a contrast to red brick at the Atlanta Club. Not that the Atlanta Country Club isn't beautiful, it's just staid and dark."

"The Nashville Country Club is exactly like Atlanta," Diane said. "Old, traditional, and a little depressing."

Ginger and Diane were both raised in the South. Diane grew up at the Nashville Country Club, but Ginger was introduced to club life only when she married Ted.

"And I love our young families. The group in Atlanta has gotten so old, but so have I, I guess! Having all those young people coming in and out on their own planes all season is so invigorating!"

At 3-Oaks, families of all ages socialized, which was very stimulating.

"Ted always loved that Treasure Beach had its own airport, not a major commercial airport, but a tiny one with its own flight school. Ted learned to fly at Air Safety."

"It's the best pilot training program in the country —"

"I know! Whether a pilot flew a Beechcraft like Ted —"

"Or a 747! Just after Bill and I came to 3-Oaks, we loved going to the Bahamas on the Beechcraft, but we *really loved* International Lumber's Big Bird."

"Oh, there's nothing like the G4!" Ginger reminisced. "I'm afraid my jet-set days are numbered."

"What do you mean?"

"Oh, Diane, it's a long story." Ginger hesitated, but only for a moment. Then she gave into her friend's curiosity and her own need to get things off her chest.

"Ted forgot to sign a second trust! So, the kids won't honor it, even though they know it reflects his wishes."

"What?! Oh, Ginger!"

"They saw the trust. My lawyer — their lawyer now! — he wrote it. With Ted. He told them that Ted wrote it. But the kids refuse to accept it. So, I have to pursue this."

"Oh, God. I guess it's time for a good lawyer."

"I just got one. Do you remember Dottie? My Atlanta friend?"

"Of course, darling lady."

"Well, she knows a lawyer in Palm Beach. He phoned and I'm going to see him in ten days. Dottie says he's the best. So, I feel a little better about it now than I did yesterday."

"What's the name of the firm?"

"Phillips, Smith & Hammond, I think."

"Ginger, do you remember when I found that Bill was having an affair? With the intern in DC?"

Just because Ginger had the tact never to bring up the subject, didn't mean she'd forgotten. Ginger remembered everything about that time, as did many long-time residents of 3-Oaks.

"Of course."

"Carl Phillips was my lawyer! Carl Phillips kept me and Bill together. You are in good hands."

"Small world!"

"Was that actually ten years ago?"

"Yes, something like that," Ginger said.

"I'll never get over how stupid men can be!"

"But what a smart secretary Bill has."

"I'll never forget *that* call. 'Did you see Cirque du Soleil twice in six months? Or should I call American Express and say there's been a mistake and a double charge?'"

Diane grimaced at the memory. But the affair had been brief, and Bill had begged her forgiveness. It was all behind them. Just as quickly as she broached it, Diane changed the subject.

"Did you hear that Missy and Richard Warren are selling their house?"

"No! But why — ?"

"Not sure. The open house is tomorrow. Sally is handling the showing."

"How can they sell? Missy and Richard love their house!" Ginger asked and wondered, does everything good have to come to an end?

"Let's go! Sally will give us the scoop. Won't that be fun — we can sneak in and out of rooms and peek in their closets . . . !"

"Okay." Anything to get her mind off Jim Donnelly and Ted's children.

"It's four to six tomorrow afternoon. I'll call when I'm leaving. And Ginger, Carl Phillips is a doll, *and* he's made of steel. By the way, in Florida, you have equal property rights. Carl taught me that."

CHAPTER 8

THE FOLLOWING DAY, the phone rang. "Ginger? It's Diane. I'm not feeling too swift. I just can't make myself get dressed. I'm going to have to pass on the open house . . ."

"I'll go and give you all the details and news."

"You don't mind going on your own?"

"I'll be fine. Hope you're just tired. I'll check on you later."

WHETHER SHE MINDED or not, going places by herself was something Ginger had to get used to. She got in her golf cart and set out for Missy and Richard's open house. Driving through the greens, Ginger took in the manicured lawns and appreciated the matching architecture of the residences. Passing members on the course, it was customary to give a wave or a nod. It was her habit to study the figures, driving their balls or trudging the rough searching for one. Then, she remembered that she would never again find Ted among them.

This was her first outing alone since returning from Atlanta and Ted's funeral. With her head high and chin up, Ginger approached the house. She didn't feel brave.

There was a great turnout. The showing was in full swing. Members came out of curiosity, of course, but it was also a social event, a chance to take note of who was around and who was out of town. And people were always looking for houses. It was a great sport for retired people: new house, new project. Everyone needed a new project.

Sally was stationed at the door greeting people. She ran the real estate office at 3-Oaks and was a member of the club. She was somewhere in her late 50s but still wore her chestnut brown hair in a bob, parted on the side, and secured with a girlish bobby pin. She greeted all pleasantly, but it was easy to tell who her favorites were. To these, she bestowed a kiss on each cheek. Naturally, these were the more influential and affluent members of the 3-Oaks community.

"Ginger, so good to see you! You're looking well. I'm so sorry about Ted."

"Thank you. I just got back from the funeral."

"You took good care of him for so long."

"I was blessed to have had him for so long."

"He's in a better place now. Let's have lunch soon — "

Sally was distracted by the arrival of Louise Baker. Louise was a Newport heiress, the club gossip, and uncontested winner of the snide-comment contest. Her lips were alternately pursed — while formulating a mean-spirited remark — or parted, flapping with the latest gossip. Plus, she was always flushed, her cheeks gave clue to her frequent indulgence in gin. When Ginger and Diane saw Louise headed in their direction, they either froze in place or made for the exit.

"Oh, Louise! You came! How are you?"

"Poor Missy!" Louise exclaimed, exchanging air kisses with Sally. "We've had so many good times in this house!"

"This must be hard for you. But I heard there are issues with Richard's fund. I hope there's nothing fishy going on!"

"Missy put her heart and soul into this house!"

"Someone will snap it up, too. It has everything, and the closets are to-die-for."

Louise spotted Ginger. They shared smiles.

"Sorry about Ted," Louise said. "You took such good care of him."

"Thank you. I miss him, but he's in a better place — "

Jennifer Stranton arrived. Sally and Louise pivoted to talk to her.

"Jennifer! Marvelous bridge tournament!"

"The prizes were adorable," said Sally. "And not tacky for once!"

Ginger had missed a lot while away in Atlanta.

"Jennifer, how's Alice?" Louise asked. "I heard Albert is drinking again."

"He just can't stay off the sauce. It's terrible. He's so attractive, but the truth is, he's more fun when he's drinking!"

"Poor Alice," Sally said.

"She's been thinking of leaving him for years," Louise continued. "But who would have her? *She's always nagging.* Her complaining probably drove Al to drink!"

Ginger walked away. Not in a state of mind for small talk, she decided to focus on the house.

It was spectacular — too fussy for Ginger, but she had to admit it was beautifully done. Mario Buatta had decorated it with his trademark touches. Yellow chintz swagged the high windows, matching the fabric on the sofas. The raspberry trim on the sofa matched the moiré ribbon and rosettes from which the dog pictures hung. Missy and Richard didn't own a dog, but Mario was known to favor English dog paintings hung on ribbons. There was a Chinese lacquer Chinoiserie secretary on one wall balanced by an antique mahogany drop leaf on another. Tasteful books were stacked on the tables: an oversized book on the Impressionists, Slim Aaron's photos of society figures, Carolyn Roehm's *Flowers*, and, of course, Audubon's *Birds of America*. In the center of the table was their Remington bronze, *Native American on Horseback.* A cabinet in the corner housed a Steuben animal collection and by it was a vintage Coromandel screen of cranes, making a private cove of the

41

lemon-yellow chintz sofa.

French doors opened onto a brick terrace and a velvet green lawn with boxwood hedges separating it from the 11th hole of the golf course. A man-made pond was alongside the hedge, rendering the 11th both famously beautiful and a challenge. Seagulls, pelicans and, occasionally, a blue heron lingered nearby. The plantation-style architecture of the Warren house was the epitome of the favored 3-Oaks style. The architectural review board considered the house the crown jewel of the club, and it was priced accordingly. Like Sally said, someone would surely snap it up.

Ginger wandered into the dining room. The long, Hepplewhite mahogany table was covered with silver trays holding tea sandwiches — tomato, chicken salad, egg salad, cucumber, watercress — 3-Oaks offerings for any occasion, from an open house to a baby shower, to receptions after funerals, of which there were many. At each end were trays with the club's signature chocolate chip cookies and chocolate covered strawberries. Ginger, suddenly remembering how little she had eaten at Ted's funeral, felt a sharp pang of hunger. She selected some sandwiches, set them on a lilac-colored plate, and sat on the sofa. Nibbling on a watercress sandwich, she studied a portrait of a man above the sideboard, wondering if he was a true relative or a 'bought at auction' ancestral painting. The painting seemed mid-1900's and was hung against lush Zuber wallpaper depicting views of Italy.

"A glass of champagne?"

Ginger looked up, expecting a club waiter. But her eyes met a man with sparkling blue eyes. Someone she had never seen before. Perhaps he was Sally's assistant.

"Well, it's a little early, but why not?"

Ginger took the glass and again she met his blue eyes.

"I don't believe we've met," she said. "Do you live at 3-Oaks?"

"No, but I'm looking. I'd left my name at the club office and asked them to call if something became available on the golf course. I'm Kevin McCoy."

"Virginia Johnson. Nice to meet you."

"How do you do, Virginia? Have you toured the house yet?"

"Actually, I haven't."

"Well, Virginia, let's get started before our bubbly goes flat."

"Everyone calls me Ginger."

"Well, then Ginger. Shall we?"

And, with that Kevin gently and deftly took Ginger's elbow, guiding her out of the dining room, across the hall, and into the library.

The library had caramel-colored wood paneling, a handsome partner's desk in the center of a window, two wing chairs on either side, and a sofa of red and beige linen opposite. A large oil of a horse hung above the sofa and a butler's tray table stood before it, both sides down. A Persian rug covered the floor, leaving a few feet of planked and waxed wooden floors. Two walls were shelf-lined, housing handsome, red-leather bound books. The third wall was more French doors leading out onto the brick terrace. The sun was lowering in the sky, making multi-colors of pink and purple, and casting shadows over the fairway.

"Play golf, Ginger?" Kevin asked, gazing out at the vista as dusk approached.

"Not really. I've tried, but it takes too long. I prefer to paint. And riding."

"I prefer tennis myself. Good exercise and fast. You ride, so you must live at 3-Oaks. The stable here is beautiful. I imagine there are great trails . . ."

"Do you ride?"

"I used to. Let's go upstairs."

Kevin turned and walked across the library toward the beautiful spiral staircase outside the door. Ginger watched him. He was about 6-feet, thin, lightly tanned, dressed in beige gabardine slacks, an open-neck light blue shirt, and a navy blazer with brass buttons, adorned with the tuft of a butter yellow silk pocket square. His feet were clad in brown Gucci loafers. No socks.

It was hard for Ginger to estimate his age, probably just beyond 50 years old. He had rather a baby face with a small nose and those blue eyes. His hair was not grey but light brown, short and brushed to the side. He had high cheekbones, prominent in this firm, youthful face. She remembered Ted when he was around 50, not at all like Kevin, yet just as self-assured. Now Ted was gone and so were the 40-plus years. Ginger did not think she looked her age — she was 68 — but no one knew that. She had always been careful about revealing her age and had been so, forever, since they first arrived at 3-Oaks.

She followed Kevin up the stairs to the second floor. She finished her champagne and set the glass down on the Chippendale chest on the landing. Another ancestor portrait hung above it. The Warrens were very traditional, be it by heritage or acquisition. Ginger had never purchased portrait oils at auction to suggest and weave the story of a patrician background. But she had insinuated it — offering bits and pieces of her life — allowing others to connect the dots and make up their own version of her story. On the landing, Kevin turned left, heading to the master bedroom. A mahogany four-poster bed dominated, with a French blue silk canopy hovering above, laced-edged linens covering the bed, European square pillows dressed it and a bed skirt also of blue silk. Swagged curtains hung tasseled and trimmed with fringe on either side of more French doors, leading to a private porch which, naturally, looked out over the pond and the golf course. A French writing desk was on the one side of the open doors, and a cream-colored velvet chaise on the other.

The blue and white linen rug with a Greek key design covered the floor, leaving a border of dark oak. Above the French commode was a gilded, Louis XVI mirror. To the left of the dresser, the door led to a dressing room, all mirrored, with a skirted vanity adorned with an array of perfume bottles and a silver comb and brush set. This anteroom led into a shell-pink, marble bathroom outfitted with a jacuzzi tub and a glassed-in shower, a double sink and two doors which led to WCs,

His and Hers. There were also two walk-in closets, also His and Hers.

"Look at all the shoes both of them have!" Ginger exclaimed, practically awestruck. "Wherever the Warrens go, it will be hard to replace this! It's certainly the advantage to designing and building your own house!"

Ginger wondered if Kevin was married. No wedding band, but he seemed to take great interest in the intimate features of the master suite.

"Look at all his sports coats! Mine would take up a fraction of the space!" Clearly Kevin was also astounded by the Warren's domestic life. He took in the shelves of shirts behind glass doors with small, brass knobs.

"Bet these are custom made," he said. "You don't find those stripes in a store!"

Suddenly, the house seemed very quiet. The light was getting gray.

"What time is it?"

He checked his watch.

"5:55."

"The Open House is four to six. We'd better hurry!"

Moving quickly, the two glanced into the three other bedrooms at the opposite end of the hall: One, blue toile, one beige and cream stripe, and a pretty, twin-bedded room done up in a peach and celadon print. They dashed back down the stairs, giggling like children about to be caught in mischief.

Sally was in the dining room and surrounded by people, presumably interested parties, and voicing instructions to the staff packing up the last of the refreshments.

"Hope you had a good showing, Sally!" Ginger called.

"The house is brilliant!" Kevin said.

"People will be calling you off the hook!"

Ginger moved out the door. Kevin followed.

"That was a workout. How about a proper drink? We could go to Eddie's, just down the road. Oh, I'm sorry. You probably have plans."

They stood on the front steps, facing one another. She felt small compared to his tall frame. Was she shrouded in grief? Could she throw it off and enjoy life again, at last? His eyes, confident until this instant, now betrayed a flash of vulnerability. She felt compelled to reassure him.

"Why don't we just go to the Tap Room at the club?" she said, surprising him, and herself, as well. She indicated her golf cart. Their steps were in unison as they turned, crossed the gravel, and climbed into the cart for a short drive on the golf path to the Tap Room.

CHAPTER 9

THE TAP ROOM was the informal restaurant at the club. There was a long bar of smooth wood, with matching round tables, encircled by green leather chairs. The walls were upholstered in green felt. Hunting prints in tortoise frames lined the walls. A blue, red, and green plaid rug helped to keep the sound down. The Tap Room was the most popular dining room at 3-Oaks.

"Good evening, Mrs. Johnson. So sorry about Mr. Johnson."

"Thank you, Harry."

"He is greatly missed. Dinner for two, Mrs. Johnson?"

"Yes."

"This way, please."

Harry led them to a table by the window. Large oak trees stood in silhouette against the star-sprinkled sky and the rising moon was full.

"Ginger, when did you lose your husband?"

"Three years ago, a few weeks ago . . ."

A perplexed look crossed Kevin's face.

"Ted had Alzheimer's. He passed away last month, but he really left me three years ago."

"Horrible disease. Sometimes, that's harder for the spouse than the victim. I mean, that's what I've heard . . ."

"Oh, I don't know. It was awful for Ted. One day you're a little forgetful. A month goes by, and you can't find the car keys. Six months later, we found him shredding dollar bills in the library totally unaware of what he was doing — just knowing he was doing *something*."

"Sounds rough."

"Anyway, then it got worse. He couldn't even find the library, so we had to take him to a facility. You spend the rest of your life in your body but out of your mind, with no recall whatsoever of yourself or anyone in your life."

"I'm so sorry. Have you lived at 3-Oaks for a long time?"

"30 years. It's a wonderful place. Have you toured the property?"

"Not yet . . . Just heard about the open house."

"And — ?"

"I beg your pardon?"

"Are you going to call Sally?"

Her eyes danced on his, and for a moment he lost himself.

"Oh, you mean and make an offer?" Kevin threw his head back and laughed. It was a delightful and carefree laugh.

"Gorgeous house. But a bit big for a bachelor, don't you think? Besides, my schedule will make me only a part time resident. Very part time."

"Well, there are smaller ones, cottages — "

Harry appeared and bowed.

"A cocktail Mrs. Johnson?"

"The house Chardonnay, please. Kevin?"

"A dry Ketel One martini. Straight up. Two olives."

"Certainly," Harry said, handing them menus. Then, he left.

While Kevin looked over the menu, Ginger pretended to do the same but really, she was mostly attempting to suppress her glee. He was a *bachelor*.

In record time, Harry returned with their drinks.

Ginger raised her glass. Kevin took a sip of his martini never taking his eyes away from hers. Ginger blushed.

"Where do you live, Kevin? And how did you hear about 3-Oaks?"

"I live in Charlotte. I'm a pilot on Northwest. I discovered 3-Oaks when I went to Air Safety for my training and licensing. I have always liked Treasure Beach. I love the water and the sense of community. So, here I am."

Harry appeared.

"Are you ready to order, Mrs. Johnson?"

"I'll have the steak sandwich, medium rare, onion rings and a side of creamed spinach. Kevin?"

"Sounds perfect. I'll have the same."

Harry nodded, took the menus, and left.

"Ginger, tell me about yourself. How long were you married? Children?"

"Ted and I were married for more than 40 years, that's hard to believe now. No children. Three stepchildren. They're grown-ups with grown up kids, and everything. They were older when we married. Ted was quite a bit older than I, but it didn't matter. He was young in spirit, always on the go — except for those last years."

"Are you close to your stepchildren?"

"Well, I thought so. Their mother died a very long time ago, before Ted and I met. I just got back from Atlanta, that's where we lived for the first years of our marriage. His children still live there, and we have the house. I mean, I still have the house. There's so much to get used to! Anyway, I don't think I'll see the Johnson children very much. There are . . . complications. Oh, I'm rambling. But that's your fault. I find you so easy to talk to."

"So are you, Ginger."

The steak sandwiches arrived. They ordered a pinot noir.

Kevin raised his glass. "To Treasure Beach."

Ginger was feeling so relaxed.

"Yes, to Treasure Beach," she echoed.

By the end of dinner, Ginger and Kevin were laughing. She hadn't felt so carefree for a long time. Nor had she had so much to drink in years. They walked outside. The valet brought Ginger her golf cart.

"Thanks for dinner, Ginger. Terrific evening. I hope I can reciprocate sometime soon."

"I'd like that."

Ginger started back to her house, feeling young, smiling to herself. She thought: *There's no fool like an old fool.* But then, what did it matter? It had been a long time since a man made her feel almost giddy. But it wasn't just that: *he listened.* Kevin seemed genuinely interested in her. How long had it been since someone really listened to her? Of course, she had lots of friends. They said the right things when Ted finally died. "It was for the best," or "God's will . . ."

At home, Ginger climbed the stairs and went to her dressing room. Slightly tipsy, she removed her clothes. But before slipping on her pale pink nightgown, Ginger paused and studied herself naked in the mirror. She was still thin. Her ample breasts had fallen and her middle had thickened. But her legs were still shapely and firm from riding, though her knees were looser and lined. Her bottom was flat and not at all tight. This didn't bother her though; she had never really liked perky fannies, preferring to wear straight skirts and dresses with no bumps. Not bad for my age, she thought to herself.

Ginger pulled on her nightgown and sat at her dressing table. She was diligent about removing foundation, eyeliner, and every trace of mascara at night. She studied herself again. Light brown freckles covered her face, too much riding in the Florida sun, even with sunblock and a helmet. Smile lines around the eyes, really crow's feet, lines around her mouth from smoking, even though she had given up the habit decades ago. Her cheeks had fallen ever so slightly but, all in all, for her 68 years she did not look her age. Makeup covered up a lot of flaws. Botox helped and, of course, the face lift she'd had at 50 by a top New York surgeon. Many of her friends had succumbed to a second face lift or laser, but she had refrained. Maybe now was the time . . . ?

Silly girl, she thought. Silly, silly girl.

Ginger crossed the thick rug and got into bed. She turned off the swing arm lamp and melted into the *Pratesi* sheets. In the dark, Kevin haunted her thoughts. The way he held her in his gaze at dinner exhilarated her. Of course, he was just being polite.

CHAPTER 10

A FTER DINNER, KEVIN peeled out of the parking lot in his red Mercedes convertible. The rental had proved a smart investment. Driving along Club Drive, he was feeling good. *Very good.* The houses were magnificent. He certainly had picked the right community, he thought to himself, turning the wheel and heading out the main gate, down Ocean Road and towards the Sands Motel. The evening had been successful. Everything had gone perfectly. He particularly enjoyed driving fast when he felt that he had accomplished exactly what he had set out to do. He had the feeling that nothing stood in his way.

IN THE MORNING, at precisely nine o'clock. Kevin made a call.

Sitting at her desk early, Ginger was startled by the sound of the phone. She was slightly hungover, but happy, too.

"Hello?"

"Ginger? It's Kevin."

A tiny pause of surprise followed, and he rushed to fill it.

"From last night?"

"Of course, good morning, Kevin. It's so nice of you to call."

"I wanted to tell you what a wonderful time I had and to thank you for dinner. Most of all, I enjoyed talking to you."

"I enjoyed it too, Kevin."

"I was wondering if I might take you to Eddie's for dinner sometime . . . I was hoping tonight."

"Well I . . . let me check my book. Hold on . . . Let me see. Hmm. Maybe I can rearrange something. May I call you back?"

"Sure. I'll give you my cell."

Kevin did not want Ginger to know he was staying at The Sands.

"I'll phone you back shortly. Bye."

She stared at her weekly organizer. Blank all week. Nothing until Saturday, the club party. Why had she not said yes at once? Or declined? Excitement stirred in her again. This is what she had gone to sleep thinking about last night; this is what she had silently wished for. How foolish! How old was Kevin? Early 50s? Well, it was just dinner. What harm could come of it? She pressed the intercom.

"Margale?"

"Yes, Mrs. Johnson?"

"I won't be at home for dinner after all. Let's do the chicken and broccoli tomorrow night."

"Yes, Mrs. Johnson."

Ginger picked up the phone and dialed. Her palms were becoming moist, and she felt the blood rushing to her face.

"Hi. It's Ginger. Tonight sounds great."

"Good! Pick you up at 7:00. Look forward to seeing you."

"Me, too. Thanks, goodbye."

She held the phone in her clammy hand and then put it down. She stared out the window at the 11th hole. For years, every Tuesday and Saturday, she used to watch Ted and his foursome play the 11th hole. All those years he had been a good husband and as attentive as a man could be who was always doing business.

She felt a pang of guilt. All of this was possible — the house, the view, Star, her beloved horse — all because of Ted. And this evening, she was going to Eddie's Grill with a perfect stranger. She was startled again when the phone rang.

"Hello?"

"How was the house?"

"Oh Diane! I forgot to call you!" Ginger had been so caught up in Kevin, she'd neglected her promise to her best friend.

"The house is divine, but no one we know is going to buy it. At our age, people are downsizing! You feel better?"

"Yes. I was thinking of heading to the stables. Do you wanna take a ride?"

"Absolutely. What time?"

"Eleven o'clock. Meet you at the stables and we can have lunch."

"See you there. Bye."

They hung up. This is just what she needed. A ride and a date with Diane would get Kevin out of her mind. Ginger went to her closet, pulled out her jodhpurs and a crisp white shirt. Would she tell Diane about Kevin . . . ? Probably not, she decided. Not yet.

CHAPTER 11

DIANE SAT TALL and erect in the saddle. Her light brown ponytail was secured with a tortoise barrette. She wore a white turtleneck under a cream cashmere sweater vest along with caramel jodhpurs and short brown leather boots with a brass buckle on the side. The ride was pleasant. Nothing hurried or fast, sometimes a slow walk, sometimes a gentle trot, and just one stretch for a brief gallop. Hunter and Star seemed just as content side by side on the bridle path as their owners.

"Ginger, what are you going to do with yourself now? Have you been painting?"

Ginger sighed. "I haven't picked up a brush since Ted died."

"I just loved your show at The Gordon Gallery. You sold out, didn't you?"

"Practically. I have to get back to it. The gallery keeps asking me to make an appearance in New York, but with Ted failing and then, well, dying — "

"I'm sure they understand."

"They do. They've been very patient, actually."

Ginger guided Star around a low branch. Diane, on Hunter, did the same.

"That branch is dangerous. It must have broken during a storm."

"We had a big rain, and a lot of wind, while you were in Atlanta. We'll let Robert know when we get back."

Robert had been stable master at 3-Oaks for years. He supervised the care of the horses and maintenance of the trails. He planned all the equestrian events, as well.

"We're so lucky to have Robert. Just knowing he was taking care of Star while I was away . . . that was a big weight off my mind."

"I have Robert take Hunter out even when I'm here," Diane said. Then, she sighed. "I wish Bill rode. He's golf, golf, golf! And business, business, business!"

"So was Ted. Ted would go on trips, but he always tacked business onto one end or the other. I guess it's better to have a man that works than not. Poor Lucy! Now that John's retired, he's always around. He golfs but then it's, 'What's for lunch?' The marriage vows should be . . . For better or for worse — but not for lunch!"

"And for Bill . . . no Las Vegas."

It was unlike Diane to mention Bill's affair and now she'd mentioned it twice in two days. Diane could forgive, but clearly, she could not yet forget. Secrets between husbands and wives fester, then bloom or sometimes explode.

Ginger gave her friend a sympathetic smile.

"Oh, Ginger, I can say anything to you. You are such a good friend. My best friend."

"You're my best friend, too."

Ginger felt a pang of guilt. Diane and Dottie were like sisters to her, but Ginger had told neither about Kevin. It was nice though to have a secret, something to herself.

"Race you to the barn," Ginger said. She gave Star a small kick and they cantered away. How she loved riding. Riding and painting. She was lucky, even if she was a widow now.

Ginger and Diane walked towards a table on the terrace of the club.

"You two girls are just galloping through life!" quipped Louise Baker, eying them from her table as they approached from the green. Louise had a following. She was funny, a little crude, very, very rich and the club gossip. True, false, or made-up, Louise always had news. "Why, with those rosy cheeks, you look like schoolgirls! I only do *indoor sports*," she said with a wink and all the girls at her table laughed, too.

Ginger and Diane took a table far away from Louise.

"Two Arnold Palmers, ladies?"

"Yes, thanks."

"Yes, and what are the specials today, Harry?"

"Blackened Mahi-Mahi and a crab salad."

"I'll have the crab salad. What about you, Diane?"

"The same. Thank you, Harry."

Unfolding her napkin, Diane turned to her friend. "Now, tell me about the Warren's open house."

Ginger went on alert. The most important feature of the Warren's open house was undoubtably Kevin, but she had decided not to mention him. She had to be strategic in her response.

"Oh, the house is beautiful. If you like all the chintz and ribbons."

"But why are they selling, did you hear — "

"Louise announced, naturally, as soon as she arrived, that Missy had referred to Richard's 'business problems'. With his hedge fund, I guess. I hope it's not another Madoff. Richard has been doing business with so many members for years — "

"Bill is not involved with Richard."

"Ted always did everything out of Atlanta."

"Oh dear. Are they staying at 3-Oaks?"

"Sally said she assumed they would. They love it here."

Suddenly, Ginger could not resist confiding in her best friend.

"Diane, I met the nicest man yesterday."

"Really? Who?"

"His name is Kevin McCoy."

"Where'd you meet him?"

"At the open house. He's a pilot . . . a captain at Northwest. Anyway, I was just sitting in the living room and having some food — "

"I hated to miss the food. How was the food?"

"Fabulous, you know. The sandwiches — cucumber, watercress, chicken salad. When I saw all that food, I realized I'd hardly eaten *in days*. I was ravenous, sitting on the sofa with a plate and — "

"Did they have the chocolate chip cookies?"

"Yes — "

"They are *to-die-for* — "

"I know. Anyway, this man walked over, offered me a glass of champagne — "

"Did they have the chocolate-covered strawberries — ?"

"There was *everything*. Anyway, this handsome man offered me a glass of champagne and we ended up going through the house together."

"Does he live here?"

"No. He's looking for a place, that's why he was there."

"How did he find 3-Oaks?"

"He got his pilot's training at Air Safety. So he knows Treasure Beach and, I guess, 3-Oaks."

"Well, the Warren house is so big. He must be married. And with a family — "

"No, he's on his own. And that's what he said. He's interested in looking at something smaller."

"I'm sure there are cottages available."

"That's what I said. We ended up having dinner at The Tap Room."

"You picked up a perfect stranger?"

Ginger was taken aback.

"He was at the club open house, and he picked me up, if you have to put it that way."

Diane hadn't really meant it the way it sounded. Ginger was obviously sensitive after Ted's death, which was understandable. Besides, a dinner at The Tap Room was harmless.

"Well, good for you," Diane said and laughed. She studied her friend. Ginger was beaming.

"Is Kevin McCoy single?"

Ginger nodded.

"How old is this Kevin McCoy?"

"I don't know. I didn't ask him."

Luckily for Ginger, Harry arrived at just that moment and lunch was delivered.

"Thank you, Harry," she said and started to eat right away. "I forgot how hungry riding makes me!"

Ginger focused on her crab salad. Diane's response made her decide not to mention her plans for the evening.

CHAPTER 12

WHEN KEVIN MCCOY pulled into the driveway at 6:30, Ginger opened the door and stepped out onto the porch. She was a vision: in white jeans, a bright blue T-shirt and white sweater draped over her shoulders. She still looked great in jeans. Thank God for riding, she thought. She had pulled her red hair back into a ponytail. This was youthful and accented her high cheekbones. Her blue eyes were almond-shaped. She was still a stunning woman.

"Ready, beautiful?"

Ginger blushed and deflected the focus.

"What a great car."

He opened the door for her. She was still pulling the seatbelt on, when Kevin roared out of the drive, gravel crackling.

"Careful. There's a speed limit at 3-Oaks. I wouldn't want you to get stopped before you become a member."

Secretly, she loved the speed, and her heart was racing.

"I called Sally," Kevin said, slightly shouting over the engine's roar and the buffeting wind. "She's showing me golf cottages on Thursday."

"Wonderful!" Ginger shouted back.

As they approached the gates, Kevin slowed, and the gate keeper nodded them through. At Ocean Drive, they waited at the light.

"They're very nice. Two bedrooms and a lanai. Plenty of space if you're alone."

"I am alone. But I have a new friend at 3-Oaks."

"Indeed, you do," Ginger smiled.

"I hope you like Eddy's."

"Oh, I love Eddy's. Great fish. Particularly, the grouper."

"Of course, you'd say that. It's my favorite, too."

The light changed and Kevin hit the gas again.

THE RESTAURANT WAS crowded. It was, after all, the most popular place in town. It was casual, noisy, and festive.

As soon as they sat at a table, the waiter arrived.

"A bottle of Landmark Grand Detour," Kevin said. "Bring an ice bucket please and leave it. We'd like two house salads and we'll both have the grouper."

The waiter gave a nod and briskly left. Ginger loved how he took charge.

"Where do you fly, Kevin? What are your routes?"

"I fly to Tokyo and Hong Kong. Northwest has direct flights. It's long but I love Asia. Very busy cities ... exciting. We usually have three or four-day layovers, so I get to explore. Have you been to Japan? Or China?"

"I was there on business with Ted. Years ago. I've seen pictures and things have really changed. When we were in China, it was all bicycles and now, it's wall-to-wall cars. But Hong Kong was fun — fun for shopping and great for Ted's business. Japan was, too."

"What business was Ted in?"

"Lumber. He started International Lumber, out of Atlanta. And now it's worldwide."

Bingo! Kevin thought.

"When's your next trip, Kevin?"

"In about six months."

"Six months?"

"I'm on medical leave. Thought this would be a good time to look for a place in Florida. I love the weather. So here I am."

"Medical leave — ? I hope it's nothing serious . . ."

"Nah. Nothing some R & R in a beautiful place won't take care of," he said, smiling at her.

"Well, if you find something you like in 3-Oaks, I'd be happy to propose you for membership. If you want to join the club."

"Thank you. I hope to take you up on it. More wine?"

Kevin looked at her again the way he had at The Tap Room. He was so attractive and attentive.

"Tell me about you, Ginger. Where did you grow up? What do you like to do?"

"Oh, I grew up in the South, in Atlanta. I went to Miss Hall's, have you heard of it — ?"

Kevin nodded no.

"Why would you — ? It's a girls' school, and then to the University of Georgia. I wanted to go to art school after that, but my father was against it. He wanted me to go to secretarial school, so I'd always have a skill and be able to find a job. I was terribly disappointed about art school. I'd been painting since I was very young. And I was good. I won awards and everything. I just knew I could make a living at it."

"Do you still paint?"

"Oh, yes."

"I'd love to see your paintings."

"I'd love to show you."

"Come up and see my etchings?"

Ginger blushed again and they both laughed.

"But I haven't been in my studio for over a month now. Three galleries represent me. One in New York, one in Houston and one here, in Treasure Beach. I sell a lot, but my father didn't know that would happen. I followed his lead, as I always did — "

"You were a good daughter."

"Perhaps to a fault. I learned the secretarial skills and my first job was at International Lumber. I met Ted there shortly after I started."

"Well, that's something to be thankful for."

"True. He'd been widowed for three years. And the rest, as they say, is history."

She seemed reluctant to say more. Kevin decided not to press her.

"Do you like ice-cream? The ice-cream next door is my favorite."

AFTER DINNER THEY walked over.

"Cup or cone?" Kevin asked.

"Cone."

"Favorite flavor?"

"Chocolate mint."

He smiled. "Of course."

"Two chocolate mint cones, please."

Kevin handed Ginger a double scoop cone. It was so much fun. When was the last time she'd had an ice-cream cone?

"Let's cross the street and take in the ocean. There's a full moon."

"Good idea," she said.

Kevin touched her arm just above the elbow, as he had at the open house, and guided her to a bench on the boardwalk. They sat side by side, looking out over the ocean. The full moon created a path of light to the horizon.

"I had forgotten how beautiful the beaches are here. I have an idea …" But then, he hesitated. "No, it's too bold."

"Well, you have to tell me now."

"Okay. For the next two days I have nothing to do until I see Sally to look at cottages. How about going to the beach tomorrow?"

"I'd adore that." The words spilled out of Ginger without her even thinking. "I have a date with Diane, she's my best friend, to take a ride. But I can reschedule. Star won't mind missing a day. Star's my horse. Do you ride, Kevin?"

"Well, I can get on and hold on. I don't know if you'd call it riding."

"You have to see 3-Oaks on a horse. The trails go all the way around the club. You get a really different view of the grounds."

"I'd like to do that. How about the day after tomorrow? Then I'll know everything about 3-Oaks."

"It's a deal. I'll ask Diane if Hunter's free."

"Hunter?"

"Diane's horse. He's a great horse."

"I hope he's gentle."

Kevin had his arm on the bench behind Ginger.

"I can't wait for the next two days, Ginger. A real vacation. How lucky I am to have met you." He leaned over and kissed her on the cheek.

Ginger stared out at the ocean. A few minutes passed before she could think of something to say.

"It will be a vacation for me, too. I haven't been to the beach forever."

And that was true. Ted didn't do ice-cream cones and he didn't do beach.

Chapter 13

Ginger opened her eyes. For a long moment she stared at the ceiling. It was pale blue, the color of an eggshell. She was forgetful of everything, including almost her name and her new station in life: a widow. Suddenly, she was startled with a shock. *A day at the beach!*

She glanced at the clock. It was nine already. Kevin McCoy had said he'd pick her up at 10:30. Ginger pushed the intercom.

"Margale! How did I sleep so long? I'll have orange juice, a poached egg on toast, and coffee, by the pool. I'll be right down."

"Yes, Mrs. Johnson."

She had so many things to be grateful for. Margale was a jewel. She had 3-Oaks and Diane, of course, and Dottie, too, even though she was in Atlanta, and Star. She was almost ashamed to admit, however, it was the thought of a day at the beach with Kevin McCoy that caused Ginger to jump out of bed. She brushed her teeth and washed her face. She caught her long red hair into a ponytail and slipped into a silver silk robe.

Stepping onto the terrace, she saw that Margale had just set breakfast for her on the glass table decorated by tulips in a vase. She threw her arms around Margale and gave her a hug.

"Good morning, Margale. Oh, what a glorious day."

"You look so rested, Mrs. Johnson. Glad to see you back to your old self. Will you be here for lunch?"

"No, I'm going to the beach with a friend, but I'll be home for dinner. Could you make crab cakes, cold tomato soup and whatever else you think?"

Margale smiled.

"Yes, Mrs. Johnson."

Ginger had a thought.

"Margale, make that for two."

"Yes, Mrs. Johnson. Would you like dinner in the dining room or on the terrace?"

"I think the terrace, thanks. Now I'd better eat. Mr. McCoy will be here soon."

Ginger's zest for life and her appetite both returned at once. Ravenous, she sat down and ate quickly. She had to change for a day at the beach.

Upstairs, looking through her bathing suit drawer, Ginger chose a simple turquoise one piece suit, a turquoise and white Paisley tunic and matching Jack Rogers sandals and returned to the terrace. She tried reading the paper, but it was a challenge. She was excited for the two-day vacation to begin.

At exactly 10:30 Margale came out onto the terrace.

"Mr. McCoy is here," she said and then retreated.

Kevin appeared. "Morning, Beautiful." He looked deeply into her eyes.

"I had a wonderful time last night."

"I just asked Margale to make dinner for us, if you'd like to have dinner here —"

"That's the best invitation I've had all day!"

"Do you like crabcakes?"

"I love crab cakes."

"Then it's settled."

"Shall we take my golf cart? There will be towels and umbrellas at the beach. Ready?"

"I was born ready!"

They walked through the immaculate, spacious kitchen and out to the garage. The site of the pair of golf carts startled Ginger. His and Hers. One was emblazoned with the letters *TJW,* and the other with the monogram *VJB.*

"I don't know why I still have Ted's cart," she muttered. "I really only need the one."

Ginger unplugged the cart with the dark green letters *VJB* on the side.

"We'll drive over the dunes. It's easier than going down the path. 3-Oaks has five miles of beach."

Surveying 3-Oaks for the first time, the grounds were even more impressive than he imagined: uniform architecture, part old world, but with the influence of the islands, pools and courtyards, manicured lawns with the squared-off hedges. These were not the high privacy hedges of Palm Beach. At 3-Oaks, members clearly wanted to show off their houses.

He took it all in.

"It's particularly nice now. We've had such warm weather for the past couple of months. The ocean seems to just get bluer. In the summer it's like the Bahamas: aquamarine and 85 degrees."

"I think I could spend the rest of my life here."

"But you have to get back to your job in six months. How about this spot?"

Kevin followed her gaze. Cream-colored canvas umbrellas were staked upright in the sand. Below them, matching mesh beach chairs equipped with attachable footrests beckoned. Nothing but the finest of everything at 3-Oaks.

"Looks good to me."

He leapt out of the cart, grabbed the bag, and set it down by the chairs. She loved his energy. Kevin wasn't ready to sit down.

"Want to take a walk?"

"Sure. It's fun to see the ocean houses from the beach."

They walked north on the sand.

"The beach is so empty."

"It's Tuesday. Most members play golf on Tuesday."

"I can't imagine wanting to be anywhere else."

"It's incredible how you get used to it."

"Used to what?"

"All the beauty. Most members only use the beach on holidays or when their families come on vacations."

They stared out at the blue sky and the bluer water.

"It's like being on a deserted island."

"I haven't been in for, I don't know, maybe a year. I love to swim in the ocean, but Ted didn't like it. Occasionally, on the rare Sunday, he'd come down, but the wind was always blowing his papers, and they got sandy."

"It's a pity."

"What is?"

"When a man can't relax. When he can't appreciate the beauty right in front of him."

Kevin wasn't looking at the turquoise water. He was looking at Ginger. She blushed. Suddenly, a shallow wave washed over their feet.

"It's so warm!" he exclaimed. "How about a swim after we get back to our spot?"

They turned and headed back across the sand.

"Tell me about Ted. He must have been a special guy to have snagged you. What was he like?"

"Ted always had a larger-than-life personality. But he wasn't tall, only a little taller than I am. We were about even when I wore heels. He was handsome.

Blue eyes and wavy hair. A reddish complexion. Ted was Irish through and through. He loved work, golfing, and boating, in that order. We had a boat, *Victory*, with a captain, and crew. In the summer we'd take it to the Bahamas. I think the boat was the only place Ted could relax. We fished, watched movies, and swam. There is nothing like the water in the Bahamas. It's so clear, you can see the bottom, all peppered with starfish. The sand on the island is so white and fine…it's like powdered sugar! Have you been to the Bahamas?"

"No. Do you still have the boat?"

"We sold it, sadly. Ted didn't have enough time. We stayed here mostly and went to Atlanta now and then. We have a house on Nantucket. We used to go, but his children used it a lot and, as much as he loved his grandchildren, all the commotion put him on edge. We stopped going there, too."

"Sounds like you had a great life with Ted."

"Yes. But those days seem like a long time ago."

"At least now you have the kids and the grandchildren."

Ginger nodded slightly, sadly.

"I'm sorry. I just assumed you're close to the kids. I mean, you came into their lives so early."

"It's complicated. While Ted was alive, even when his mind was gone, they were nice. Emily, the youngest, was warm and fun, too. We had a good relationship, at least I thought we did. Things have changed since Ted died. It's come as a surprise, but maybe not. There are issues with the estate. But I have a new lawyer, he's very highly recommended, and he assures me he can straighten things out. Still, it's a headache."

"Things will work out, Ginger." When he took her hand, Ginger didn't resist his touch.

When they arrived back at their spot, and sat, side by side, in their chairs. The beach was still empty.

"Let's rest for a moment, before swimming," he said. "I love talking to you, Ginger. I love just being with you."

"I'm enjoying you too, Kevin, only I've done all the talking. Tell me about you, and your family. When did you learn to fly?"

As he spoke, he was in profile and Ginger found herself captivated. He seemed to flicker between man and boy, and this fascinated her.

"I always liked airplanes even as a little kid. I had toy planes and then I made model airplanes. I have a brother, John. Two years younger. Our father is a doctor and John's a doctor, too. Dad always wanted me to be a doctor, only I had no interest. My interest was planes. I wasn't a great student. John was though. I think my father always favored John. Once, he walked in when I had just shoved John, and he fell. Dad heard the noise, I guess. John had started playing with a model I had just finished. The glue wasn't dry. I grabbed it and pushed John aside, just as he walked in. Dad got a hold of me and shouted, 'Don't you ever do that again . . . ever. In this household we do not push people down, we share!' He took the model out of my hand and gave it to John. Then, he stormed out, disgusted. In our house, I felt as if I was a visitor. And that made no sense. I was there first and yet I always felt like I was only visiting. John did everything he was supposed to."

"What happened then?"

"He said, 'I shouldn't have taken your plane. I knew the glue was still wet.' He was such a sweet kid. He idolized me. Big tears rolling down his cheeks. I gave him the plane and said, 'Keep it.'"

"That's sad. Where's your brother now?"

"He works out of a hospital in Atlanta. I think. I haven't seen anyone in my family for a long time."

Sitting under the umbrella, they grew silent and listened to the waves.

"Look at the ocean. It's . . . unpredictable yet constant. The ocean always moves in one direction, and we do, too. We reach our shore when we are called home. We either break and crash like big waves or end in small ripples, peacefully."

"Called 'home?' Ginger, do you believe in God?"

"I do. I believe each life has a purpose and our job is to find that. God is always there for us, but man has free choice. We know that from what happened in The Garden of Eden. What about you Kevin? Do you believe in God?"

"I do and I don't. My mother was religious. My brother and I went to Sunday school and then when we were older, we went to church, Lutheran Church. We were raised to believe that the Bible was the word of God and all true. My father, however, being a doctor believed that everything begins and ends with science. I was torn, until I was 12. Then something happened that made me believe only in science."

Ginger waited for Kevin to explain but he said nothing more.

"How can one *not* believe in God when you spend all your time thousands of feet above the ground? I always find the view from above inspiring. Oh, I hope I haven't misspoken. It's just that . . . I don't know what I would have done without prayer throughout my life."

"Flying is all science. The plane does it all."

"When did you start to fly?"

"When I was 16. I used to take a bus to the airport and just watch the planes. Come on. Let's swim."

He jumped up and pulled off his shirt.

"Got lotion?"

Ginger nodded and reached into her beach bag.

"Will you do my back? Then, I'll do yours."

She flipped off the cap and squeezed the white lotion into her palm. Kevin had turned his back towards her. His muscles were taut, and his shoulders were strong. She rubbed the lotion into his back. He certainly had a great build.

"This red mark on your shoulder . . . Is it a burn?"

"It's a birthmark. I don't see it often. Only when I look in the mirror. It's kind of the shape of Florida, whatever that means. Maybe it's an omen. Thanks, now, let me do yours."

Ginger turned, anticipating his touch.

"Your shoulders are beautiful," he said.

At his first touch, she shivered. As he massaged the lotion into her back, his large hands were so strong, she had to resist and brace herself. She was relieved when he was done.

"Let's go! Race you to the water."

Kevin burst into a run and dove into the soft waves.

"How is it?" she shouted.

"*So warm! Come in!*"

Ginger followed and plunged in. Kevin caught her on the other side and held her up. Her heart was in her throat. She looked at Kevin.

"You look good all wet," he said.

Then, he tossed her lightly into the next wave and started swimming.

"Catch me if you can!" He shouted out, over his shoulder.

He was a powerful swimmer and swam way out. Exhilarated, Ginger threw herself on the surface and raced after him. When she caught up to him, he rolled over, laughing joyously, and floated on top of the water. Ginger did the same. He found her hand in the waves. For a while they floated, holding hands.

"I don't know when I've felt so relaxed. I love flying but it's stressful. It's good to have a break. I'm out for six months now. I might as well change my lifestyle and shed the stress. 3-Oaks seems like a good place for that."

"It would be wonderful having you here."

Oh, so, so wonderful, Ginger thought to herself. If only I could feel like this for the rest of my life.

"Let's race back," Kevin rolled over and started back. Ginger followed him to shore.

Breathless, they staggered out of the water and onto the sand. They sank into their chairs on the beach, panting in unison. Then they grew quiet. It was a long time before either of them spoke.

"I'm so glad you suggested a two-day vacation."

"Me too," Kevin said. "But I'm starving!"

They walked towards the cabana bar.

The cabana bar was open all afternoon until four. Members ordered burgers, hot dogs, or salads, the special being the 3-Oaks Cobb salad, fresh turkey, ham, and hard-boiled egg with bacon, chopped tomatoes and chopped iceberg lettuce topped with Thousand Island dressing. It was delicious and deserved its fame.

"I'll have the Cobb, please. And an iced tea. Kevin?"

"Make that two, except — " He looked at her devilishly. Already, the sun had reddened his nose and cheeks. "Let's have a couple of Bloody Marys. After all, we're on vacation."

Ginger laughed.

"Two Bloody Marys. Thanks." Then she turned to Kevin. "You twisted my arm."

WHEN THEY RETURNED to the beach, they read and rested. Kevin looked over her *Town & Country* magazine, while Ginger read a novel. Now and then, her eyes left the page and sought out his. She noticed that he did the same. They seemed to share the same contentment in one another's presence. It was uncanny. It was wonderful. They spent the day like this.

After, Ginger let Kevin drive the golf cart back to her house.

"Thanks again for a brilliant day. See you at seven."

"Yes," Ginger replied, dreamily.

She took a long shower and dried her hair. She pushed the intercom and spoke to Margale.

"Mr. McCoy will be here for dinner at 7:00. Surprise me with dessert."

"Yes, Mrs. Johnson."

GINGER WAITED FOR Kevin on the terrace. What a lucky woman I am to have been married to Ted, and now to have met Kevin. Her heartbeat fast at the thought of him.

"Good evening, beautiful. A beach day suits you. Stand up, let me see all of you."

Ginger stood. She was wearing a strapless, sapphire blue, at-home dress that went to the ground. She wore lapis and gold earrings, and gold sandals. Her long red hair was pulled back into a ponytail.

"Wow."

"Stop, Kevin. You're embarrassing me!"

"What is there to be embarrassed about?"

Ginger pivoted. "You know where the bar is. Help yourself to a drink and pour me a little vodka on ice. There are twists and olives already out. I'll take a twist."

Kevin went into the library. He felt at home in her house, and he liked the feeling. How long had it been since he had a home? He had left his family, gone off to flight school, and spent his career crisscrossing the globe. For years, he was always on the move. Even so, at Northwest, he never made captain. He was always in the third seat. When would he land somewhere? Kevin made Ginger's drink, a hefty one for himself, and went back to the terrace.

"Just look at that red and purple sky."

They stood gazing out and Ginger explained which hole they were looking at, the landscaping features it was famous for, and the challenges. Kevin finished his drink quickly. Too bad he hadn't taken up golf like his dad and his brother. It sure would come in handy here.

Margale was at the door.

"Dinner, Mrs. Johnson."

With a glance, Ginger invited him to the table. He pulled out her chair. The air was warm. The lanterns on the terrace were lit and the hurricane lamps sparkled with candlelight. Margale served them.

I could get used to this, Kevin thought. She's not half bad for an old broad.

How nice to dine at home with a man, Ginger thought. It's been over four years. Kevin was handsome, caring and so attentive. Kevin was kind with words. His words seem to erase decades off of her. He was wearing a navy linen shirt opened at the neck, white pants, and red moccasins with no socks. How natty he looks.

After serving them, Margale left.

"Are we going to ride tomorrow? I'd love to see 3-Oaks as you described, on horseback, before I look at the golf cottages."

"Of course. Diane said you can ride Hunter."

"Great. Then we can swim, that is if I'm still alive!"

He laughed and threw his head back. There was something lovely about the way he laughed, Ginger thought to herself.

Expertly opening a bottle of pinot, Kevin surprised her with a question.

"Do you have a secret?"

Ginger hedged.

"What do you mean?"

"I'm just so curious about you. Tell me more about your life."

"I've led a vanilla life. After college, I went to secretarial school — "

"Per your father's wishes — "

"Yes, exactly, and got a job. Then I met Ted. You know the rest. At least then my mother didn't have to work, and my father retired. I think it had been hard for her. No one else's mother worked, maybe one or two. Ted was very generous with them. He was that way with everyone. He bought them an apartment in Stewartville, and they were very comfortable to the end. I had a modest upbringing, but with lots of advantages."

"Did it bother you being less affluent than the other girls at Miss Hall's?"

"Definitely. That's why I painted all the time. It was something I was good at. It made me feel special. And I guess it was sort of an escape, too."

"The feeling of not belonging, or fitting in. That's something I know about."

"I remember one incident. Julia Kent was a girl at Miss Hall's. She invited me for a sleepover. My father took me to her house. We drove up a long drive to the front door. The house was enormous. It was white with large columns. I had never seen anything like it. It looked like The White House! My father put my small bag by the front door and rang the bell. An elderly man answered the door. He was wearing a white jacket and white gloves. 'Miss Julia is in the playroom. Follow me, please.' We crossed a black and white diamond marble floor to a spiral staircase. A small woman in a black uniform, with a white organdy apron and cap, was waiting for me. She took my bag, and we climbed up the stairs. I expected to see angels at the top of the stairs! 'Miss Julia is very excited to see you, Miss Ginger.' She led me down a hall to the playroom. There were more toys than at *Toys R Us*. The rug was a deep green and thick, like grass. 'I'll unpack your things, Miss Ginger. You two play until dinner and you'll eat in the children's dining room.' Then Julia came in and said, 'Oh, I'm so glad you're here! My nurse Eleanor was going to make me practice the piano!' Julia and I had a grand time. But the next day, she said to me when I was leaving, 'When may I come to your house?' I never invited her. How could I? I was ashamed. Then I felt ashamed of being ashamed. I never told that story to anyone. I guess I did have a secret. Julia Kent."

Kevin was finishing Margale's apple crisp and yet another glass of wine. His cheeks were flushed.

"Do you have a secret, Kevin?"

His eyes held hers. Then he seemed restless, got up and paced. He circled round the terrace, then came back to her chair and put his hands on her shoulders. As he talked, he started to massage her back.

"I was 12 years old, and my hormones were going crazy. I wasn't the easiest preteen; I couldn't sit still in school. My brother, John, was an A student and good at sports. An all-around model son. I was . . . I suppose you could call it, a prankster. I excelled at, you know, the Gentleman's C. I only liked track, because when I ran I felt powerful and free. Anyway, I was in my room — it was after dinner — I started downstairs to get myself a snack."

Kevin's hands moved to her arms. She felt herself flush and didn't dare move. Was she under his spell or his hostage?

"My parents were in the living room talking. My mother said something about getting a call from the school. Then I heard his fist pound the table and I stopped on the stairs. 'Damn,' he said, 'It's his genes! What do we know about his parents!? Nothing!' My mother was upset and said, 'We agreed *never* to talk about that. He is our first son, and he always will be. You can't ever let out that he's adopted. Everyone's different. John will probably go through the same things when he's 12. Remember when you were a boy. Don't be so hard on him. I'll talk to his teacher.' Who were they kidding? They both knew John would never be like me. I turned and tiptoed back up the stairs. I had been abandoned and adopted. I didn't belong. My father was right. They were different and DNA doesn't change. From that night forward I was a stranger. I went through the motions of being part of it all, but I withdrew. I felt tormented, unloved, and now abandoned — not once — twice. John couldn't figure out what was wrong. He asked me all the time what the matter was. But I shut him and everyone else out. When I wasn't at school I was in my room. When I wasn't in my room, I took the bus to the airport and watched the planes taking off. There was speed. There was excitement. I was going to fly. I would escape into the air. I decided to learn as soon as I was old enough. One day when I was getting off the bus, John saw me. 'Where have you been, Kev?' None of your business, I said. 'Oh, come on. You can tell me. I won't tell mom and dad.' 'I won't. Leave me alone.' But he persisted. 'Kev, I'm your brother. You can trust me. Come on, what's eating you?' I stopped. I looked at John. 'You're not my brother and mom and dad are your mom and dad, not mine.'"

"What did he say?"

"He didn't believe me. 'Oh, come on Kev. You're crazy. Just because they're on your back about school doesn't mean they don't love you.' So I said, 'John, I'm adopted.'"

"What'd he say then?"

"He was in shock. 'What do you mean, adopted?' I said, 'Adopted . . . Somebody . . . that is, my real parents, they didn't want me and gave me away. Your parents adopted me, but I don't belong to them. I heard dad say so. 'Not the same genes' he said."

"He loved you. You were his big brother. I can't imagine it made any difference to him."

"It didn't. 'I don't care what you heard, or they said. You're my brother. Do they know you know?' 'No — and if you tell them, I'll kill you.'"

"Rough conversation. Hard on both of you."

"He was just trying to take it all in. 'Kev, I told you, you can trust me. I promise and I'll never break my promise.'"

"He idolized you."

"To this day, I think of him as my brother. I actually felt better after telling him."

"I guess he kept his promise."

"We never spoke of it again."

Kevin dropped his hands from her shoulders and fell silent. He seemed spent. The candles in the hurricane lamps had lowered. The two bottles of wine stood empty. He hadn't planned on telling her his secret. He had to collect himself.

"Guess it was my turn to talk your ear off."

She wondered if he regretted his disclosure.

"We both had a secret to share."

"I've had a lot of wine, and sun. I think now I'll leave, Ginger. We've another busy day tomorrow."

"Riding, and the beach," she said and stood.

He kissed her on the cheek. He could tell she was succumbing to his charms. He'd felt her shiver under his touch at the beach and again at dinner.

"Good night, Ginger."

Ginger sat alone in the dark. She watched the candles dwindle down to the last inch. Her life had shifted, from the recent years of seeming to live in slow motion to now. Suddenly everything was in quick time. Her emotions were on high alert, agitated and exhilarated. His words stirred her, and so did his touch. She was starting to truly care for him. How to account for how quickly these feelings had developed? Was it due to years of emotional deprivation? A hunger for connection that she had forgotten was even possible? Or was there something real resonating between them? So much had happened to her since she met Kevin.

Now, she sprang out of bed in the morning and opened her drawers looking for alluring outfits. Sitting in the near dark, she felt elated, a kind of dizzy happiness she hadn't felt since, well, since she was a teenager and in love with Frank Pierce. Even now, so many years later, this memory returned vivid and pulsing. She'd put it aside, stashed it away while Ted was alive, but now that he was gone, there was nothing to keep her from remembering Frank. Kevin's secret caused her to recall her own.

CHAPTER 14

A GOOD NIGHT'S sleep seemed to have restored and steadied them both. In the morning, Kevin sauntered into the living room and greeted her with a kiss on either cheek. She felt confident and looked attractive in her crisp white shirt and her crème-colored riding jodhpurs.

"Hope I can ride in jeans. I don't have proper riding clothes."

"Hunter won't know the difference. Just hang on with those tennis shoes. We're going to walk the trail around the grounds."

"No galloping?"

"Not even a canter."

"Okay, that's a relief. If I move here, I guess I'll have to get a horse."

"Don't worry about that. They're plenty of people who'd be delighted if you'd exercise their charges."

Kevin was looking steadily at Ginger, as if his mind was somewhere else.

"What — ?"

"About last night — "

"I had a lovely time."

"I think I imbibed a little too much — "

"Long day . . . lots of sun."

"I'm sorry — "

"Nothing to be sorry about."

"I can't wait for the ocean."

"Me too," Ginger said.

"And maybe a beer at lunch."

They laughed.

"Hair of the Dog," they said in unison.

When they got to the stables, Robert had readied the horses.

Kevin closely watched as Ginger got on Star's back and into the saddle. He followed suit and climbed aboard Hunter. He had heard how horses can tell when you're nervous and tried to act nonchalant. He had to let Hunter know who was in charge. High up, and slow walking out of the barn, Kevin felt surprisingly at ease, mainly because Ginger was by his side.

His mother had signed him up for some lessons, so he knew the basics. Keep your feet tight in the stirrups, gentle pulls on the reins tell the horse where you want to go, and yank both reins to stop. But Hunter knew what to do. He was going wherever Star was going. Kevin felt the same way, but with his eyes on Ginger. With her velvet helmet and deep blue shirt, she looked like the cover of *Town & Country.*

"Want to try a trot?" Ginger asked.

"Sure."

"Let's go."

They turned onto the bridle path that made a loop around the grounds. Ginger was quiet, in a meditative mood. She smiled at him now and then and set the pace. Kevin caught on. He was free to look around at the old growth trees, the manmade ponds with mallard ducks and herons.

I could get used to this, he thought to himself. All of this, he thought, glancing at Ginger.

AFTERWARDS, THEY SWAM. Kevin kept touching her. Easily, he lifted her, carried her in both arms, and tossed her, releasing her lightly. She dove under, as exhilarated as a girl, grinning from ear to ear, her nostrils exuding a stream of bubbles. They raced and splashed and then ran back to their chairs, breathless. It really felt like a vacation.

"Ginger, I want to ask you, do you think there are any rooms at the club? Something I could rent for a few days through this real estate thing? I've been staying at The Sands, but they have a wedding party coming in tonight through the weekend. I checked the hotel in Treasure Beach, but they're booked too. Same wedding."

"Well, there are rooms. Not many though, and they go quickly. Why don't I check with Sally."

"That would be great."

"There's a party at the club tonight. It would give you a chance to meet some members and an idea of what 3-Oaks is like. It's just drinks but there'll be heavy *hors d'oeuvres* . . ."

She didn't want him to leave, not until he at least looked and hopefully found something at 3-Oaks.

"Why don't you stay in my guest room? It's downstairs, off the library."

"Are you sure it's not too much of an inconvenience? I'd love it and of course it would mean more time with you . . . breakfast, lunch, and dinner."

"It's a big house. It needs more life. You go to your hotel and collect your things. I'll tell Margale and we'll meet at 6:00. Just wear a blazer and a tie."

"I'll be there. Can I leave my car out front?"

"Why don't you return it? You can use Ted's Lexus. Or put the other golf cart to use. It's just sitting there."

"Perfect. Thanks!"

Maybe a little too perfect, Kevin thought.

"I'll grab my few things and be back . . . ready at 6."

Ginger could not believe she had invited him to come stay. But why not? she thought. It's only for a few days.

AT SIX, GINGER was waiting out front. She wore a sleeveless, white silk dress, and high heeled red alligator Manolo Blahnik sandals. Her hair was pulled into a knot on the top of her head. Her amethyst and peridot earrings hung down from her ears. Her skin glowed with a slight tan.

Kevin gamboled towards her.

"You certainly scrub up well."

It was true, too, he thought. She wasn't bad for an older broad.

They had a brief embrace.

"My chariot awaits, or shall we take yours?" Ginger said, with a playful smile and he understood that she meant Ted's golf cart.

"The keys are on the floor."

Kevin moved to Ted's cart, snatched the keys and took his place in the driver's seat, like it was made for him.

The main room of the clubhouse was closed on three sides except for the accordion glass doors to the terrace. These were open most of the time as the weather was almost perfect year-round. There was an easy and lovely flow between the bleached wood floors of the interior and the cream-colored stone of the terrace.

"Let's go out to the terrace. I'll introduce you around."

Ginger was slightly self-conscious about bringing Kevin, but only slightly. For a moment, she had thought to tell Diane and warn her that she'd have a date in tow, but then decided against it. She was allowed to have a life, wasn't she? After all she'd been through, did she have to run her every move by her friends? Having Kevin at her side made Ginger feel liberated, free of the need to rely on others.

Unfortunately, the first person they encountered was Louise Baker.

"Hi, Ginger," she said, blatantly ogling Kevin. Like most women in the 65-plus set, she had a keen radar when a younger, handsome stranger came within range.

"Hello, Louise. Kevin McCoy, I'd like you to meet Louise Baker."

He offered his hand.

"Good evening, Louise."

Louise ignored his hand and leaned into him, as if to smell the scent of his aftershave. Already, she was unsteady. Louise liked her martinis.

"How do you do. What brings the likes of you here, to 3-Oaks?"

"Kevin is looking at properties. He's looking to buy."

"Is that so? There's lots to look at around here. What do you do, Mr. McCoy, was it Ken?"

"Kevin. And I'm a pilot."

"Oh, what kind of plane? We have a G4, but Henry doesn't fly. Henry has pilots. Two pilots, to be exact."

"I fly Northwest."

"Oh, where do you live? Do you know Florida well —"

Ginger grabbed Kevin's arm and pulled him away. It wasn't maternal, but she had an instinct to protect Kevin from the drunken innuendos Louise Baker was famous for.

"She's often in her cups," she murmured, steering him away.

They moved to the next cluster.

"Diane! Kevin this is Diane Butler. Kevin, you rode Diane's horse today."

"Hello, Diane, I'm glad to meet you. Thanks for loaning me Hunter. He's a wonderful horse. Very gentle."

"Kevin is looking at golf cottages tomorrow with Sally."

Diane seemed surprised.

"You're moving to 3-Oaks?"

"I can't think of a place I'd rather be."

Diane looked at Ginger, who was especially dressed up and radiant, and then at Kevin. It was as if she was doing an equation in her head.

"Ginger, I haven't seen or talked to you for days. You just disappeared."

"That's my fault," Kevin said, smilingly.

"We've been having a vacation. Kevin suggested it. You know, the ocean is *so warm*. I don't think I've been in for years. It's divine."

"I see." Then, she cast a glance at Bill. He was holding court to a group of men, eagerly hanging on his every word. "Bill is with his usual cronies. They just gather around and lap up his Washington Report. He thinks he's a big deal, so they think he's a big deal, and everyone's satisfied. That's our life, I suppose." Diane sighed and turned back to Kevin. "How long are you here?"

"Well, I'm looking at properties in the morning —"

"Oh, that's right. Ginger, do you want to ride? And then we'll have lunch?"

"Lunch? When were you thinking?"

"Tomorrow."

Ginger glanced at Kevin.

"No worries," he said. "I'll have lunch with Sally or grab something. Lots of questions and decisions to make."

"Good. Ginger, I'll see you tomorrow. Ten o'clock, the barn? Or is that . . ." She paused, giving Ginger a significant look. "*Too early?*"

Diane's meaning registered with Ginger.

"Ten is perfect."

Ginger and Kevin pivoted and continued their tour of the room.

"There's Philip Baker. Let me take you to meet Philip. He's Club President, and then we'll just twirl through and go."

"Sounds great."

85

"Philip, this is a friend, Kevin McCoy. He's thinking of buying at 3-Oaks."

"Well, welcome, Kevin. It's a great spot, and you've met one of the top residents, I see," Philip smiled at Ginger. He had been a CEO of a public company before retiring and moving to 3-Oaks. Philip famously maintained his CEO habits. He rose at dawn, read a stack of newspapers while on the elliptical and was very disciplined about food and imbibing. He was an excellent president, appreciated all around for his leadership and tact.

"What do you have in mind Kevin? Going for the Warren place?"

Kevin laughed.

"That would be a lot for a single man, don't you think? Ginger and I walked through it the other day and . . . I don't have nearly enough suits!"

The men laughed. Kevin is so personable, Ginger thought to herself. It was a pleasure being with him. For years she went everywhere alone.

"Maybe one of the golf cottages is more your speed."

"That's what I had in mind. Sally is showing me around, tomorrow."

"You a golfer?"

"Yes, but I could use a brush up. The last few years I've spent more time in the air than stomping around on the green."

"A pilot, eh? Who do you fly for?"

"Northwest."

"We like pilots around here," Philip said, smiling approvingly. "We've got one or two of those."

Clearly, Philip liked Kevin. He was easy to like, for sure. Glancing around, she noticed the Millers looking over. It was bold of her to arrive with a man on her arm. Kevin's presence was creating a stir.

"Give me a ring, Kevin, if you decide to buy. I'll rush your application through. A friend of Ginger's is a friend of mine."

The men shook hands.

Millicent and Keith Miller arrived at their side, as did Jean and Don Li and the Stuarts. Ginger introduced them one by one, and Kevin shook each hand heartily in turn. It had been a long time since she had a man by her side. She admired his social finesse. She could tell that the women were especially impressed.

Finally, after another half hour of pleasantries, Ginger and Kevin were inching towards the door. Diane intercepted them.

"Leaving so soon?"

"Margale defrosted a couple of steaks — "

Diane raised an eyebrow and Ginger instantly regretted sharing this information.

"Can't wait until tomorrow. We have *a lot* to catch up on."

Oh boy, do we ever, Ginger thought to herself as Kevin got the cart. While Kevin talked to the valet, Ginger wondered just how much she'd share with Diane in the morning.

Kevin drove the cart as if he owned it. He parked with ease, as if he'd done it a thousand times before. They entered the house.

"Can I make you a drink, Ginger? I know where everything is."

"I'll just have a glass of white wine. I'll tell Margale we'll be ready soon. Thirty minutes?"

"Thirty minutes, perfect."

Kevin went into the library. He'd never seen such an elegant room, books all leather bound, a partner desk of rich mahogany with a bright green leather top and set apart from the wall, with a pair of armchairs, upholstered in leather, on each side. With awe Kevin wondered, what would it be like to command such a desk?

Now, now, let's not get ahead of yourself, he thought, as he poured Ginger's wine. He made himself a vodka on the rocks. He strolled through the hall and waited for Ginger in the settee at the base of the stairs and sipped his drink.

Upstairs, Ginger took her time dressing. Pale blue tonight, she thought.

Palazzo pants and a tunic top. Perfect. Sitting at her makeup mirror, she noticed her hand trembled as she re-applied eyeliner and mascara. Her thoughts were *Kevin, Kevin, Kevin.* An intimate at home dinner was exciting and scary.

Ginger descended the stairs.

Moon River was playing. Perfect he thought.

"Dance?" he said and pulled her into his arms.

They moved slowly. Ginger placed her cheek on his shoulder and closed her eyes. They moved and swayed. The music was transporting. For a moment she felt as if she was young again and in the arms of Frank Pierce. Frank held her just like this when they danced. Their song was, "*Fly Me to the Moon.*" In Kevin's arms she felt a vague ache. But was it for Kevin? Or for Frank? Confused, she pulled away and stood slightly apart.

"I think we've forgotten about dinner," she said. And then, calling in the direction of the kitchen added, "Margale, we're ready when you are."

"Everything's ready, Mrs. Johnson."

"We'll be right in."

Ginger went to the bar refrigerator and took out a bottle of Burgundy. Kevin took it from her and opened it. Then, side by side, they walked through to the dining room. At the table, Kevin held the chair for her, and she slipped into her seat.

Please, don't let this ever end, she prayed.

"Tomorrow's a big day. Sally and the cottages. After the Warren's manse, I am very curious about the cottages . . . Although it's hard to imagine being happier than I feel here. Thank you, Ginger, for making me feel so at home."

What would Diane say when she realized that he was living in her house? A shiver went down her spine. Kevin kept on talking.

"You're so generous. You're also smart, warm, kind — and beautiful."

He filled her glass with red. But who needed wine? Ginger was imbibing his words and felt drunk on them.

"And you're an athlete. An accomplished rider, and fast in the water, too —"

"Swimming was heavenly. I forgot how much I love the ocean —"

Ginger was about to say something about how Ted was not a beach person, but she stopped herself. She dared herself to throw away the old scripts and live in the present. A new life, with new interests — and maybe love.

"There's only one thing you haven't shared yet with me." His eyes danced on hers. She looked at him steadily.

"What's that?"

He paused, she shivered.

"Your paintings."

"Oh, I'd love to show them to you." Relieved, she started to ramble. "I have so many. But I have to get canvases ready for my galleries in New York and Houston. They are very demanding, not that I mind. Not at all, I love my time in the studio."

"It's a shame your parents didn't get to see how successful you are."

"Oh, they'd never believe it! They did recognize my talent, my grandmother especially, but being an artist to them was a guarantee of poverty! It came so easily. I just picked up the charcoal or pencil and images took over the page. My grandmother said I had a gift. She said I was '. . . a child of the angels!'"

Kevin raised his glass.

"To Ginger, a child of the angels!"

"Well, I don't know about that," Ginger took a sip of her wine. "But it's very important to have someone appreciate you. I know that. It makes a difference."

"How true," Kevin said and drank some more.

"Actually, she was my angel. You know, I have more memories of being with my grandmother than I do with my mother. When I was with her, I felt special. And I felt special drawing. Thank you, Kevin."

"For what?"

"For reminding me of what makes me feel myself. Like swimming in the ocean. Like my art. I guess this a good time for me to remember what makes me feel special."

"You're very special. In fact, I can't think of anyone as special as you. I am the lucky one, Ginger. I'd like to know you forever."

Margale entered with a tray.

"I've made your favorite, Mrs. Johnson," she said clearing the plates. Then she set down before each of them a small *chocolat pot de crème*.

Kevin laughed, throwing his head back in his delightful way.

"It's time to throw caution to the wind, don't you agree, Ginger? Let's just enjoy ourselves," and with that, he plunged his spoon into the dessert.

He was right. She had set aside her passions, and followed her parents' wishes. She was obedient and said yes to Ted as soon as he had asked her. His proposal was a lifeline and the chance of a life beyond her wildest dreams — not just security but luxury, multiple homes, a boat anchored in the Bahamas, and travel on private planes. She had loved him, yes. They'd had many wonderful times and years, but she had never felt for Ted the delirious passion she knew was possible. And now, it felt right to be daring, to set aside what anyone else thought. She was 68 years old. Didn't she deserve to live life on her own terms?

"*You must remember this, a kiss is still a kiss,*" Kevin sang along with the song. He rose and offered her his hand. "*The world will always welcome lovers, as time goes by.*" He held her in his arms and turned her slowly. He was a superb dancer. How was that possible? So much was unsettled, concerning Ted's affairs and the children, but dancing with Kevin, Ginger felt that everything was going be fine.

"Ginger, I can't remember ever feeling like this before," he murmured in her ear. She stopped and stood still facing him, shocked to hear him say the words she was thinking. She studied his face. He was serious.

"I know. We don't really know each other that well, yet . . ." She hesitated. His heart was in her hands, and she didn't want to say the wrong thing. "Only once

90

before have I felt the way I feel about you — ”

“I can't compare to Ted — ”

“Not Ted. Someone else. Before Ted — ”

Ginger felt she was being disloyal to the man who had given her everything.

“This was someone else. I was very young, a teenager! A very long time ago. I'm older now and wiser — ”

He cut her off.

“Never mention age, okay? It means nothing to me.”

His tone was jarring. It ripped the delicate mood between them. She took a step back. The song played on: “*Moon light and love songs, never out of date, hearts full of passion, jealousy and hate . . .*”

“I'm sorry, Ginger.” With her, he had the disturbing instinct to speak from the heart and tell her about his life. “I was married, too. A long time ago, to someone exactly my age. Everyone said we were right for each other, perfect for each other. Only it wasn't true. She was immature and spoiled. She was my ideal, or so I thought. But a pilot's salary wasn't enough for her. I wasn't enough for her. She had an affair and we split, after only a year and a half.”

Abandoned twice. No wonder he was so vulnerable, and volatile. She had been long married, but now she understood that she had always felt lonesome. Was it possible that in one another they each found what they had been missing?

They were still in the hallway. Kevin looked deeply into her eyes.

“Ginger, right now, there's nothing I want more than to follow you up those stairs . . .” Her heart was racing. “I want to spend the night — the rest of my life with you.”

“Oh, Kevin, Kevin, darling. Talk to me tomorrow, let's discuss this when there's been no wine. One more night like this, and I might have to go to Betty Ford!”

One minute she was elated at the idea of throwing caution to the winds and the next minute, she was clinging to the railing of everything that was familiar in her life. But he looked crestfallen, like a child.

"Kevin, I . . . I . . ." she stammered. Just as she was about to take his hand and lead him up the stairs, he interrupted.

"I can wait."

He kissed her. On the forehead, sweetly, tenderly.

"Good night."

Ginger turned and walked up the stairs alone.

For once, she abandoned her evening rituals. Ginger dropped her clothes in a puddle on the floor by the bed, pulled on her yellow silk nighty and slipped into the safety of her sheets. She was filled with excitement, with dread. Was it sexual excitement or anxiety? After a half an hour of consternation, Ginger took 5 milligrams of Ambien and went to sleep.

CHAPTER 15

IN THE MORNING, but later than usual, Ginger rang for Margale. "Is Mr. McCoy up yet?"

"Oh, yes, Mrs. Johnson. Up and gone. He had an appointment with Sally, he said, and would see you midafternoon. He mentioned a swim and maybe Eddie's, for dinner?"

"That's right. Take the night off, Margale. Did you give Mr. McCoy breakfast?"

"I offered, but he said he didn't want to be a bother. I told him it was no bother, but he said he'd just get a bite in town — "

"Well, you can make breakfast for me, I'm starving."

"Yes, Mrs. J."

"I'll have coffee, juice, two eggs and toast."

"Yes. Mr. McCoy took Mr. Johnson's car."

"I told him to use Mr. Johnson's car while he's here. I'm going riding with Mrs. Butler."

But that wasn't for an hour. Ginger needed to talk. When she hung up with Margale, she dialed Dottie in Atlanta.

"Oh, Dottie! I'm so glad you're there. Can you talk?"

"Ginger, I was just thinking I hadn't heard from you *for days*. You dropped off the edge of the earth! I'm about to take my daughter shopping. Is everything alright?"

"Yes. As a matter of fact, I'm more alright than I've ever been in my entire life!"

"Well, of course, you are. You have to be terribly relieved about Ted. He's in a better place, at last."

"This isn't about Ted."

There was a speechless silence on the other end of the line.

"Dottie, I've met someone! I'm in love!"

The confession was a relief. All the feelings and the words that she and Kevin had said to each other last night became more real and flooded her with joy. She knew Dottie would be happy for her.

"What did you say?"

"I said, I think I'm in love. In fact, I know I am. Dottie, I haven't felt like this since Frank Pierce!"

"Frank Pierce? You haven't mentioned that scoundrel in decades."

"I know, and he was a scoundrel. But Kevin, that's his name Kevin McCoy, reminds me of Frank — "

"That's a good thing?"

"I mean, he reminds me of how I used to feel about Frank Pierce!"

"Ginger, your husband is newly ensconced in heaven and you're taking up with someone who reminds you of Frank?"

"Oh, no, I didn't mean it to sound like that — "

"Are you free to talk later today? At 5?"

"I can't. Kevin and I have plans for a swim."

"What about this evening?"

"He's taking me to dinner."

"Is Mr. McCoy completely monopolizing your calendar?"

Ginger laughed.

"I'm free tomorrow morning."

"Are you sure you don't already have plans with Mr. McCoy tomorrow morning?"

"I'm sure. Are you free at 9?"

"Yes, and you're going to have to tell me all about Mr. Kevin McCoy."

"I'll tell you everything. I promise."

Ginger hung up the phone and sighed. Talking to Dottie was such a relief. There was no need to be guarded. Suddenly, she remembered her plans with Diane. She jumped out of bed, threw on her riding clothes, hurried through breakfast, and left for the barn.

DIANE WAS IN the stall and readying Hunter for their ride. Adjusting the strap of a stirrup, Diane looked over her shoulder at Ginger.

"You're very chipper this morning. Good night's sleep . . . ?"

Ginger sensed Diane's curiosity and focused on readying Star right away. But she was so happy, it was hard to suppress her excitement.

"Not really. I took an Ambien though and that helped."

"I thought you didn't take those anymore."

"I don't, only sometimes."

"You're processing Ted's death. You were married forever, you don't get over such a loss in a month."

"Actually, it wasn't about Ted . . ." She was veering towards the subject and couldn't stop herself. "Something wonderful has happened and I was so excited I couldn't sleep!"

"Something exciting? At 3-Oaks? Tell me!"

"I'll save it for lunch," Ginger said, slyly.

"Such self-control."

Hunter was ready and so was Star. The women hoisted themselves up.

"I'll tell you everything at lunch."

"All?"

"All," Ginger said, laughing. It made her feel special to have intriguing news. She gave Star a little kick and off they trotted. Diane and Hunter followed close behind.

It was amazing to Ginger how, now that Kevin was in her life, she was empowered to make decisions for herself. She felt calm, not always looking to others, even her dear friends, for advice or guidance. She had Kevin now. Would she really become Mrs. Kevin McCoy? Riding Star along the path of 3-Oaks, through tree-lined trails and on the stretch along the manmade lake, Ginger hardly noticed her surroundings. She was entertaining visions of her new life. Diane wasn't a chatter box, like so many women she knew. They enjoyed riding without talking. The easy silence between them was another bond.

BACK AT THE stables, Robert, the stable master, took the reins for Star and Hunter, and escorted the horses back to their stalls for a curry comb and water.

"Ready for lunch?"

"You bet. I only had coffee and toast for breakfast."

At the entryway of the clubhouse restaurant, they surveyed the boisterous crowd.

"Louise is holding court, as usual," Ginger said.

They came to the same conclusion.

"Let's sit in the corner," said Diane.

"Agreed. She not only has a big mouth but big ears."

As soon as they took their chairs, Alfredo was by their side. If only the club members were half as discreet as the staff.

"Good afternoon, ladies."

"What's the special, Alfredo?"

"Today we have a French dip and shrimp Louie."

"I'll have the shrimp. What about you Diane?"

"The same. And, an iced tea, please."

"I'll have an Arnold Palmer," Ginger said. Ted had introduced her to Arnold Palmers. He always had one after golf. On the trails Ginger had felt the liberty to imagine her life. Now her thoughts were complicated by Ted. How much shall I tell Diane? she wondered.

"I hear the Warrens got a bid on their house."

"That's yesterday's news, Ginger. I want to hear about whatever it was, or *whoever it was*, that made you so excited you took an Ambien! Come, on! You look like the cat that swallowed the canary!"

"Okay. Well, I'm in love."

"You're what?!"

"In love . . . with Kevin McCoy."

"Ginger, have you lost your mind? In love with *Kevin McCoy*? You just met Kevin McCoy! Have you known him even a week?"

"Diane, I know. I know I sound like a crazy old lady, but I have never felt this way in my life. I mean, not since I was in my teens."

"Ginger, what do you know about him? How old is Kevin McCoy, anyway?"

"I know a lot. And I know that Kevin says he wants to spend the rest of his life with me and that's the way I feel about him. At least I think I do. I don't think, I'm certain I do."

Diane sat stunned and staring at her.

"I don't know how old he is. He refuses to discuss age. He forbids me to even talk about it! We haven't made any plans, but I will be talking to my lawyer next week and as soon as the estate is settled, I want to move on. I don't care what other people say or think. Diane, you know better than anyone what the last three years have been like. Please, be happy for me!"

"Okay, okay. But we need to get to know this Kevin McCoy better. How about coming for dinner Saturday? Just the four of us. I'll postpone any lectures until we've all had a chance to get to know him."

"Thanks, Diane. We'd love to."

"Where's he staying?"

"At my house."

"*Oh, my God.*"

"In my guestroom, Diane."

The two shrimp Louie arrived just in time.

CHAPTER 16

S ATURDAY EVENING, they took one of the golf carts to the Butlers for dinner and Kevin drove.

Ginger had been giddy through the past 48 hours. Kevin couldn't stop talking about their life together. She yearned to have him next to her upstairs, to have his clothes in the closet, and his toothbrush next to hers in the sink. By his side, she felt a constant feeling of exhilaration, simple bliss. Had she missed all this in her years with Ted? With Ted, she had felt safety and a strong bond. He loved her, adored the very ground she walked on. But most of all he took care of her and in a way that nobody ever had before. This had many advantages; indeed, it had propelled Ginger into a world she'd only glimpsed at through her friends at Miss Hall's School. But there were also the negatives. She was learning this late in life, and only because of her feelings for Kevin.

"You're quiet tonight," Kevin said. She loved the way he noticed her moods.

"Just content." She smiled and he smiled back.

"Is this house the Butlers'?"

"No, no. Two down, same side."

They drove along.

"Someone around here sure knows how to make every house look like the next one."

"The Architectural Review Board. It's better than having a hodge-podge of houses."

"That's true," he said.

"You'll get used to it."

"I'll get used to it."

Soon he would be living with her at 3-Oaks, and she would be Mrs. Kevin McCoy. From now on, this is the way it was going to be — for the rest of her life. Going to parties, dinners and events with Kevin. Planning trips with Kevin, and not alone like all the other widows at 3-Oaks. How lucky I am, she thought. Could anyone be this happy?

As they pulled up on the lawn in front of the Butlers, she prayed Diane and Bill would see Kevin as she did. But if not, she simply didn't care. For the first time, Ginger felt secure and accepted for who she was. She was not judged based on where she came from or how much money her family had. Kevin was enough for her — his love, his understanding and acceptance was all she needed or wanted. She felt a pang of guilt about Diane and Dottie. Did her friends think her love for him was disloyal to Ted? Or, maybe, to them? She also felt guilty about her secret. He had spoken so openly and about so many things. Like his childhood and his wife leaving him. But she had not shared as openly with him. Ginger promised herself to tell him everything as soon as they were married.

Bill answered the door. He kissed Ginger on the cheek and shook Kevin's hand, then put his hand on Kevin's shoulder, drawing him in.

"Well, well. A rare sighting. You two have certainly been in hiding. Come out to the terrace. Let's have a drink. Ginger, pinot grigio? And Kevin, what may I get for you? It's still summer and summer rules are observed around here — that means you make your own. Or allow me. What's your fancy?"

"A vodka on the rocks, thanks Bill."

"How's Grey Goose?"

"My favorite. Thanks, yes."

Bill always talked broadly, as if addressing a whole crowd. His goal was to claim centerstage at the outset. He took the lead and held court. He usually succeeded, especially with new blood. Everyone wanted to hear about insider Washington.

Ginger stepped outside to find Diane. The terrace overlooked the golf course and the lake. The wrought iron and glass tables, always pristine and sparkling, were surrounded by white wrought iron armchairs with matching cushions. The Old Chicago brick was a contrast against their pale stucco house. Red geraniums in pots adorned each table, reflecting the red of the brick. Cocktails at the Butlers was a popular invitation. A dinner date was a rare honor. The table was set for four, and everything was so inviting. Would it be a successful intimate dinner, or would it be an interrogation?

Diane walked over to kiss Ginger and Kevin arrived at her side.

"How's my best friend? Kevin, so nice to see you again. I do hope to get to know you more. Everything is always on the fly here at 3-Oaks. We must make a point of seeing a lot of you. Ginger is a treasure. Our treasure. We have known her for over 30 years. Is it that long? Bill?"

"What?"

"How long have we known Ginger?"

"Since we moved to 3-Oaks. So, 30-plus years. Ted and Ginger were the first people we met, became best friends. It's such a loss. Did you know Ted, Kevin?"

"Kevin never met Ted," she said, attempting to pre-empt the topic.

"Of course not, Bill," Diane chimed in. "Kevin only arrived here recently."

"When was that, exactly . . ." Bill said.

"Almost two weeks ago," Kevin offered.

"Is that so? Well, that *is* recent — " said Bill with his back toward them. He was at the bar, pouring the drinks.

"Bill forgets everything. Kevin was here looking for a house. To move here.

They met at the Warren's open house."

"Big spread for a man on his own — "

"That's for sure," Kevin offered. "The cottages are more the ticket."

"Oh, well. Yes, that's more like it. Ted . . . he was a great golfer, a special friend. We played every Saturday."

Bill handed Ginger a globe of wine and passed a cocktail to Kevin.

"You play golf, Kevin?"

"I'm not really a golfer, no."

"Well, you can learn. You're so young. Great pros here, at 3-Oaks."

"I'll definitely try it out, if I move here."

"Good idea, great group of guys, a few your age, too. Although there are more old-timers like me clogging up the greens."

Why was Bill harping on age? Ginger wondered. Probably, this was just the beginning of this sort of talk, either to my face or behind my back. I'd better get used to it. I really don't care though. It is what it is, and this is what it's going to be.

Everyone was looking at Ginger. Was it possible they'd heard her thoughts? Diane saved her.

"Do you ride, Kevin?"

"I'm not an equestrian."

"But he did take Hunter out on the trails!"

"Thank you for lending me your horse."

"Sure. How'd he treat you?"

"Gentle. I managed to stay on board. But there's a lot of room for improvement."

"Well, you can learn," Bill said. "Wonderful riding master Robert, and you're young enough."

Ginger rolled her eyes. Diane noticed and changed the subject again.

"Ginger, I won at bridge today. 1.5 master points. At this rate, I'll be 90 before I become a life master. Do you play bridge, Kevin?"

"No, but I'd like to. And I'm young enough to learn."

Everyone laughed. Kevin most of all. He threw his head back and laughed freely, fully. Every time he did that, she was fascinated. Bill and Diane also seemed surprised. His congenial response was a victory. But Bill liked to win, especially on his own turf.

He pivoted and changed the subject.

"Next fall might be dicey," Bill said. "Going to make for a nasty election. What's your position, Kevin?"

Ginger watched Bill anticipate Kevin's answer. Alarmed, she realized that Kevin's political position was utterly unknown to her. Had she just made certain assumptions? They were so caught up in their deep conversations and so fixated on their future, they had never talked politics.

"My position is, may the best candidate win."

How diplomatic, Ginger thought. Her eyes flickered from Bill to Diane. But what did they think?

"Now that's what I call noncommittal," Bill said, and he jumped up from his chair. "Kevin let's go into my study, and you can tell me the real ins and outs of your thinking. I'll show you my humble collection of golfing trophies. Might inspire you to join in – that is, *if you move here.*"

Kevin stood and, again, Bill put an arm on Kevin's shoulder and steered him towards the study.

"I thought they'd never leave. Ginger, how are you?"

"Diane, I've never been happier in my whole life."

She raised an eyebrow.

"What have you been doing?"

"Just spending time together. Talking, having meals. We've been swimming every day. Diane, I haven't been in the ocean forever!"

"But you seem a little tense — "

"I guess it's seeing Kevin with Bill. Bill and you are Ted's old friends, and it makes me a little nervous — "

"That's understandable. Bill's protective of you, you know. He can't help it. We all are."

"That's nice, but the constant mention of age! Is that necessary? Kevin and I have discussed age, and it makes no difference to him. I already told you that. And I believe him, so please just drop it."

"Alright. I'm sorry."

"There's something I want to tell you. Only you mustn't repeat it."

"Girl Scout's honor."

"Kevin is spending the summer at my house."

Diane's face registered shock.

"I thought he was looking at real estate — ?"

"He is. He was. Sally showed him golf cottages. He likes them, but he needs to think about it. He told me how he feels about me, Diane. He said he wanted to spend his whole life with me. I asked him to spend the summer here at my house — "

Diane was dumbfounded, but Ginger's euphoria was unleashed.

"We have so many plans to make! Everything is so new. We need time to think together. The summer should be perfect. It's so quiet here in the summer."

"Have you spoken to anyone else about this? Like, your lawyer?"

"I know, I should probably get some legal advice about marrying Kevin, Dottie mentioned it. But first I have to get this estate situation settled with Ted's children. I haven't lost my mind completely! Kevin hasn't asked any questions about income or anything. I have plenty, only I don't know if he'll be flying because of his health."

"His health? But he's young — "

Ginger glared at her.

"Forget I said that. What about his health? What's wrong with him?"

At that moment, Aggie announced dinner. Ginger was spared from further interrogation.

Dinner with roast chicken, mashed potatoes, and peas, followed by Aggie's specialty, peach pie. As usual, Bill held court with monologues on politics and his meetings with this senator, that congressman, and even an hour in the Oval Office with POTUS himself. Diane had probably already heard these stories, maybe a dozen times. She appeared engrossed, but Ginger noticed how she fixed her gaze on Kevin. He didn't notice. Kevin was caught up in Bill's Beltway name dropping. Now and then, Kevin managed a secret wink in her direction and that warmed her. But dinner seemed endless. Ginger looked forward to it being just the two of them again, and for a postmortem on their first outing as a couple. Diane and Bill obviously assumed she and Kevin had turned her home into a love nest. What would they think, she wondered, if they knew the truth?

When Diane reminded Bill he had an early flight to Washington, dinner finally came to an end. Bill and Kevin walked to the door, and so did Diane and Ginger.

"When I get back from DC, we'll get together for golf."

"I'd like that."

"When are we riding Ginger?"

"Anytime."

"Let's talk tomorrow."

Bill and Diane gave Ginger a goodnight hug.

"Good night!"

"Good night!"

"Thank you!"

"See you soon!"

They closed the door and Kevin and Ginger were alone again. Ginger sighed with relief. In the golf cart, they were silent. They seemed to need a moment to recover. Was there a space between them, she worried. Or was she imagining it?

"Sorry about my friends."

"What do you mean? They're delightful. And dinner was delicious."

"Aggie is a great cook."

"Too bad I didn't take up golf, like my dad and my brother."

"It doesn't matter."

"They sure like their games. I think Bill forgot I don't know a putter from an iron. I guess you forget little things like that when — "

"When what?"

"When you have a big job in DC."

"And a big mouth. Maybe we weren't ready for that."

"What are you talking about? No one can touch us."

"That's right. No one can touch us."

They entered the house in silence and stood facing each other at the foot of the stairs.

"Night cap by the pool?"

Ginger broke into a yawn.

"No, but you go ahead."

He kissed her on the forehead. They both seemed to like their secret: they'd agreed to wait for their ultimate intimate moment. It was so important to them both and everything had to be perfect.

CHAPTER 17

IN THE MORNING, Ginger sat at her desk sipping coffee and watching the clock. At nine o'clock sharp, she picked up the phone and dialed Dottie. Ginger was excited for a heart-to-heart talk.

"Good morning, Dottie. How are you?"

"I'm fine. I'm sitting in my kitchen with my morning coffee. How are you?"

"I am sitting at my desk with my coffee."

"Good. We got all that out of the way. Now, tell me about Kevin McCoy."

Ginger laughed.

"Where do you want me to begin?"

"How did you meet?"

Ginger took a deep breath and began.

"I met him at an open house at 3-Oaks. He was interested in the property. I was there just looking — "

"Okay . . ."

"We started talking, he handed me a glass of champagne and, there was not a lot of time, so we ended up going through the house together. We instantly hit it off. After, he invited me to dinner. I said, 'Sure, why don't we just go to the club?'"

"You invited a stranger to dinner."

"Yes. But no. It didn't feel like that. He didn't feel like a stranger. We started talking and didn't stop. For hours and hours. The next morning, he called and asked if he could reciprocate. I'd taken him to the club, of course. At first, I said no, but when I looked at my calendar and saw day after blank day — and because I enjoyed his company, I thought, why not? We had another wonderful dinner. It was like we'd known each other for years. Then he asked me if I would consider spending the weekend with him — "

"That's rather forward. But you said, 'yes'?"

"I did."

"Doesn't he work, have a job?"

"He's a pilot with Northwest. But he's on leave. He had to wait to look at cottages here. We went to the beach. Dottie, *I hadn't been in the ocean in years!* You know what the last few years have been like. But Kevin and I went swimming! We just talk. And he listens! He cares about me and everything I do, everything I am. But it isn't just me doing all the talking. He tells me things he's never told anyone else."

"And what else do you do with Mr. McCoy?"

"I took him riding. He borrowed a friend's horse, and I was on Star. I am actually in love. You'll probably think I'm nuts, but Kevin is living in the guest room for the summer. We're going to work it all out and I want your advice. But, please be happy for me. Please support me. Dottie, please, please, please!"

"I don't know anything about this man! How much do you know about him?"

"I want you to meet him."

"Tell me you are talking with lawyers — "

"I'm going to Palm Beach next week to see Carl — "

"About a pre-nup. Tell Carl what you're thinking. Ginger, as your friend, I am advising you, you must be careful. Ted isn't around to protect you anymore — "

For a moment, Ginger was flummoxed. Ginger hated to think that Dottie was referring to the fact that there are men who prey on rich widows. But Kevin hadn't preyed on her. He hadn't even been upstairs and in her bed!

"I have to wonder if he did protect me, Dottie."

"Hush, child. You know that's no way to think."

There was a moment of silence between the friends.

"Don't let your heart run away with your head. Now, my time is up. I can hear my daughter out front, madly honking her horn. She must think I'm deaf! I love you, Ginger. Talk to Carl."

CHAPTER 18

"LET'S TAKE A VACATION today and go to the beach. It's my birthday."

"Your birthday? What's today?"

"May 15th."

Ginger was shocked. Her romance with Kevin had made her entirely forget the approach of May 15th.

"Kevin McCoy, or Baby Boy as the agency probably put it, born 50 years ago today. So you see, Ginger, I'm a half century today. A bonafide old man."

A puzzled look crossed her face. Hadn't they agreed not to talk about age? Kevin changed the subject.

"What a wonderful day it is too, to spend it with the future Mrs. Kevin McCoy. Someone gave me away once, but the one thing no one can do is take you away from me."

From now on, May 15th would be the best day, the day Kevin was born.

"What is it, Ginger?"

"Oh, nothing. Let's swim. Do you want to go to Eddie's for dinner?"

"Perfect. Jeans, fish, ice-cream — and the future Mrs. Kevin McCoy."

"And I want to swim all day with my birthday darling."

"WHERE'S THE COPPERTONE?" Kevin asked when they dropped their things in a pair of empty chairs.

"In my bag. Want me to do your back?"

He pulled off his shirt and turned away. Ginger unscrewed the bottle and began applying the lotion. There it was, the mark, the State of Florida.

"I'm rubbing the State of Florida . . ."

"Don't rub it away. It's a symbol now that the best is yet to come."

She concentrated on doing a thorough job and kept it to herself how curious her hands were about the muscles on his back and the slight taper from his broad shoulders to his waist.

"Give me the lotion, I'll do yours."

She turned away from him. First he warmed the gooey lotion in his hands, and then smoothed it on her shoulders and forcefully down and all around her back and arms. His touch was expert and powerful. Had Ted ever put lotion on her body?

Kevin finished and tossed the lotion on the chair.

"Let's catch a wave," he said and dashed towards the water's edge. She set down her hat and followed.

"Come here," he said, holding out his hand. "Let me dance with you in the ocean on the best birthday of my life." He twirled her around and around. She laughed. No, Ginger giggled. She had never felt so young and happy. When she closed her eyes, she was that young girl with Frank Pierce.

Kevin dropped her into a wave, then swooped her up again. He darted off in a freestyle and she chased after him. Soon they were both breathless and headed back out of the water. They walked across the sand and lay down exhausted under the umbrella. Kevin reached over and took her hand. He squeezed it three times.

"That's my signal. It means, 'I love you,' in case I want to tell you when we're in public. At that endless dinner at the Butlers, I winked at you, once or twice. Did you notice?"

"I wondered if you had something in your eye," she said, laughing.

"It was my way of saying, I love you. Now, we have a real signal."

Ginger squeezed his hand back, three times. The swim had been so refreshing. Had she ever felt so content? Before, she had always thought she was content, but nothing could touch the comfort and compatibility she shared with Kevin. He is my soulmate, she thought. They had spent the last two weeks together, almost every day and every evening. She glanced over at him.

"Why the faraway look?" she asked.

"You must be tired of seeing me in the same old bathing suit. I didn't bring many clothes when I came to 3-Oaks. I didn't expect to fall in love and stay. Is there a store somewhere around here? In Treasure Beach?"

"Yes, the Village Shop. They've great clothes for men." She was about to mention Ted, and how he ordered most of his clothes from The Village Shop. Luckily, she caught herself. "Why don't we go shopping?"

"You don't have to do that."

"I know I don't have to. But I want to. Let me spoil you on your birthday. We can look for what you might need for the next three months."

"It sounds wonderful."

"It's settled then. Lunch first at the beach cabana?"

"Sounds good," he said.

"Let's go now so we can get to the shop."

AT THE CABANA, they sat at their regular table.

"A Planters Punch?" Kevin asked.

"Well, why not? Though it might make me sleepy."

"After birthday shopping you can take a nap. Wait and see. You might be so excited by my new wardrobe; you won't need a nap. What are you having for lunch?"

"A Cobb salad, chopped."

He nodded, "Let's get two."

Kevin signaled for a waiter passing by. He certainly felt right at home. He seemed to like taking control. He was almost a little aggressive. No, that was negative. He just took charge. Ted had always taken charge. Men took care of women, but Kevin was so young, well, not that young. Her thoughts were going around in circles again. Why even think about it?

It is too bad Ted's things weren't smaller, she thought. Then, instantly, she felt guilty. Ted would have wanted her to be happy, right? Didn't people always say you could tell a happy marriage if someone remarried after a spouse's death? Ted would not want her to be alone. Or would he? He had been possessive but only in the nicest ways. He wasn't jealous, but he was proud. He always let people know she was his wife. The ease she'd felt frolicking in the water was gone again. Diane had said you don't get over a long marriage in a month . . . Maybe she was right. Was everything happening too fast?

"Now who has the faraway look?"

"Oh nothing. Just thinking about Ted. I mean, his clothes."

"What about them?"

"I mean, I haven't touched a thing in four years. It's time to let go."

"Don't think about that now. Not today. Just think about us. Not the past, just the future. That sounds selfish. But I am selfish when it comes to you. I want all of you."

She couldn't think of what to say. Not that this declaration didn't thrill her, it did. Only Ginger didn't know how to respond. What did he expect from her? It had been a long time since she had been wooed or courted. That sounded old fashioned. Maybe, pursued? She was hopelessly out of practice at romance. Was he impatient for sex?

Kevin seemed to read her mind.

"There's no hurry, Ginger," he said. "Let's take our time. From now on, we have forever." He squeezed her hand three times. Ginger blushed and gave him three pulses back.

After lunch they decided to take her BMW and Kevin offered to drive.

"Just tell me where we're going. I actually don't own a lot of clothes because I'm always in uniform, even on the layovers."

And those uniforms do a mighty work with the ladies, Kevin thought. They were a first-class ticket. No woman could resist him in uniform, that, plus his charm. Kevin was completely aware of his assets, and he knew just how to make them work for him. His brother always marveled at that.

Kevin opened the door for Ginger and off they went. When they were out of the gate, he pressed his foot on the accelerator and raced along Ocean Drive. It amused him to watch the old dame try and keep her hair down as the wind tossed it every which way.

Frank Pierce used to drive this fast in his convertible, she thought. Her hair was blowing around as it had with Frank, so long ago when she was young and in love. Why was she thinking of Frank so often? And Ted? Ginger closed her eyes and prayed to just be in the moment and enjoy herself. And from now on, May 15 would be a day to look forward to, not a day to dread.

"You're away again," he said, shouting over the engine and through the wind.

"You're a mind reader."

"I try."

"Well don't read all my thoughts. There have to be some surprises."

THEY ARRIVED AT the Village Shop and went in. A bell on the door announced their arrival in the quiet shop. Randy, the store manager, standing by his desk, looked up. His short dark hair was parted on the side, carefully combed, and secured in place with product. He was the epitome of preppy and perfectly modeled the clothes in the shop. When he saw Ginger through his tortoise-rimmed glasses, he smiled. Seeing Kevin, he seemed surprised. She could almost read his thoughts, but she ignored them.

"Hello Randy."

"Mrs. Johnson, it's so good to see you."

"This is Kevin McCoy. He's visiting and short on a few things. We'll just look around a minute."

"Of course, Mrs. Johnson. Just so you know, Al is in today."

Ginger tried to will Randy not to mention Ted, only it didn't work.

"Mr. Johnson always enjoyed a tailoring session with Al."

"Thank you, Randy, let's wait and see what Mr. McCoy needs."

"Mr. McCoy, feel free to use the second door on the right. It's the larger dressing room."

Ginger and Kevin shared a glance.

"Thanks," Kevin said, already engrossed by the stacks of gorgeous shirts in every hue. The two of them got to work, walking around the shop, gathering armloads of clothes. Ted had never ever let her choose his clothes.

"Do you think we have too many things?"

"Best to get it all at once, and not have to come running back for this or that."

"I don't need to try the shirts, just the pants. Maybe the trunks, too. just for size."

"Randy? I think Mr. McCoy is ready for Al."

Al appeared from the back.

After an hour of measuring and fitting, they were done.

Randy stood at the cash register, ringing up the pile of items.

"Let's see, we have two white jeans and two khakis. One Nantucket red slack and one in yellow. Is that correct?"

"Correct," said Ginger.

"Also, two navy polos, two blue stripe polos, and one yellow polo. Correct?"

"Correct," said Ginger.

"Dress shirts: two pink, two blue button downs, one white and one navy linen. Correct?"

"Correct," said Kevin, and gave Ginger a wink.

Randy went on. "One woven belt, one brown alligator belt, one tassel loafer and one docksider. Four bathing trunks."

"Do you think that's too many bathing trunks?"

"You love to swim and they're great looking."

Randy continued. "Which jackets are you taking?"

"The navy cashmere blazer. The beige linen. Oh throw in the white cashmere, too. Might as well."

"Yes, Mrs. Johnson."

"Good. When will Mr. McCoy's things be ready?"

"How's a week from now?"

"Fine. And, put it all on my account."

Randy raised his eyes over his tortoise frames, hesitated, then said, "Yes Mrs. Johnson, of course."

"It's Mr. McCoy's birthday."

"A most happy birthday, sir."

"Thank you, Randy."

"Would you like help to the car, Mrs. Johnson?"

"Not necessary," Kevin said, and Randy nodded.

They exited swiftly, the bell on the door jingled after them. As they crossed the parking lot, Ginger imagined Randy and Al watching as they filled the back seat with black and white striped bags, packed with shoe boxes, belts in tissue paper and brimming with shirts. Kevin held the door open for her, closed it and dashed around to the driver's side of her car. Soon they'll have to call me by a new name, she thought.

Kevin grabbed her hand, squeezed it three times, and then kissed it. Did he have a tear in his eye?

"You'll never know how much this means to me. I never had this many presents from my parents! This was like all my birthdays and all my Christmases rolled into one. I'm so lucky I found you. I'm so lucky you love me."

She squeezed his hand three times.

He peeled out of the lot.

As they drove along, now it was Kevin who was brooding.

Even my own birth mother would never have done something like this for me, he thought. Why think of her? I have no idea where she is, and I don't care. He never wanted to think of her again. But the old surge of anger flared and the pain ached. He hated her, that's all he knew about her.

CHAPTER 19

"**I** AM GOING to my studio for a while, then I'll lie down, and be ready at seven."

"Seven it is."

At the foot of the stairs, he watched her ascend. He hated to see her leaving, retreating into this whole other world that she had not yet shared with him.

"Ginger! When can I see your work?"

She turned on the stairs.

"I need to finish a few pieces first."

"Deal. We have so much to celebrate. First my birthday and then your art. You're going to turn me into a culture vulture!"

"Kevin. I don't want to turn you into anything. You are glorious as you are. Particularly in your new swimsuits and showing off the map of Florida."

Her eyes sparkled at him in a new way. Imagining him in all his new clothes, seemed to have had an effect on her. Soon he would achieve his goal.

"You're frisky," he said.

"Uh-huh," she said looking over her shoulder on her way up the stairs. She felt his eyes in her back, and it thrilled her.

CHAPTER 20

AFTER DINNER AT Eddie's, they were by the beach again, on the bench on the boardwalk, facing the ocean and a black field full of stars.

"Someday I want to put all those stars around your neck. And I will if I have to hijack a 747."

"I don't need diamonds. I like having them in the sky and looking up at them, especially with you. I have everything I ever wanted now and more."

"I have an idea. Let's get married on the beach!"

"Oh, Kevin I can't think of that now. I'm going to Palm Beach soon to see my lawyer. I have to get that settled, if I do, which I'm sure Carl can, he's the lawyer, then we'll go forward and make our plans. First, I need to wipe this slate clean. You understand."

"I hope you don't think I'm pushing. Well, I am pushing, but I understand. Is there anything I can do to help? Do you want me to come with you to the lawyer?"

"I have to do this by myself." Ginger changed the subject. "Should we have ice-cream?"

"What does my lady fancy?"

"A chocolate chip cone. Double dip."

"I'll be back."

Ginger felt tipsy. She could never tell if it was because of Kevin or the wine. They drank a lot of wine. Oh well, he's on leave. He can't drink when he's working. She wondered whether alcohol was bad for his stomach. Anyway, he certainly wasn't a complainer. Medication probably helped. Oh, she was lucky. Ginger had enjoyed watching her future husband being fitted for a new set of clothes. He cut such a handsome figure. Already, she was the envy of the women around her. The widows certainly, and the married ones, too. There was a little guilt swirled in with her excitement. She wasn't cheating on Ted. He was dead. Gone. But was this all too soon? No, she told herself. It was her time to live fully. Still, everything she had was from Ted. But why had he not signed that second trust? She had to call Dottie. She needed to talk through things with her friend.

Kevin returned with two cones, both double-dipped in chocolate.

"Is your cone chocolate chip, too?"

"Uh-huh."

Kevin always ordered what she did, and she wondered why. But the thought was a fleeting one.

"Hey! You're about to lose a drip!" Ice-cream was leaking out from under the crust of chocolate. "Lemme grab it for you." He leaned in towards her and made a clean swipe of her cone with his tongue. They burst into laughter. His boyishness delighted her.

"Just what I thought."

"What?" she asked.

"Yours tastes better than mine."

He put his arm around her on the bench.

THEY RODE HOME with the top down in thoughtful silence. Or was it a fraught silence? She'd had a similar feeling as a teenager. As the end of the date got closer, the tension as the boy drove her home. Would he park and turn off the car? Would he reach for the door handle to get out of the car and walk her to the door? Or would he turn the car off and turn towards her? When would the first kiss come? Or would it not? What did Kevin expect from her at the end of the evening on his birthday?

Inside, she headed at once for the stairs.

"How about a nightcap out by the pool?"

She sighed.

"Do you want me to spend the final hours of my birthday by myself?"

"Too much fun and sun — and wine!"

He took her hand, lifted it to his mouth and kissed it.

"Thank you for the best birthday of my life."

"I'll see you tomorrow."

"I'll see you tomorrow."

"Help yourself to anything."

Ginger wanted to go to sleep. She could hardly wait for May 15th to be over. It was not her favorite day. But for the rest of her life, May 15 would be a good day. From now on she would celebrate it with Kevin. She went through her nightly rituals. Put on her coziest nightgown, slipped in between her sheets, and instantly fell asleep.

AT FOUR IN the morning, Ginger woke and found herself drenched in perspiration and shaking. What had she been dreaming? What sort of nightmare? Ginger got up, went to her dressing room, and peeled off her damp nightgown. Was she sick? But the chill that ran through her body was not a flu chill, but a feeling of foreboding. She climbed back into bed, but sleep evaded her. She tried to remember her dream. There was a car, a convertible, a man driving, and his head thrown back laughing, but it wasn't Kevin. The face was blurred, and the car was going fast. The woman's hair was flying, it must have been her. She was the woman in the car, and she was laughing . . .

Why was this so frightening? The next image of the dream was all arms and legs, naked, and entangled. Did this scene represent Ginger's excitement or anxiety about having Kevin in her bed? It had been a long time since she had slept with someone. Ted had moved to the Memory Unit years ago, and before that, while he was tender with her, his interest in sex had fallen off. Besides, he had usually slept in the side bedroom because of his unsettled sleep and snoring. What would it be like to have a man in her bed? Her anxiety was understandable. She lay there and pictured the bodies in the dream. It wasn't her though because her body would be an older body. Dreams made no sense. What would it be like for Kevin to hold an older body? His love and obvious attraction to her would overcome that. At least she hoped it would. How could she best ready herself for the moment he was waiting for?

She reached for an Ambien.

CHAPTER 21

GINGER SLEPT UNTIL nine. Even in the morning, the dream haunted her. But whatever had possessed her seemed to have passed, and she felt normal and rested. Lolling around late in bed helped. Ginger rang for Margale. A morning alone should set her aright, she thought. It was a good day to catch up on things. Tomorrow she was going to the lawyer. It was an unpleasant thought, but Carl seemed confident.

"Margale, bring me a tray, please. In the studio. Tell Mr. McCoy I'll meet him for lunch. I have to finish some work."

"Mr. McCoy is gone."

"He is? Where did he go?"

"He took Mr. Johnson's car and went out for breakfast. Said I needed some time off. He's a nice man, so considerate."

"Did he say when he'd be back?"

"12:30 sharp, he said. And 'Tell Mrs. Johnson I'm going to explore Treasure Beach.' He told me he learned to fly here, at the Air Safety."

"That he did," Ginger was relieved. "I'll come downstairs quickly before I start painting and check his room, the flowers and everything. Then, I'll take the tray in my studio."

Ginger walked downstairs and into the guest room. The flowers could be refreshed a little. The room was neat. She walked over and opened the closet. Except for a few shirts, it was empty. She saw Kevin's red tennis shoes. Ted would never have worn those shoes; but they looked stylish on Kevin, with his white jeans and striped shirt. Soon, all of the new clothes she had bought for him would fill this closet. The striped bags from their shopping spree were untouched on the couch.

In the bathroom, there was a collection of prescription bottles on the counter. Ginger was curious. What exactly was his medical condition? He was rather evasive about it, but men never like to admit it if they were sick. She picked up the bottles one by one and read the labels. There was nothing she recognized. She went to the bedside table to get a pen and pad. She'd write down the names and ask the pharmacist. If it seemed that something serious was wrong, she would insist that Kevin see Dr. Marcus. Opening the bed stand drawer, Ginger saw some newspaper clippings. She lifted the one on top, looking for the pad. Then, she glanced at it, uncomprehendingly. The next one also bewildered her, but the third registered. The clipping read, "Theodore W. Johnson." It was Ted's obituary. She replaced it and closed the drawer. Forgetting about the prescriptions, she left the room. Why would Kevin have Ted's obituary in his drawer? He hadn't known Ted, or had he?

She walked back upstairs and into the studio. Agitated, she picked up her pencils and pale charcoal and began sketching on a canvas. A beach scene emerged, with a male figure in the foreground, his back to the viewer, looking out to the sea. She mixed her colors, then started on the head, the taut neck and the strained muscles of his back. Ginger painted quickly, mixing several tones, and using various brushes. It was always a challenge to get flesh color right. She turned off her mind, investing all thought and energy into making the figure's back into a strong, tense surface. Then she mixed blues and started on the sea beyond. The tension in the back was a contrast to the field of sea. The viewer would feel the contrast and sense the conflict. Would the ocean bring tranquility to the muscles? It was so good to be painting again. She channeled her anxiety into energy, and to bringing the canvas to life.

After a few hours, she stepped back and looked at the canvas. Unless it was a commissioned portrait, she never had anyone in mind when she painted. Pondering the figure, she knew it was familiar, but not Kevin. She closed her eyes and remembered the bodies in the dream. The back in the dream was the one on her canvas. The dream remained so vivid, both the first part in the car and then the naked bodies. Again, she viewed the dream in her mind's eye. The back, no face. There was a red mark on the back between the shoulders. She stepped away and left the studio.

It was almost lunchtime. But she needed more time to think. Ginger pushed the intercom.

"Margale, tell Mr. McCoy I'm not feeling well, a touch of the flu maybe. I'm going to stay upstairs today. He can take the golf cart and go to the beach for lunch."

"Anything I can do for you Mrs. Johnson?"

"No. Thanks. And Margale? No visitors. I'll ring later."

The dream didn't leave her. The man with the blurred face was Frank Pierce. Why was Frank in her dreams? It had been decades since she had been with him. Was it because Ted was gone, that images of Frank came to her again? She lay down and fell asleep again. When she woke, the shadows were low over the golf course. The clock said 6:00.

Maybe she was sick. She looked out the window, wishing she would see Ted, in this foursome, waving up at her. She knew for certain though that the figure in the painting was Frank. But the birth mark was Kevin's. And what about the clipping, what did it all mean? She thought of how totally in love she had been with Frank. Their song, *Fly Me to the Moon*, played in her head. They danced in his apartment. They danced before bed. They danced naked, after making love.

Her confusion was overwhelming. She had to talk to someone. How long could she stay up in her room? She needed Dottie. But Ginger had left so much unsaid to her friend. And, for that matter, to Diane as well. Would they forgive her? Who could she talk to?

Then, she walked back to her studio. She would lose herself in her painting, just as she had done her all her life. She pressed the intercom.

"Margale, make a tray for me in about an hour or so. Chicken, rice and vegetables. I'll have it upstairs."

"Yes, Mrs. Johnson. Mr. McCoy has asked several times if he could go upstairs and see you. I told him you said no visitors. He's worried about you, but he doesn't want to cross me."

"Thank you, Margale. I'm leaving early for Palm Beach. No need to tell him until I'm gone. He knows I have an appointment. But in the morning, I'll only be seeing you. About 7:00 am. I'll just take coffee in a to-go cup."

"Yes, Mrs. Johnson."

Ginger walked down the hall and opened the door to the studio. She studied her painting and knew just what to do. She started furiously with her brushes and lost track of time. The intercom interrupted her.

"Mrs. Johnson, I'll be bringing your tray up in 15 minutes."

"Make it a half hour. I'll shower first and *60 Minutes* will be on."

Ginger stepped back to assess the canvas. The painting was finished. The tension in the figure mirrored her own. Now, just one more night, one more Ambien night, and she would see Carl. She remembered Dottie's words: *Everything you say to a lawyer is confidential.*

After her shower, Ginger walked into Ted's office and went straight to the safe. She opened it, reached at the back and extracted a large envelope. Pulling it out, she looked at the front: *PRIVATE* was stamped in red. She put it in her tote bag. Tomorrow she would go over *everything* with Carl. She went to the bar, chose a crystal glass, filled it with ice and poured a stiff scotch from Ted's favorite label. There were two beige leather recliners. His and Hers. Ginger and Ted often had a cocktail watching the evening news. With Ted, things were uncomplicated. What you saw was what you got. What was she seeing now? What was she getting? Waiting for Margale to knock with her dinner tray, she clicked on the remote. Anything on the news was better than the thoughts in her head.

CHAPTER 22

IT WAS STILL dark when Ginger got up. She took her time bathing and getting dressed. The combination of White Label and Ambien had done their work. She had slept soundly. She had dreamed but was grateful she couldn't remember her dreams. Quietly, carrying her tote bag, Ginger slipped down the back stairs to the kitchen. Margale was waiting.

"Morning, Mrs. Johnson. Here's your coffee in a carafe. And I made you toast."

Ginger was about to ask Margale about Kevin, but she anticipated the question. They spoke in whispers, like conspirators.

"Mr. McCoy is not up yet. He was out by the pool, long after midnight."

"Thank you. Tell him I'm in Palm Beach and will call him later."

Margale opened the door and Ginger went out. The garage door opened noiselessly, and Ginger drove slowly, as if tiptoeing on the gravel drive. When she approached the gates, the guard waved her through, and Ginger felt relief.

She pulled onto highway 95 South towards Palm Beach. Ginger was doing her best to postpone thinking. She didn't want to think until she had to, until she was in Carl's office. It was about an hour and a half drive and coastal Florida unfurled along the familiar road. She admired the sea grape bushes, native to Florida, which stood as high as the trees. She loved their round leaves which grow larger than a hand. The roadside creeks and rivers were banked with tall, wild grasses. Australian pines lined the highway. They reminded her of the Bahamas and her idyllic days and nights on *Victory* with Ted. In the fields between the exits marked Ft. Pierce, St. Lucie, and Jupiter, cows grazed lazily. She passed the Jupiter exit, with the Mobil Gas Station and its bright red sign of the flying horse, Pegasus. Another half hour and she'd be there. Ginger wondered. Would she receive guidance, solutions, and closure? Or would more complications present themselves?

She needed to talk to someone, but who? She felt so unsettled and talking things through with friends always made her feel safe. Dottie could always diffuse emotion. But Dottie had no idea what was going on. Neither did Diane. Caught up with Kevin, she had isolated herself. There was her secret and the uneasiness that made sleep impossible. Was it excitement or was it dread? Were her fears real or phantoms? Dottie had great intuition about people. On impulse, Ginger pushed her direct dial to Dottie, and, to her amazement, she answered.

"Dottie! I'm heading South on 95 to Carl's office and wanted to say hi."

"Well, hi, there. You will not believe it, but I was just thinking of you. My children swear I'm a witch. They mean the good kind, I think. Carl called me over the weekend. It's his birthday tomorrow . . . a big one, and he wants me to come. So, I thought why not? No one is getting any younger. I called and got myself a plane — a King Air — and a couple of pilots. I leave for Florida in the morning. Thought maybe Wednesday afternoon I'd ride up and see you if that's convenient?"

"That would be wonderful!"

"You know, Carl has to work, work, work . . . Even with Carl Jr. there. Well, you don't know him yet, but you will."

"Come as soon as you can. But do you mind the upstairs guest room? Actually, it's Ted snore room. Kevin's in the guest room downstairs."

"Sure."

"Good. It'll be just us girls upstairs."

"Sounds like fun. Still on cloud nine?"

"Oh, Dottie, I really have fallen in love. And he has too, I think. But, I have so much on my mind. Ted's will, the estate, the stepchildren! I'm feeling rushed and —"

There was a pause on the line. Ginger thought she might burst into tears.

"Ginger? Are you all right?"

"Yes, yes. I think. Some moments I feel happier than I ever have. But, other moments, I'm confused and not sure of anything."

"Good timing for a visit from an old witch like me."

Ginger laughed, then protested. "More like a fairy godmother!"

"I like that better. Ginger, try to be happy and enjoy yourself."

"I know, but sometimes I worry —"

There were worries that Ginger was not willing to admit to or talk about.

"Like, what would Ted think — ? Ted would have wanted you to have someone. He always knew you would survive him."

"Yet he didn't sign the second will. Why didn't he? And now the children are fighting me, like I'm the enemy!"

"Well, I don't know. But you're on your way to see Carl and CJ. Talk to them. You can trust these two."

"Okay. I will. Thank you Dottie. Let me know when you're coming Wednesday. I hope it's in time for dinner. I'll have Margale make her peach cobbler."

"That's all you had to say. Carl's loaning me his driver and the plane will pick me up in Treasure Beach."

"Stay as long as you can, please."

"You know me, I always have to rush home. God knows why. You'd think the children were in diapers."

"I want you to get to know Kevin. It's important to me."

"I'll stay a couple of days."

"Good. Thank you, Dottie."

"Good luck with Carl and don't worry your pretty little red head. Enjoy yourself. It's later than you think."

Dottie laughed and that made Ginger laugh. Dottie added, "Much later. Bye! My daughter's honking in the drive — !"

Dottie clicked off. Wasn't that just like her? She is always there when I need her. She'll love Kevin. Carl will straighten everything out. And, at last, she will tell someone her secret. The sign said Okeechobee, 1 1/2 miles. She glided off the exit ramp. It was a little after 9. Ginger was right on time.

"GOOD MORNING, MARGALE! Wow, is it really 10:30? I guess I stayed up pretty late. I need Mrs. Johnson to keep me honest," Kevin laughed. "Has she come down? Is she better? Is she in her studio? I know she had to finish some paintings for her galleries."

"Mrs. Johnson's not here."

"She's not?"

"She left early for an appointment in Palm Beach."

"Oh, right. That's right. She's meeting with her lawyer. What's his name again — ?"

"I don't know his name. She said she's not sure when she'll be back, said for you to do whatever you like and enjoy yourself."

"Okay. Thanks for the message. Well, another beautiful day in paradise. I think I'll start with the late breakfast. How about eggs and bacon, juice, and coffee?"

"Yes, Mr. McCoy. Would you like that in the breakfast room or on the terrace?"

"Terrace. Thanks."

"Would you like a special baked good with that? Mr. Johnson always liked a sweet treat with a late breakfast."

Kevin thought about it, but not for long.

"Love it. I guess Ted and I have that in common, too. A sweet tooth. Newspaper on the hall table?"

"Yes, Mr. McCoy."

"Thanks," he said and left her to her work.

Margale thought to herself. He sure acts like he's master of the house. Only been here a couple of weeks . . . nice enough, sure good to Mrs. Johnson. She needs someone around, just wonder how long he's staying. Mrs. Johnson said three more months. He ought to be set by then. Still, something's not right. What's a young man doing tarrying with an old woman? Well, Mrs. Johnson isn't old, not like Mr. Johnson, but she's no spring chicken.

Margale went to the deep freeze and looked around. Between the frozen peas, corn and broccoli she found what she was looking for: a frozen block wrapped in foil, labeled with her own handwriting. "Mr. J's Banana Bread," it said.

"Uh-huh," she said unwrapping it. "We'll see if he likes this."

CARL PHILLIPS' OFFICE was on the 22nd floor. A pretty assistant, Lily, escorted Ginger down a long hallway. She carried her pocketbook and her tote bag. Lily ushered Ginger into a spacious corner office with walls of windows. After squinting a moment, she saw two impeccably dressed men. The older man was on the phone at an impressive partner's desk, and the younger man sat on a leather couch. Carl Sr. hung up the phone and both men stood to greet her.

"Ginger, how nice to meet you."

"How do you do, Carl — ?"

"Yes. And, this is my son, Carl, Jr."

The young man extended his hand. "Hello, Mrs. Johnson."

"Call me Ginger, Carl Jr."

"I go by CJ. Makes things easier."

"Hello, CJ — glad to meet you both."

"These days, CJ and I work closely on everything. If you ever need something and I'm not available, he's your man."

CJ offered her a chair.

"Here, let's sit. Dad's going to take the lead here."

When they were all seated, Carl began.

"First thing off the bat, let us assure you, there's not too much to worry about. As I mentioned on the phone, Florida law protects you. I have gone over all of Ted's papers and shared them with CJ. Everything's in order — "

"Except for the signature on the second trust — "

"Yes, Ginger, that's true. Except for the signature on the second trust. Yet, to us, Ted's intention is strong and clear, Ginger, and the law says — "

"I was married over 40 years and we're talking law? Ted would be very upset. I know he would. Ted would be just as bewildered as I am."

The men exchanged glances.

"Ginger, you're not the first woman who has run into stepchildren problems. Nor will you be the last."

In the recent dizzying days of Kevin's company, Ginger had almost forgotten her problems. They had seemed distant, like the affairs of some other woman. But in Carl's office, all the hurts and betrayals came back to life. She had tried so hard with the children from the start: birthdays, Christmas and every other holiday, and always including them on vacations. She knew she couldn't replace their mother, nor did she want to. Nor had she tried, no one could do the impossible. She was sure this was all Emily, not the boys. Everyone knew Ted's intentions. Ginger was lost in the swirl of her own thoughts, then realized that Carl was still speaking to her.

"It's just the nature of things. Divorce may be worse on kids than death.

But neither is good. The kids need to latch onto something, some target for their grief. While the grieving spouse seizes an opportunity to move on, begin again, and finds a new object of affection, finds new love — "

Was this need the cause of her instant connection with Kevin? Had she just latched onto an obsession to distract herself from this hurt?

Carl continued.

"Usually, it's nothing more than plain old jealousy and ordinary posses-siveness. They've lost one parent, and the kids don't care to share the one that's left. A new spouse presents a real threat to parental attention which was, suddenly, just halved. They're torn, of course, because their remaining parent is happy. So it goes, until there's another death. Then, it's all about the money."

"The root of all evil and greed," said CJ.

Ted had trusted Jim Donnelly and the two of them had created the second trust. Yet Jim made excuses for why Ted had not signed it. Was he, in fact, less trustworthy than Ted had assumed?

CJ seemed to guess at her panic.

"We'll work it out. We just want you to know it's not uncommon *and* it's not personal. Especially given the surrounding circumstances, a jury would most likely rule in your favor."

"What circumstances?"

CJ continued. "The precedent of the first trust. While, no doubt, a signature is a critical detail, in the context of the surrounding notes of your former lawyer — "

"Jim Donnelly — "

"That's right. Think what we might of Mr. Donnelly, he took copious notes as he worked with your husband on the second trust — "

"And the dates of these documents well precede your husband's arrival in the Memory Unit."

"So, these reveal Ted's true intentions?"

"To our minds, absolutely. It is hard to believe a judge would not rule in your favor."

Ginger sighed deeply.

"By the way," said Carl, Sr. "I have spoken with Mr. Donnelly, and he has talked with the kids. I get the feeling that all parties would like to settle as soon as possible."

"We think they want to avoid a trial. Trials are expensive. Hours and depositions take a lot out of everyone's pot, including his."

It still hurt her how Jim had taken sides with Ted's children. Did everything come down to money? In a flash, she remembered the clipping in the nightstand.

"Well that's reassuring. Thank you. How long will this take, do you think?"

She was thinking about Kevin, about his push to have her "all to himself."

"A couple of months maybe, not too long. Of course, you're in a good position financially. Our accountant looked things over. He assured us that you were fine in that regard."

"You'll be more financially 'fine' when all of this is sorted out," CJ added, smiling.

Looking back and forth, and listening to the pair, Ginger felt reassured.

"Thank you, both. And thank God for Dottie!"

They shared a moment of appreciation for the doyenne of Atlanta.

"Why, Dottie is headed our way; did she tell you?"

"Yes, she told me you have a birthday tomorrow."

"That's right, a big one. My wife Mary is putting something together — "

"For 100 of Dad's closest friends — " added CJ.

"Glad Dottie's going to fly down. That woman made her husband happy every day of his life. Dottie said that you did the same for Ted. I bet there are lots of people who would gladly come forth and testify as such — "

Instantly, Ginger pictured herself on the stand, maybe in her black Chloé suit and her Chanel spectator pumps: like a witness in a television drama on Lifetime.

"But you don't think it will go that far, do you — ?"

"We doubt it will come to that." CJ glanced at his watch and stood. "Dad, I've got one more meeting before a conference call at noon."

"We're about through, I think. Ginger, I'll have Lily send notes on everything we talked about. Look it over and call me back with any questions. Go ahead, CJ."

"Thanks, Dad, I'll check in with you later."

CJ crossed to Ginger and extended his hand.

"Lovely to meet you, Ginger."

"Thank you for everything, CJ."

"Of course," the young man said and left.

"You're invited to our gathering tomorrow evening. Any way you could stay on over a night? Mary would love to meet you, and Dottie would be delighted if her friend was there."

"Thank you. But I have a house guest."

Kevin had been on her mind the whole time she was there.

"Carl, I was wondering if I might talk to you about another matter. Do you have time now or should I make an appointment and come back down?"

"I was just about to ask Lily to order a salad for me. Why don't you join me? We can talk over my mid-morning lunch. My next appointment isn't until 11:30."

"I'd love that."

Carl pushed a button on his desk.

"Lily, we're going to order from Trellis."

"Yes, Mr. Phillips."

He looked at Ginger. "Nothing fancy, but decent enough."

"Sounds perfect. Carl, the matter I'm about to discuss with you is very delicate."

"Anything you say to me, or to CJ, is confidential. 100 percent."

136

Lily entered with menus.

"I always have the same thing, chicken salad plate and iced tea with lime." Ginger waved Lily off, without glancing at the menu.

"I'll have the same, except I'd like lemon in my iced tea. Thank you."

"Certainly." Lily left them.

"I know you'll think I'm crazy but hear me out."

Carl gave her a small nod, her cue to begin.

"About a month ago I met a man. His named is Kevin McCoy. He's a pilot and was in Florida looking for a place to live. We met at an open house at 3-Oaks. We started talking and then toured the house together. Instantly we were having a wonderful time. Like we already knew each other. I'm not making that up. We both felt it and ended up having dinner. He's on leave, and I was so stressed — "

"Your husband had just died, the funeral, and issues with the kids."

"Right, so one of us, honestly I don't remember if it was Kevin or myself, we decided to spend two days together. Like, a mini vacation. Well, two days has turned into weeks. In fact, at the moment, he's living at my house. Let me be very clear, he's in my guest room."

"Okay. You said he's a pilot?"

"He's with Northwest, on leave for six months for medical reasons. Carl, we have fallen deeply in love. I have never had anyone who felt like this about me, and I feel certain he's never had anyone care for him as much as I do. You must think that I'm a fool, vulnerable after her husband's death, but remember, I have been alone for a lot longer. Ted's funeral was last month, but really, long before that, his mind was gone because of the Alzheimer's — "

"It's terrible for spouses. Like two deaths, just different kinds."

"Yes. So, the point is, Kevin and I plan to spend the rest of our lives together."

There was a pause. "Do you mean to marry Kevin McCoy?"

"He has asked me to, yes."

Carl was quiet again and looked down at his hands folded on the desk.

"Well, congratulations are in order. Very best wishes to you both."

"Honestly Carl, I may be a fool, but I don't care. I have never felt this sort of happiness before."

"Has Mr. McCoy been married before? Does he have children, a family?"

"Yes – and no. He was married once. A long time ago. It lasted a year, I think? No children. And he's estranged from his family."

"Do you mind if I ask a question?"

"Please."

"How old is Kevin McCoy?"

"50 years old. Obviously, he's a good deal younger than I. We have discussed this, but he assures me it makes no difference to him. He's said that on more than one occasion. He is adamant on this point and won't tolerate any reference to the issue of age."

"I see. And what can I do for you, Ginger?"

"It's all been so wonderful, but fast. My friends, like Dottie, caution me."

"They want your happiness."

"Yes, and we're on the brink of this momentous thing. I trust Kevin completely, but my friends are unanimous with their concerns. So, I'd like you to find out everything you can about Kevin McCoy. I want to know about his life from beginning to this moment. He was born in Jacksonville."

"We have some very good people in the Jacksonville area. And they work quickly."

Ginger nodded calmly, but her heart was racing. She never imagined she was the sort of person who would hire a private investigator.

There was a knock at the door.

"This must be lunch. Come in, Lily."

Lily set the salads on the small table by the window.

138

"Anything else, Mr. Phillips?"

"No, thank you. But maybe, well, why not put a few chocolate mint cookies on a plate. Mrs. Johnson might enjoy them. They're in the credenza. And no need to mention it to Mrs. Phillips."

Lily smiled. Clearly this was a frequent request.

"Shall we, Ginger?"

They stood and took chairs at the table.

"Hardly Cafe Europa, but the view is better."

Ginger looked down at Lake Worth, at the magnificent yachts down below in the marina. The scene reminded her of Ted. What would Ted think of her speech to Carl? And what would he think of the contents of the envelope?

"Ginger?"

"We had so many glorious days on our boat in the Bahamas. Oh, why did that awful disease rob of us of our final days together?"

Ginger had spoken so freely, that only now her feelings were emerging. And Carl was practically a perfect stranger. But he was her lawyer, and his manner was kind. He seemed to care about her as a person, not just as a client.

"And then, there's this."

Ginger reached into her tote and brought out the envelope marked *PRIVATE*. She handed the envelope to Carl.

"What's this?"

"It's a secret I've never told anyone."

"And you wish to share this with me?"

Ginger nodded, then she said, "But do you mind waiting to open it until after I leave?"

"Of course. I'll set it aside for the moment."

Carl stood, crossed the room, and opened a side drawer of the partner's desk.

"It's taken me decades to share this with someone. No one knows," she hesitated. "Not even Dottie. I was planning on carrying the secret with me to the grave. Thank you. Only now do I realize how heavily it has weighed on me."

Carl smiled at her. They lifted their forks and began their lunch.

"Delicious chicken salad. Thank you so much."

"Oh, it's fine. Saves me an hour or so. CJ is on top of everything, but I like to be on hand and know what's going on, the ins and outs on all the cases. Now, why don't you tell me more about Mr. Kevin McCoy."

What could she say? Could she tell him about the walks and talks, the dinners and dancing, in the ocean and on the terrace. The long, long conversations, the comfortable silences, the way he squeezed her hand three times. Could she explain how she loved his energy and ease, the way he threw his head back and laughed? No, these were their secrets.

Instead, she spoke about his career, about his love for flying, and how he had trained right there at Treasure Beach, how he was estranged from his father who was a doctor. And that he had a brother who was also a doctor. How he'd learned he was adopted.

She was aware that Carl was paying close attention to the facts she offered. He would relay these to his people in Jacksonville.

After salad, they shared the mint cookies. Carl talked about his birthday gathering. Then, he walked her out of the office and towards the elevators.

"Don't worry, Ginger. We'll solve everything. In the meantime, take my advice. Get plenty of sleep."

Ginger traveled down the 22 floors in the elevator. Stepping out into the day, she exhaled, and felt relief from the pressure of these issues for the first time since the funeral. Carl seemed more like a doctor or a priest than a lawyer. He was right. All the drinking and the late nights had tired her out. She'd lost her equilibrium. She would call Margale and ask her to make an early dinner and she would go straight to bed. The last few nights had been tormented by fitful sleep and disturbing dreams. She realized that a part of her dreaded going back home. It was a full two days before Dottie would be there.

CHAPTER 23

G INGER was halfway back home and stopped at the Mobile station
when her cell rang. It was a New York number.

"Ginger — ?"

"Yes?"

"It's Avery, at Gordon Gallery — "

"Avery! How are you?"

"Oh, I'm fine. Very well, as a matter of fact — "

"I've been meaning to call you and apologize. I've just been consumed by
my personal life — "

"Your husband died, Ginger. There's no need to apologize — "

"With Ted, first, of course, and then other things — "

"I trust you got the flowers?"

Ginger had no recollection of the flowers, so many people had sent flowers.

"The flowers were exquisite. Thank you so much. I wanted to tell you some
good news, I've finally gotten back to painting . . ."

"Gordon will be glad to hear that."

"I finished a canvas last night. I'll send you a picture."

"You can show me when I see you."

"Are you coming to Florida?"

"No. Ginger, that's why I'm calling. I've got some news. Yesterday, one of our clients bought a painting of yours."

"That's wonderful."

"And she insists on meeting you. She's our best client, so this is me and Gordon begging: Can you fly up? And meet her?"

"Of course —"

"Guess which piece."

"No, not —"

"Yes —"

"You sold *Sand and Surf*?"

Sand and Surf was a painting Ginger had done for Ted, inspired by photos of their last time together in the Bahamas. Avery had seen it in her studio and insisted on featuring it in the window at the gallery on Madison. Ginger agreed, but only if the price was sky high so that no one would buy it.

"The Countess of Edington did not bat an eyelash at the price. She wants *Sand and Surf* for her estate."

"The Countess of Edington? She's the buyer?"

"Yes! Congratulations, Ginger!"

"Goodness. We thought that painting would never sell."

"I hate to impose, but can you come?"

"Yes. When?"

"Today? She's leaving for England tomorrow on her private jet and she's taking the picture with her. The countess is not used to the word *no*. Please, Ginger. We'll take care of all the arrangements. In fact —"

"What?"

"I've already booked you a flight out of Treasure Beach —"

"For today?"

"On the 2:00. It gets into JFK at 5:00. Martin will meet you and drive you to the gallery for a quick glass of champagne with the countess. That's all we ask."

"Avery, I'd love to. But I've a house guest."

"I booked you a room at The Plaza. I wouldn't ask if it wasn't important to everyone. The gallery, the countess, and you."

What would Kevin say about her sudden change of plans? What would he think of the impressive sale of her painting to a countess?

"What do you say, Ginger?"

She glanced at the clock. She could easily make it to the Treasure Beach airport in time.

"I say: *I can't wait to meet the countess!*"

"Wonderful! And congratulations on the biggest sale of your career. This definitely calls for champagne. We'll see you at about 6:00, depending on traffic."

Avery jumped off and Ginger called the house. Margale answered.

"Margale, it's me. Is Mr. McCoy in?"

"Why Mrs. Johnson, you just missed Mr. McCoy. He was having a late breakfast — "

"Breakfast?"

"Yes, uh-hum. He was on the terrace and Mr. Butler drove by in his cart. The two of them got talking and talking and then, off they went!"

"Bill and Mr. McCoy drove off in Bill's cart?"

"That's right."

If Bill took him along for 18 holes, Kevin would be gone for hours.

"Okay. Well, who knows how long he'll be. Margale, I'm going up to New York. Just for the night. Please throw a black dress and heels into a carry-on for me, a nightgown, too, and underthings, my 3/4 coat, and a scarf. Oh, and my grey travel cosmetics case and any other essentials. Call Paul and ask him to pick these things up and bring them over to the airport before 1:15. I'm booked on the 2:00."

"Ooh! You better get yourself there right quick."

"I'm halfway there already."

"What shall I tell Mr. McCoy?"

"Tell him I've sold a painting to a countess!"

"Now, how grand is that? Congratulations, Mrs. J."

"Thank you. Now I'd better go. Call me with any problems."

Ginger got back onto 95 North and drove intently. The day was full of breakthroughs. She had hired lawyers and they assured her that everything was going to work out with the trust. She had instructed Carl to hire a private investigator to look into Kevin's history. And Carl's 'people in Jacksonville' would fill her in on everything about him and put her foolish fears to rest. She had handed over her most private secret to Carl, a first step before sharing it with Kevin. Their relationship had to be based on transparency and trust. To top it all off, a countess had bought *Sand and Surf*. It was going to Devonshire, and she was going to New York! All this good news made Ginger indulge in the ultimate happy ending: soon she would be Mrs. Kevin McCoy. Who knows, Kevin might even learn to play golf. Ginger speeded north.

CHAPTER 24

EVERYTHING WENT SMOOTHLY that afternoon. In record time, Ginger exited 95 North for the main road which led to Airport Way. She followed it, driving along the field where the private planes were lined up, side by side, looking almost like toys. Delta's 30-seat Northeaster was sitting on the runway. She parked and went inside. Paul was waiting for her.

"Hello Mrs. Johnson. Your belongings are already on the plane."

"Thank you, Paul."

"Sure thing, Mrs. J. Oh, and Margale said I should give you this." He handed her a smart looking cooler. "She thought you might be hungry. I believe there's a sandwich, coffee, and cobbler. She gave me a piece of her cobbler."

"There's nothing better than Margale's cobbler."

"Have a great trip. Will you be gone long?"

"Only till tomorrow."

"Give a holler if you want me to come out and pick you up."

Ginger walked onto the tarmac and ascended the silver steps to the plane. She chose a window seat and settled in. Usually, the empty seat beside her made her think of Ted. But today, she fantasized that Kevin was by her side. She imagined how he would squeeze her hand three times during take-off, and she would do the same back. After the obligatory announcements, the plane taxied down the short runway and soon was airborne. Ginger looked out the window at Treasure Beach below. The plane banked and circled over 3-Oaks. If she'd wanted to, she could have spotted her house by the tall stand of oaks. But instead, Ginger scanned the smooth and rolling, pond-studded greens for a golf cart which might contain Bill and her future husband. When the plane reached cruising altitude, she adjusted her seat back. The hum of the engine was hypnotic, and she closed her eyes. Not even the idea of Margale's cobbler could keep Ginger awake.

CHAPTER 25

O N THE STEPS of The Plaza, Ginger marveled at the urban mag-
nificence of 59th and Fifth Avenue. The grand fountain gushed lively
white and silver water upwards, then it cascaded downwards with a splash. Horse-
drawn carriages lined the street, waiting for tourists to climb in for a ride through
Central Park. Traffic, dominated by giant, bullying buses, roared by. Taxis jockeyed
for position and weaved across lanes. People of all ages, types and sizes moved in
every direction, crowded at corners waiting for a green light and the right to cross.
Exhilarated to find herself in New York City, Ginger decided to visit her favorite
store. Bergdorf Goodman, the iconic store, the epitome of fashion, style, and luxury,
is just steps away from the entrance to The Plaza. BG has three entrances, 57th
Street, 58th and the golden revolving doors on 5th Avenue. But Ginger didn't enter
immediately. She treated herself to a viewing of the store's famed display windows.

Faceless mannequins struck unnatural poses, hips protruding forward and
elongated arms with hands in articulated gestures. They were swathed in shim-
mering tulle and lustrous leather. They wore skirts heavy with beads, topped by
Nehru jackets in silk brocade. Famous from the Sixties, the jackets looked positively
new in the windows of Bergdorf's. Color combinations she would not dream of
assembling, or dare to wear, arranged in a window of BG by their inhouse, sartorial
savants, suddenly make sense. There was nothing at all like this in Treasure Beach,

or anywhere else. The windows were as stimulating as ever. Ginger entered the golden revolving door and pushed her way into the *ne plus ultra* of fashion, style, and luxury.

Walking through the jewelry department, she paused before the pristine cases to survey the designers on display. Bergdorf's always championed new designers and featured the established ones, as well: like, Ben-Amen, Jamie Wolf, and Anita Ko. Beyond jewelry were handbags of all types: day bags, totes, and evening purses of all sizes and by the top designers. Valentino with the iconic *V*. Chanel, quilted with a chain shoulder strap, and Judith Lieber's signature jeweled animal evening bags. Ginger was partial to Lieber's dogs: a Doberman, Spaniel, or Poodle. The cats were incredible, too. Made of tiny rhinestones, with colored glass to depict the nose, eyes, and mouth. She loved how the clasp was hidden. Inside, there was room for a lipstick and a handkerchief. Sometimes, Ginger asked to see a Lieber purse, marveling at the intricate design and turning it in her hands with awe. She had never purchased one. The price of a Lieber purse was $500 to $10,000, but it cost nothing to look at such delightful, whimsical pieces. She was about to take the escalator so she could peek at what was on each floor on her way up, when suddenly she remembered the Bergdorf's Men's Store across 5th Ave. She hurried out and crossed the street. What would she get for Kevin? She was thinking of gold cufflinks, with initials. She would see if there were any ready-made with the letter K, she didn't want to wait to have them engraved. She wanted to give them to Kevin tomorrow, when she returned. But did Kevin ever wear French cuffs . . .? Ted had only worn shirts with French cuffs. Sometimes it shocked her how little she knew about him. Oh well, she'd buy him a couple shirts too.

She was in the European dress shirt boutique when she heard her name.

"Virginia? Is that you?"

Ginger turned and saw a not-terribly tall, handsome man, with silver hair. She didn't remember his name, but she remembered his eyes. They were azure and the exact color of his shirt, which was not a coincidence.

"It's wonderful to see you. After all these years — "

Suddenly, she remembered.

"Charlie Taylor, how are you? Are you in the city now?"

"No, still in Greenwich. I'm just in for a meeting. You and Ted haven't moved to The Big Apple, have you?"

"Heavens, no — "

"No, you two have the perfect set up. Shuttling between paradise at Treasure Beach and your stately place in Atlanta. That is, when you're not boating in the Bahamas. Do you still have your boat? What was she called? *Conquest?*"

"*Victory.* No, we sold her long ago."

"Good times."

Charlie and his wife, Ann, had been their guests on *Victory.* But it had been years since they were in touch. He probably didn't know about Ted.

"What brings you here?"

"I'm here just for the night. I came up because my gallery sold a painting — "

"That's right, you're an accomplished artist. I remember."

"And they asked me to come up at the last minute — "

"Ted's not with you then?"

"Charlie, Ted passed."

"What? When?"

"About a month ago."

"I had no idea. This is terrible news."

"Believe it or not, it's for the better. He'd been in a Memory Unit for years."

The genial expression on his face changed.

"I'm so sorry."

"It was heartbreaking, but he was well taken care of. And I was with him every day."

Looking down, Charlie nodded. "I'm terribly sorry. Ted was the best. It's incredible that we ran into each other. And at Bergdorf's."

Ginger felt speechless. Was she supposed to play the role of a grieving widow? What if Charlie guessed she was shopping for the new man in her life? She flushed. Kevin was her secret, and she was not about to share his existence with a distant acquaintance, like Charlie Taylor.

"I am just as amazed to find myself in New York. I was in Palm Beach this morning, but my gallery called and asked me to fly up for a drink with a countess."

His expression turned warm again. He smiled.

"A countess?"

"An English countess bought a picture of mine, and they asked me to come up at once, before she left on her private jet — "

"Your story gets better and better."

"But when I arrived at JFK, the driver informed me the countess had already left the country."

"A flighty countess."

"She had an emergency. There's terrible flooding in Devonshire."

"I see, so you never met her?"

Ginger nodded her head. "No."

Her story brought a bemused look to Charlie's azure eyes. He gazed at her, and she blushed.

"So instead, the driver delivered me to The Plaza. I went to my room and fell asleep."

"Like Eloise."

Ginger laughed. She remembered from their nights on *Victory* how Charlie was famous for his sense of humor, and infamous for being a flirt.

"Look, if you have no plans, how about a drink and dinner — ?"

"I'd love it," the words came out of her mouth before she gave it a thought.

"8:00 at St. Ambrose? It's just a couple blocks up Madison. I often go there when I'm in town. It's a decent bistro."

"Wonderful, see you there."

They had the briefest embrace and he dashed into an elevator.

Really, it had been the most amazing day. Ginger quickly found a pair of cuff links engraved with a lovely font. Waiting for the girl to wrap them, she calculated she had just enough time for a brief bath before changing into the clothes Margale had packed for her. Later, in the bath, she went over her conversation with Charlie. She felt badly when she realized how she had neglected to ask about Ann, his wife.

CHAPTER 26

PROMPTLY, AT 7:45, Ginger exited the revolving doors of The Plaza, and stepped onto the sidewalk, becoming one more person crossing the teeming city streets. The evening air expanded her lungs. She enjoyed the anonymity of the city. Ted used to bring her to New York for his board meetings. Once, when she was a bride, they came at Christmas to shop and watch the tree lighting ceremony at Rockefeller Center. But now, here she was, a widow.

But striding up 5th Avenue, Ginger felt like a woman on the brink of a new life. She walked on the park side, along the high wall that corralled a thousand leafy trees. She turned onto a street in the early Sixties passing fabulous townhouses, lined with ornate wrought iron gates, and punctuated by the occasional urn, graciously brimming with flowers. Reaching Madison Avenue, she turned left. Madison Avenue is the address of the best, the best grocer, baker, bookstore, undertaker, boutique, or gallery. The Gordon Gallery was at 63rd. Standing before the windows, she studied the pair of portraits hung there. How strange that her champagne with the countess had never occurred. She'd received gorgeous flowers in her room and a note from Gordon and Avery, apologizing profusely and explaining about the rains in Devonshire. Why was she in New York? Was fate keeping her away from Kevin for one more day, until Dottie arrived? Until Carl's 'people in Jacksonville' put her at ease? When would they grant her the green light to look forward to her life as Mrs. Kevin McCoy?

Wherever she was, Kevin was never far from her mind. In fact, he was always on her mind.

Passing the windows of Brooks Brothers, the male mannequins posed, handsome in their uptown, preppy attire. The tweeds and corduroys and silk dressing gowns all reminded her of Kevin. Now and then, a fearful thought crept into her mind and accosted her. Why would a man of fifty be ready to commit to a life with a woman nearly two decades his senior? Had the drink, the late hours and the giddiness of their infatuation caused her to forget herself? Or had she found herself in his laugh, his attentiveness, and his love. He assured her that he was happy to wait, but for how long? Soon the affairs of Ted's estate would be settled, and she could no longer put off his desire to make plans. Or his desire to make love. Here, far away from home, Ginger studied her own reflection in the windows. Whatever was ahead of her, she wanted to be ready and to be sure. It had been a very long time since she made life decisions for herself. To hire her own lawyer to wrangle with his children about Ted's estate, to share with a man she just met her life's most closely guarded secret, and to ask the lawyer to investigate a man who swore his love for her — this, in itself, felt like a betrayal. But the newspaper clipping in his nightstand drawer had opened a Pandora's box of worries. Honestly, she was grateful to Avery, the countess, and the rains in Devonshire for keeping her away one more day. Before entering St. Ambrose, Ginger prayed that soon all questions would be answered and the tension of unknowing would be behind her.

The restaurant was dimly lit. A pretty hostess greeted her. "Good evening, do you have a reservation?"

"Virginia Johnson. I'm meeting —"

"Yes. This way. Mr. Taylor is waiting for you."

The dark interior was brightened by impeccable squares of thick white table cloths and lit by small candles. The lighting was muted and so were the voices.

Charlie stood to greet her. He seemed different, rather subdued, and not the *bon vivant* he had been on the boat. She was perplexed.

"Oh, Charlie, what a lovely place."

"I'm glad you like it. It's been a long time since I've shared it with someone."

As soon as they settled into the corner table, Ginger remembered to ask about Ann. However, the waiter descended on them, inquiring about their drink order.

"Negroni?" Charlie offered.

"Love it," Ginger answered, and the waiter departed.

"Ginger, I honestly feel we were fated to meet today. There was something I wanted to talk to you about, only I couldn't bring myself to broach the subject at Bergdorf's, especially after hearing your news, of Ted's passing. Then, it hardly seemed appropriate to change the subject. You must be suffering greatly from such a loss."

Before she could answer, the waiter returned and presented two short glasses, each with one large, perfect cube of ice, with a lemon twist floating in amber liquid. Charlie lifted his glass.

"To our reunion." They toasted and sipped. Ginger was full of suspense for what Charlie was about to disclose, but the waiter appeared and recited a long list of specials.

"He's very eager," said Charlie, bemused, when the waiter left.

"Indeed." She sipped her Negroni and waited.

"It's about Ann. Four years ago, Ann was diagnosed with Parkinson's."

"Oh, Charlie, I am so sorry."

"To make matters worse, she's been in a home for the last eighteen months."

Ginger nodded with compassion. "Oh, dear."

"It's nearby, in Wilton. It's a great place, the best in the Northeast. I am working a lot from home now, so I can visit her many times a week."

Ginger paused and then dared to ask the most sensitive of questions. "Does Ann know who you are?"

Charlie looked down. Ginger connected it to the inexplicable expression that had overcome him earlier. Now, she understood.

"Charlie, I'm so sorry. That's just so hard. I know."

"One day, I'm her brother. Another day, I'm the fellow she dated in high school. I love her. She's there. I can hold her hand. But she's not there."

"It's the worst disease."

"It's killing me."

There was a deafening silence. Charlie looked at Ginger, his eyes moist and Ginger smiled a slight smile, her eyes also full of tears. The waiter returned.

"Are you ready to order?"

"I'll have the sole, please."

"Very good, Madame. And, to start?"

"The burrata looks lovely."

"Thank you. And for you, sir?"

"I'll have the wedge salad. And the filet, medium."

"Very good, sir." The waiter gathered the menus and left.

It was startling dining with a man who ordered a completely different dinner for himself. Kevin always mimicked her order. What did he order when she was not there, she wondered? She also wondered how his evening was going. Who was getting the better of whom, Bill of Kevin, or Kevin of Bill? Diane had certainly joined them. She imagined how her friends at 3-Oaks would learn about the Countess of Edington from Kevin and, without Ginger's protective presence, how they would contrive to learn everything they could about her younger suitor.

"Thank you, Ginger."

"For what?"

"For listening. I have no one to talk with about her. People are nice, of course. But everyone has their own life, their struggles. This has been going on for a long time — "

"I know. People forget."

"I don't blame them."

"I visited Ted every day for three years."

The sorrow of those visits came back to her. Charlie remained quiet for a while. He had been so flirtatious before, long ago, in the Bahamas. Now, she was seeing him in an entirely different light. Clearly, his feelings for his wife were very deep. His reputation as a flirt belied his genuine devotion to her. Ginger broke the silence.

"Ted and I had such a wonderful time with the two of you on *Victory*. I remember how you made Ann laugh. You made everyone laugh. Especially — " She stopped herself.

"Especially?"

"Especially me."

They both blushed.

"Too much champagne, I'm sure I got carried away."

"You were hilarious. It was the only time I ever saw Ted jealous."

"He was a gracious host. And, in a way, a mentor to me."

"He loved sharing the boat with friends. And everyone wanted Ann as a partner in bridge. She was so good at bridge."

"Yes, she remembered everything then."

The waiter arrived with appetizers. Confusion about a lost napkin and then the grinding of fresh pepper lightened the mood between them.

Charlie ordered a bottle of a California Pinot Noir and, with the tough subject out of the way, the two of them were free to enjoy their dinner like old friends.

AFTER, THEY WALKED down Madison together. It wasn't very late, but the avenue is mostly shops and all of them were shut. So, besides the occasional dog-owner and their leashed pet, the two of them had the avenue to themselves. In front of a lovely dress shop, Charlie came to a halt. Just as the male mannequins had made Ginger think about Kevin, these figures in artistic prints made Charlie pause. She guessed he was thinking about Ann.

She touched his shoulder, breaking his gaze. "Charlie, you have loved your wife for a long time, and obviously you have loved her well. But there comes a time when it is best to let go. If there is one thing Ted and Ann teach us, it's that life is short."

He turned to her. His eyes met hers.

"I apologize for being so glum, and you've just lost Ted. It's just such a relief to see you, someone who understands."

He remained subdued until they arrived at The Plaza. Ginger was preparing to say good night when he surprised her.

"I'm here, too, by the way."

"You didn't mention that — "

"The corner suite on 16. It was our home away from home. Of course, it's been three years since Ann's been."

"You'll never believe this. I'm on 16."

He smiled. Crossing the vast lobby, he steered her towards the elevator.

"Our meeting today has nothing to do with chance. It was the Fates at work!"

In the elevator, they were alone.

"My whole day has been about coincidences. My head is spinning."

"I proposed to Ann in The Palm Court."

The elevator came to a standstill and Ginger stepped out first onto the plush floral carpet.

They shared a look.

"Which way are you?" he asked.

"To the right."

"I'm to the left. The northeast corner. I don't suppose you'd like to see the view. It's beautiful at night."

It was clear that he dreaded being alone.

"Sure, I would," Ginger replied, and they both turned left.

"It's just spectacular. You'll see. There's the park, and everything."

At the door, Charlie nervously fumbled in his pockets for his key card. After some searching, he came up with it.

"Phew!" He said, charmingly.

They laughed and entered his suite. Ginger crossed the spacious room towards the broad windows, dropping her coat on a chair. Charlie went to the phone.

"Good evening. This is Charles Taylor in suite 16NE. I'd like a bottle of Veuve Clicquot. On ice. Thank you. What — ? Oh, two glasses."

Ginger gazed out, taking in the dark park. Now, her own sadness engulfed her.

"We used to drink Veuve Clicquot on *Victory*."

"That's why I ordered it," he said.

Charlie joined her by the window. Standing side by side, they gazed out. The perimeters of the park were brilliantly lit. The interior rectangle was startlingly black, the dense population of trees.

"It's amazing that in this vast city, I should run into Virginia Johnson. And of all places, in BGM. Why were you in the men's store at Bergdorf's, by the way?"

"My day started in Palm Beach. A meeting with my new lawyer over Ted's estate — "

"Everything's in order, I hope?"

"Yes, but there are issues. In this case, three. Ted's stepchildren. My lawyer is doing extra work for me. I wanted to get him a small gift to show my appreciation."

Room service knocked. Charlie admitted a young man who pushed into the room a white-clothed table with a silver ice-bucket and a pair of champagne flutes.

"Good evening."

"Good evening," they replied in unison.

"Would you like me to open it, sir?"

With the business of opening and pouring, Ginger had a moment to recover from her fib, and to think. It was 10 o'clock. She had turned her phone off hours ago when she got into the bath. What was Kevin doing? What was she doing? She wasn't sure, but she felt curious and strangely ready for whatever might happen next. She would drink champagne with this handsome man, a colleague of Ted's, a man who was her age, and who, like her had proven his devotion to an ailing, incapacitated spouse. She noticed a difference in herself with Charlie. With Charlie she felt in command of herself, whereas with Kevin she often felt off-balance. It was a new feeling, unfamiliar but empowering.

The champagne bottle popped and emitted vapor. Ginger and Charlie shared a smile. The waiter swiftly poured two glasses. Then Charlie walked him to the door and pressed a bill in his hand.

"Thank you, sir. Good night, sir."

The heavy door shut, and they were alone again.

Charlie handed Ginger a glass.

"To old times," he said. They clinked glasses and sipped champagne. They each eyed the other through the lens of their glasses, and they both got caught.

"Another toast. To letting go," he said, and they each took a deeper drink.

Charlie took her glass from her hand and set both on the table. His gaze told her his next move. Holding his gaze, she allowed him to move closer. His face was near, and she breathed in the smell of his skin. Her hand moved to touch his face. Their lips met.

A countess, champagne and now a kiss. The day had been full of surprises, and she was under the spell of the day. She was living in the moment in Manhattan, and her whole self was breathtakingly ready for whatever the next moment brought. His hands fell on her shoulders and traveled down her arms, sliding along the satin of her sleeves.

"So lovely," he whispered, his face nuzzling in her neck.

She took a breath and initiated the next kiss. It began as a question, until they both yielded to their impulses. The kiss became complex, a wordless dialogue between a woman and a man, both of whom had been imprisoned in aloneness and now felt the relief of another. In tandem, they moved awkwardly to the couch. They sat down, side by side, and the kiss continued. Then, Charlie pulled back.

"Are you okay?"

Ginger nodded.

"Is *this* okay?"

"Yes."

Searching for words, he paused.

"I have a confession."

"Okay."

"I always had a reputation of being easy. I always acted the flirt. But that's all it was. Swagger, an act — "

"You don't have to explain anything."

"But the truth is different. For forty years, Ann's been the only woman in my life — "

"That's beautiful."

"I've haven't been with another woman since I was 25 years old."

"It's the same for me with Ted."

He was quiet for a moment, and Ginger was suddenly unsure of what would happen next.

Finally, he spoke. "Let's make another toast." He filled their flutes. "To the days on *Victory*. To Ted and Ann."

"To Ted and Ann."

"Whom we cherish."

"Yes," Ginger said. They each drank the full glass. Then Charlie took his glass and hers and set them down. He took Ginger's hand, and, with wordless consent, they stood. And the two of them, old friends, went into the bedroom and with rapturous resolve, they made love.

CHAPTER 27

"GOOD EVENING, MRS. JOHNSON," said the figure in uniform, leaning out from the window in the gatehouse at the entrance to 3-Oaks. "Welcome home."

"Thank you, Max. Beautiful evening," she said as her car slowly rolled into the enclave. He nodded and waved her through.

Kevin would be waiting, no doubt. Nearing the house, she felt the familiar anticipation. She prayed she had just been overwrought and overreacted to those clippings. It was a stressful time in her life. She was vulnerable and had let her imagination run away with her. Kevin adored her and she adored him. But then there were those dreams . . .

She opened the garage door and parked. The closer she got to him, the more she felt the imperative to rush to him. Her heart was beating excitedly as she entered the house. Margale was by the door, as usual.

"Margale, I neglected to call. I'm so sorry."

"I had an idea you'd be here soon."

"Thank you. My things are in the car."

"I'll gather them right away."

Yet neither woman moved. Margale anticipated her next question.

"Mr. McCoy is on the terrace."

Ginger could not suppress a smile.

"Thank you. I'll go see him."

"And Mrs. Johnson, congratulations. About your painting and the countess."

"Thank you, Margale." And seeing Margale beaming with pride, Ginger wondered if it was possible that all her dreams might manifest at last: success as an artist and success in love.

She stepped out onto the terrace. It was not yet dark, and Kevin was reading a magazine. "Ginger!" He jumped up and his embrace felt like home. Of course, he was exactly who she thought he was. How could she have doubted?

He kissed her forehead. "I haven't seen you for two days, but it feels like two weeks. How was Palm Beach? How was New York? I want to hear everything!"

"Such a whirlwind! Everything happened so suddenly. One moment I was meeting Carl and discussing the legal problems, you know — "

"How did that go? Was he able to resolve anything — ?"

"I'll tell you at dinner. Shall we go to the club? I'm famished."

"Wherever you like. Only I am not letting you out of my sight — "

Ginger laughed. "We had an early lunch and a conversation. Then I left Palm Beach. I was halfway back here when Avery called from the gallery. They needed me to fly up because the Countess of Edington had bought my painting — "

"I know. Margale told me and I told Bill, and Diane told everyone! 3-Oaks is buzzing!"

"Oh, God! And the countess wanted to meet me before she left the U. S. *They'd booked my flight.* I could hardly say no — "

"I wish I had known; I would have met you at the airport and flown up with you."

"You were on the golf course — "

"When you go around with Bill, you are OTG — "

"OTG?"

"Off the grid. No one's allowed to have their phone on. What was she like?"

"Who?"

"The countess of . . . wherever!"

"Edington."

"Where's Edington?"

"I don't know. Somewhere in England. I never met her — ! She bought the painting but then left New York before my plane landed."

"What?"

"She had to leave. There were rains in Devonshire. She had to go — "

"So, what did you do in New York?"

"How was the golf . . . ? Did he convert you?"

Kevin threw his head back and laughed. Just like he always did. The two of them were joyous to be together again. "It's such a gorgeous course. Finally, I get the appeal. I watched mostly. I took a few swings, and left my share of divots, but Bill and his crew put up with me. When word got around that you'd been kidnapped by a countess, they insisted on taking me to dinner."

"Speaking of food, are you hungry? Can we eat early? I can't stay up late."

"I'm ready. Let's go."

"Great. I'll just have a quick shower and change."

"I'll throw on a jacket and make you a drink."

Before she could leave, Kevin took her hands and gazed into her eyes. "I'm so glad to have my Ginger back."

This was the Kevin she loved. He was so caring. And he was proud of her, too. Feeling happier than she'd been in days, Ginger went upstairs to change. She'd been silly to let anything bother her.

WHEN SHE HEADED down the stairs, Kevin held a balloon wine glass towards her. "Gin and tonic . . . ?"

He knew everything she liked. All drinks in stem glasses. She took a taste. "Perfect."

"That will take the edge off, after your meetings and traveling."

They both drank. But Sinatra was singing "*All of Me, Why Not Take All of Me?*" Kevin offered his hand and they set their glasses down. He took her in his arms and moved her to the music. Ginger felt all the familiar trembles. A gin and tonic, Sinatra, and Kevin. A perfect combination.

After, Kevin drove them to the club in Ted's golf cart.

"Before you left, I was worried about you. Margale was like a Navy SEAL commander: *No disturbing Mrs. Johnson.*"

"Margale can be very intimidating."

"I didn't dare climb the stairs, not until I move up there . . ."

They shared a smile. As Kevin maneuvered the cart, the wind ruffled his hair. He was so handsome.

"I wasn't myself. I wasn't sleeping. My dreams were strange. One night, I had chills and a fever. But by yesterday morning, I felt fine enough to drive to Palm Beach."

"When did you find out about the countess?"

"Right away. The driver who met me at JFK told me to call Avery."

"I hope they were apologetic."

"*Very.* And they took good care of me. I had a huge bouquet with a regretful note waiting in my room at The Plaza, which they'd arranged."

"That's the least they could do after inconveniencing you like that. So, what did you do?"

"I went to the Men's Store at Bergdorf's. I did some shopping for a very special someone."

"Really?"

"Yes," Ginger smiled mysteriously and stepped out of the cart.

INSIDE, CEDRIC ESCORTED them to a cozy, corner table. It was early. There were just a few diners, and luckily no one she knew.

"Thank you, Cedric."

They sat. Kevin gazed at her, and she savored his attention.

"I guess I just needed some time . . . I felt overwhelmed . . . We agreed on two days of vacation, I mean I think I may have overdone it. We've been burning the midnight oil for weeks! I'm afraid I'm not going to be that available this week either. Painting matters, legal papers. And tomorrow, Dottie Morris arrives! I can't wait for you to meet her."

"It will be wonderful to meet her, particularly since I know she's your best friend."

Kevin was hurt. Ginger couldn't be setting up roadblocks, could she? No, of course not. He had felt her surrender in his arms, all the tension had left her body. But now, a friend was coming. For how long? He would wait to ask.

Cedric returned.

"I'll have the chicken salad plate."

"Sounds great. I'll have the same."

Cedric nodded and left.

"I had one yesterday with Carl sitting by the window on the 22nd floor, overlooking Lake Worth."

"Tell me about that. I want to hear how your meeting went."

Ginger hesitated; she was not yet ready to share her affairs with Kevin. There would be plenty of time when things were settled. Kevin sensed her hesitation and made a pivot.

"Tell me about Dottie."

"Dottie was the first person I met with Ted. She was married to Bert Morris, a very close friend of Ted's. She's older than I am. She smoothed the way for me and helped me navigate Atlanta's top tier. Dottie is the top; everyone always falls in line behind her. She's been President of the Garden Club for so long, no one can remember who was president before she was!"

That's just grand, Kevin thought. I'll have two biddies on my arm. But he smiled at Ginger, and she took that as a cue to continue.

"We've been through a lot together in our many years."

"Does she have a place in Palm Beach?"

"No. She's coming down for Carl's birthday. Dottie is the one who assured me that Carl could handle anything the kids threw at him. I think she's right. I felt so at ease with Carl. I talked to him about all sorts of things. Like an old friend."

Kevin took this in. He sure wished he could have been a fly on the wall for their *tête-à-tête*. He could just imagine how her young lover had come up in the conversation. In time, in time. Best not to rush things. Focus on her best friend, that was his strategy. He asked Ginger so many questions about Dottie, by the time they finished dinner, Kevin knew everything about Dottie except her blood type.

"Well, I'm excited to meet her but take all the girl-time you need. Maybe I'll sign up with Captain Jim and go deep sea fishing for a day."

"Do you mean Captain Jim on television?"

"Exactly. That fellow who runs ads on TV. I've always wanted to try it. It'll give you ladies some space."

Kevin is so sensitive, she thought. Only he would think of that.

This promises to be a tedious time with old Dot around, Kevin mused to himself.

"By the way, how long will Dottie be staying?"

"I hope through the weekend. We'll do dinner at home and maybe I'll ask some people over for drinks on Friday. Dottie's been coming to 3-Oaks for years. Everyone adores her. It will be nice for you to meet more people at a smaller gathering. I'll probably be busy most of tomorrow. I have to get on the phone and call everyone."

He took her hand. "We have all summer to plan our life together. What are a few days or even a week?"

"Thank you for being so understanding. Dottie's going to love you!"

THAT NIGHT, GINGER slept soundly. Her reunion with Kevin had pushed aside her qualms. Also, she had successfully put aside her talk with Carl and his promise to 'look into matters.' She was not brooding about what she would do with the new information, probably it would just go back into the safe. Once she and Kevin were married, she would tell him everything. Not about hiring a team in Jacksonville, and not about her time at The Plaza. It was surprisingly easy for Ginger to compartmentalize these things. What happened at The Plaza was, in part, her way of readying herself to be his. She didn't expect Kevin to understand. She was proud of herself for the last two days. That night, Ginger had no nightmares.

Chapter 28

FIRST THING IN the morning, refreshed, Ginger called the catering desk at the club.

"Wendy? Mrs. Johnson. I'm having friends for drinks on Friday. Can you ask Sam to help with the bar? There will probably be 20 or 30 people, tops. I'd like the club to send over *hors d'oeuvres*? Great. Ready? Thank you. I'd like shrimp with your wonderful Russian dressing . . . the jumbo cheese puffs, onion puffs, and miniature burgers. Then, let's pass beef tenderloin on silver dollar buns and ham on biscuits. Also, make some vegetable tempura. That ought to hold everyone, those who want to make it dinner."

Wendy repeated the menu, then added, "Yes, Mrs. Johnson. What time?"

"I've invited people for 6:00, so maybe Sam should arrive at 5:00. You'll have to bring ice as I only have a small ice maker in the bar. Sam knows. I have Margale, but I'll need a girl from the club to help pass — "

"Amy is available. I can have Amy help."

"Wonderful, and she's good in the kitchen too. Good. I'll phone you with the exact number later today."

"We'll take care of everything. Thank you, ma'am."

It had been a long time since she'd entertained. Still, she felt a little uneasy realizing everyone would know that Kevin was living at the house. She would be sure to mention that it was a temporary arrangement, while he looked for a place of his own. It was good, she told herself, to have friends meet and get to know Kevin. Nothing about their serious plans, however, but just that he was staying with her *and* in the guest room. Dottie had taught her long ago that getting out in front of gossip was the best strategy. To herself, she admitted that she seemed to teeter between two positions. One moment she was sure of him, like when she was in his arms, then another moment, she was waiting for word from Carl and 'his people in Jacksonville.' This back and forth between contentment and her qualms meant that she didn't feel as confident as she had when she told Diane and Dottie about him. Anticipating the arrival of Dottie and throwing a party were excellent distractions.

Ginger pulled out the 3-Oaks directory and made another call.

"Sally? Dottie's coming to visit. Drinks and heavy nibbles at 6:00, Friday? Wonderful. I'm so glad you two can come. What? Oh, thank you. Yes, the countess bought my painting, but I never got to meet her. There was flooding in Devonshire!"

Ginger glanced again through her 3-Oaks directory.

She loved Kevin and Kevin loved her, and that was that. The sooner the community got used to him the better. Eventually they would know that he was here to stay. And they would like him. He was handsome and charming. And he was smart. There were a lot of tests to pass to become captain of a 747. All those long flights over the Pacific. Actually, they scared her. If Kevin gave up flying permanently to be with her — and they had touched on this — then he could really take up golf and tennis. Bill promised to include him in his games. He would meet some men and they would like him. Maybe he could do something at Air Safety. Maybe teach, just part time. She needed to help him reduce his stress. Chronic stomach issues were not good. Ginger realized she had forgotten to check the prescription bottles she found in his room. The clippings in his bedside table had made her completely forget.

Ginger went through the book. Her thoughts were just a delaying tactic.

She had to make the big call. No one dared to have a party of ten or more without Louise. It wasn't worth it. She took the plunge and dialed.

"Louise? Drinks, Friday, at 6:00? Dottie's coming from Atlanta. Yes, yes, plenty of food if you and Henry want to make a dinner on the *hors d'oeuvres.*"

"Will your Ken doll be there?"

"Yes, my friend, will be there. Not Ken, it's Kevin. By the way, Kevin is using my guest room downstairs. All the hotels and motels were full for a wedding. Just as easy for him to look at real estate from my house."

"I thought Dottie stayed in the guest room?"

A conversation with Louise could feel like a cross-examination.

"Dottie will be upstairs, by me. We're going to have a fun girls' visit. I've got to run, lots of calls to make. See you Friday!"

Why did Ginger feel compelled to explain everything to Louise? *"Never complain, never explain."* The Duchess of Windsor was famous for that phrase. In fact, Louise had it in needlepoint on a pillow. Louise, she was the Duchess at 3-Oaks. She always aroused the old feelings Ginger remembered from her days at Miss Hall's. The feeling of being inferior to the people around her and, therefore, strangely beholden to them.

She sighed, thinking, I guess I'll always have those feelings.

But maybe they would go away when she married Kevin. When she was Mrs. Kevin McCoy everyone would be jealous, including Louise. Ginger smiled. It was good she had been up front with Louise. Even though she was certain that long before sundown all of 3-Oaks would know that Kevin was living with her. Louise, as the messenger of this juicy information, would surely derive power and importance. After an hour, she was finished making her phone invitations. Everyone was a Yes. She made one more call.

"Wendy, Mrs. Johnson again. We'll be 26 for Friday. So please add the chicken in chutney and some smoked salmon on pumpernickel. Thanks."

After the flurry of phone calls, Ginger returned to the sanctuary of her studio. She was grateful to Kevin for respecting her as an artist. As Ginger began to paint, she became transported and lost in her thoughts. Just like when she was a girl. What would her life have been like if her father had allowed her to go to art school? Would she have moved to New York and lived in Soho? What would it have been like if she had achieved her dreams and become a widely known artist? But now, on the threshold of a new life, why bother about the past? Even if she could, she would not redo her life. She was content. She would settle the dangling threads of Ted's estate and live happily ever after as Mrs. Kevin McCoy. Painting helped to make the time pass quickly until Dottie's arrival. From now on, whenever Dottie visited, they would have a man to share. Even though Dottie was a full ten years older, she showed no sign of her age. She was a vivacious Southern belle, with wonderful wit and was everyone's favorite. Even Louise bowed to Dottie. This was going to be a celebration, the happiest time in years. Ginger painted into the night.

CHAPTER 29

GINGER AND KEVIN were on the terrace reading while waiting for Dottie to arrive. Ginger put down her book.

"Kevin, you've been marvelous for the past couple of days."

He looked up from *Forbes Magazine* and smiled.

"You mean by making myself scarce?"

"I mean for allowing me to focus to get everything organized. Tonight, it will be just you, me and Dottie and we'll eat out here. Unless she's exhausted and would rather have a tray in her room. We'll see. Tomorrow, we're going to Diane and Bill's. They want to hear everything about the countess, and I want to hear about your golf game from Bill. Friday is my — " she almost said *our* " — drinks party. Saturday, we'll play by ear. Dottie loves the fish at Eddie's. Maybe on Saturday we'll go out."

"Maybe I'll go out fishing on Thursday. And, if it goes well, I'll go out on Saturday, too, and bring home fresh catch for dinner. Captain Jim said he'd clean up whatever I caught, and Margale can cook anything."

"Oh, Dottie and I love fresh fish right out of the ocean!"

This idea really hit the bullseye with Ginger, Kevin thought.

"Captain Jim said pompano and tuna are running."

"Margale does pompano in a bag. Surprise us."

"Oh, I will."

Women go crazy when a man 'brings home the bacon' or, in this case, the fish. If I'm unlucky on the boat, there's a fish market in the village. Kevin would impress them one way or another.

The phone rang. Ginger listened and waited. Margale come out onto the terrace.

"Mrs. Morris is at the gate."

"Why don't you go greet her. I'll stay out here. See if she's up to company after her long trip before you spring me on her."

"Oh, that's very thoughtful. I'll go see."

Kevin had a sinking feeling. But he would survive this. He could survive anything. He always had. He picked up his magazine and stretched out on the chaise lounge. Before long, he could hear the squeals of delight. Nothing like a couple of Southern women, he thought. He had to give old Dot a chance. It was only a few days.

Inside, after Dottie's driver rolled in Dottie's suitcase, Ginger and Dottie exchanged rounds of hugs. Dottie was short, slightly plump, with a peaches and cream complexion, and a crown of silver hair. She was in her Dottie uniform: a dog collar of pearls, a loose buttoned blouse in pastel, slacks, and Belgian loafers with tassels.

"Margale would you please help Mrs. Morris unpack and help her get settled upstairs."

"So nice to have you here, Mrs. Morris."

"Margale, such a treasure, just like my Dessie. But don't send me upstairs just yet. Not when I've been waiting to meet Mr. Wonderful."

"Kevin's on the terrace."

"Lead the way!"

The old friends walked out arm in arm, like schoolgirls.

175

"Kevin McCoy, may I introduce my dearest friend in the South — "

"Only the South — ?" Dottie corrected her, and Ginger laughed.

"In the world!"

"Much better!"

"Dottie Morris."

Coyly, Dottie extended her hand.

Kevin took her hand, bowed, and kissed it. She didn't appear to be a force to be reckoned with. But he was sure she was a steel hand in a velvet glove.

"I'm so happy to meet you, Dottie. Ginger has told me so much about you."

"Likewise, Mr. McCoy."

His suave move made the older lady's eyes glisten. She surveyed Kevin. Then, she looked beyond him at the splendid scenery.

"My, I just forget how lovely it is at 3-Oaks. I'd be right here with you if I didn't have all my people in Atlanta."

"I hope you'll be here for many, many days. But I am sure you'd like to start off with time with Ginger. I promised Margale I'd run into town before dinner. Seems we used up all the tonic water. It'll give you girls a chance to chat. Need anything?"

"I don't need anything, do you Dottie?"

"Can't think of a thing."

"I look forward to tonight."

"Drinks at 6:30, dinner at 7:15," Ginger said.

"Wonderful. See you two girls then."

Dottie watched Kevin as he left the terrace. Ginger watched Dottie.

"Well?"

"He certainly is attractive, charming, and considerate. Maybe I will go upstairs, get settled, and have a little toes-up before dinner."

"Come, I'll go up with you, then leave you. I'm right down the hall so just come see me anytime, like a sorority! Oh, I'm so happy you're here."

AT 6:30 THE MUSIC was playing. But there would be no dancing in Kevin's arms tonight. Dottie was holding forth before dinner.

"Fly Me to The Moon ... that song takes me back. I used to love dancing to that. Bert, that's my deceased husband. Bert and I were married for 50 years. We met during my coming out season. We used to dance until dawn. My feet just couldn't stop. By the end of our first summer together, my feet had to be bandaged. Now, tell me Kevin, where are you from?"

"Jacksonville. My father is a doctor. He was with St. Martin's hospital."

"Is he retired?"

"I really don't know. I left home years ago. He didn't approve of my career choice and so we parted ways."

"Oh, now isn't that too bad. Family is everything. Why, I don't know what I would do without my clan, unruly though they be."

"My brother became a doctor, so that filled in both filial requirements, I'm sure."

"I see. And your mother?"

"I just don't know. I may contact them in a few months now that I plan to really settle down."

The remark registered as significant to Dottie. Ginger hadn't realized how delicate and problematic this line of questioning might be. She was grateful when Margale came out onto the terrace.

"Dinner is served, Mrs. Johnson."

Saved by the bell, Kevin thought. Yes, family is important. That is, if you have one that loves you, not one that gives you away.

Ever since the hour Kevin learned that he was adopted, he had mentally separated himself from his adoptive family and thought only of his birth parents — his real family, the ones who had given him up and abandoned him. He would steer clear of all of that with Dottie. Ginger would probably fill her in. Women confided in each other about everything. Obviously, he had to be circumspect. He knew full well that a Southern woman is sharp as a tack, despite the shrieks, the giggling and acting the coquette. Luckily, dinner conversation was light. A lot of Atlanta catch-up, Garden Club gossip and all the goings on in Dottie's family. When the subject of Carl, the lawyer, came up, Kevin paid close attention. But the women mostly focused on his 75th birthday party, about the festivities, the food, and the toasts. Ginger told the story of flying to New York to drink champagne with the countess who bought her painting, *Sand and Surf*, only never meeting her. It wasn't until coffee that Dottie turned the spotlight back on Kevin.

"What do you do Kevin? You mentioned that your family did not approve of your career choice."

A strange tack thought Ginger. Dottie knew Kevin was a pilot.

"I'm a pilot."

"But how wonderful. Where do you fly?"

Dottie had had a few glasses of wine and was becoming more Southern.

"I'm with Northwest Airlines. We fly to Asia."

"I love the Orient. That's what my generation calls it. I've seen so much change in China, and Japan and Thailand. I just love it there, or should I say loved. I haven't been over there for years. I mostly travel where I can charter, it's easier now."

"Kevin's a captain on a 747, he's just too modest to say so."

"My, my. That's a big plane and a big responsibility. I would think your parents would be proud of that."

Dottie was circling back to Kevin's least favorite subject: family.

"Well, I didn't start out on a 747. I started at the bottom, naturally, and trained for years with no guarantees."

"He trained right here, at Air Safety. He knows the area and loves it."

"I love everything about it," Kevin said, staring boldly at Ginger. She blushed. Dottie carried on, as if she didn't notice.

"I visited Ginger and Ted here for years. I have always said if ever I move to Florida, it would be to right here in Treasure Beach, not Palm Beach. Now, if you kids will excuse me, I'm going up. I've had a long day of traveling and, boy-oh-boy, did we have a party last night."

Dottie stood. Ginger and Kevin did so, too.

"Dottie, I think I'll join you," Ginger said.

"No dear, you stay here. I'm going to watch the news and turn out the light."

"I have a busy week. Kevin, you don't mind?"

"Of course not. I'll see you tomorrow in the afternoon. I leave early."

"Teeing off at dawn?"

"Kevin doesn't play golf."

"That's interesting. Yet you chose to look for a house on a golf course."

"Kevin plans to play."

"That's right. But tomorrow morning, I have to see a man about a fish," he said and laughed.

"Kevin was going to surprise you by making a fresh catch of pompano or tuna."

"Yes, wish me luck!"

"Good luck," the two friends said together, and giggling went up the stairs.

Dottie opted for sleep over a late-night gossip session. Best to let her sleep, Ginger thought, closing Dottie's door. They'd have the whole day tomorrow to shop and talk.

CHAPTER 30

L ATE THE NEXT MORNING, Dottie came into Ginger's room. "Morning, honey," she said.

"You've had a good long sleep."

The friends kissed one another and settled in the chairs by the window.

"I was up with the sunrise. I slipped out onto the terrace. Margale knew I was awake."

"Goodness aren't you the early bird. Did she feed you, I hope?"

"Margale made me a tomato omelet, it was divine, fresh orange juice, and wonderful coffee. I had such a good sleep. I forgot how comfortable your beds are, and the sheets are sublime!"

Ginger smiled. Dottie always appreciated luxury.

"I'm very up to date on your household. Your lovely young man has gone fishing. Your catch is going out to make a catch!"

Dottie laughed at her own joke.

"He's already a provider."

But both women knew who would be footing the bills. That's all right, Ginger thought. It comes with her new status as a widow, and a wealthy one. As the saying goes, "You're either born into it, made it, or married it."

"I'm glad you enjoyed your morning. I just had juice and coffee early. I wanted to do my desk, and free up the day for gossip, lunch, and whatever. There's not much shopping here, it isn't Atlanta. Still, we can give it a whirl if you like."

But Dottie had not come to 3-Oaks to shop. Ginger was her best friend; it was Dottie's solemn responsibility to make sure Ginger had her head on straight. She had to tread lightly and start slowly. Clearly, Ginger was deeply smitten. All morning Dottie had promised herself that she would have an open mind.

"Let's wait and see. It's lovely to just relax. Somehow you never do it at home — with the phone, the house, mail, the usual, kids everywhere and everything. Why, later today I might even read a book! I recall one time being here and reading a book by the pool and just loving it. But first, let's gab. I want to hear more about Kevin McCoy."

"I've never felt like this, Dottie. At least not since I was in my 20s — "

"I know, since that cad. What was his name?"

"Frank Pierce. I loved Ted, of course, you know that. But this is different. I don't know how to describe it — "

"It's called romance. *Butterflies, adrenaline highs, life on Jupiter and Mars,* just like in the song. You feel like you're playing *among the stars.*"

"Sometimes I am breathless when I think of him. But just so you know, Dottie, Kevin lives *downstairs.*"

Dottie hoped this was true.

"It is getting harder though to keep him from following me upstairs. But we agreed to wait. There's a lot to straighten out. I'm preoccupied because of the estate issues with the kids — "

"Was Carl helpful?"

"Oh yes."

"Good."

"And Kevin's been very understanding. The thing is, we both want it to be perfect."

Dottie had to work quickly. There was still time to find out if Kevin was sincere and to make sure Ginger was using her head, and not just her heart, and other parts of her anatomy.

"Well, you know I want your happiness above everything."

"Thank you, Dottie!"

"Now, tell me what you know about him."

"Like he said, he's from Jacksonville. He loves flying and always has. The thing about his family is, well, when he was 12, he overheard his parents talking, and found out that he was adopted. It was an awful shock. They didn't know he heard. He didn't tell them. That feeling of betrayal just ate away at him. And the feeling of abandonment has never left him. He feels safe with me, and I feel the same with him. We both have our wounds."

"You're a grieving widow, after all. How long after Ted died did you meet Kevin?"

"It was the same week. But Dottie, you know that Ted had been gone for a lot longer than that. For years . . ."

"Yes. This is true. But the open house was right after you got back from the funeral?"

"Yes, but — "

"Surely you were feeling extremely vulnerable . . ."

"I was used to being alone. For two years, Ted didn't even know my name."

Charlie Taylor flashed in Ginger's mind. It has been only a week since The Plaza. She had not contacted him, nor had he reached out to her. It was their unspoken understanding that their tryst had occurred as if in a separate, or parallel, reality. Their night together at The Plaza had answered questions they had in common. They each needed a signal to move on in their lives.

"Yes, all the same, you had to have been in shock."

"What are you suggesting? I've never had anyone listen to me or care for me the way Kevin does. I mean a man, of course. You always listen. I had no idea one could have this type of a relationship with a man, until Kevin."

"A man like Ted, building his business to support his family, doesn't always have the inclination to talk, or describe the wounds from his childhood, even if he was aware of any."

"I always thought that Ted took such good care of me, but — "

"But what?"

"I just don't know why he didn't sign the second trust."

"With Ted, you never lacked for anything, and never will."

Why was Dottie so fixated on Ted? Ted was gone, why was she arguing on his behalf? She said she wanted her to be happy, but did she really? Ginger sighed to herself. Were all her dear friends threatened by a new person in her life?

"It's just different with Kevin. I had no idea what I was missing."

Dottie bristled at this. Ginger was far gone indeed if she was so quick to disparage Ted. Dottie shifted to another line of questioning.

"How did he find 3-Oaks? How did he wander into the Warren's open house?"

"He learned to fly at Air Safety. He's always loved Treasure Beach."

"But how did he hear about 3-Oaks?"

"I think he said he saw an article in *Town & Country*? And then he just called the real estate office, and they told him about the open house. Obviously, he was looking for something smaller. But now he's here. It's just incredible how things work out. My father used to say, 'Good things just come out of the blue, particularly when you're not looking.' Well, Kevin just came out of the blue! Dottie, he wants to spend the rest of his life with me."

Dottie raised an eyebrow.

"Have you made plans?"

"He wants to take care of me. He even offered to help me with the estate problem."

"I bet he did."

"I'm sorry — ?"

"Ginger, I am going to say something you might not like to hear. You are a beautiful woman, smart and fun, with an envious figure, but you are in your late sixties. Let's get to the bottom line here. How old is Kevin McCoy?"

"Fifty. We celebrated his birthday last week. But Kevin will not tolerate any conversation about age. 'The subject is closed,' he said. 'Let's never discuss it. Age doesn't matter to us.'"

The situation was more dire than she'd thought. It was time to be direct.

"Ginger. Florida is loaded with rich widows, and you are now one of them."

"That's an awful thing to say. This is not like that."

"What man reads *Town & Country*? Men read *The Economist*. Can you see Ted or Bert or Carl reading *Town & Country*?"

"I'm sure he reads those, too. He's very well informed."

"I just don't want anyone taking advantage of you. I will be here to pick up the pieces, you know, but let's try to avoid that."

"I know you feel protective towards me. I thank you for that. Maybe you are even a little jealous of Kevin in my life . . ."

Dottie stayed quiet and tried very hard not to roll her eyes.

"You know how love arrives — unexpectedly and it changes everything."

"Years and years ago, during the debutante season, I was madly in love with George Parker, or I thought I was. My parents liked George, but they had other things in mind. In those days, as you know, marriages were arranged. My parents had picked Bert Morris and Bert Morris had picked me. When George left for the military, the families took over. The Stuarts, another old Atlanta family, gave a dance. Bert danced with me all night and I found that I really cared about him. He was attractive, easy, even though I wasn't breathless like I had been with George — but

Bert said he had always loved me. Bert courted me and proposed. And eventually, I fell in love with him. I never looked back. It was a good match and lasted for 50 years, as you know. I could not have had a better life. When George died, he was on his fourth wife. By the way has Kevin been married, any children?"

"He's been married, but no children. It was a short marriage, the daughter of someone, I can't exactly remember. But it didn't last. She left him for a very wealthy man. Kevin has been abandoned twice. He is very strong and vulnerable at the same time."

"Why isn't he working?"

"He's on medical leave. Six months, he said. Something to do with his stomach."

"I think we ought to find out the particulars, don't you? You don't want to be a purse and a nurse."

"Dottie, you think I'm just a foolish old woman. Well, I'm not. That's why I've asked him to stay here. We have all summer to be together and really get to know each other. After all we've been together day and night for a month now. Well, part of the nights," Ginger added with a giggle.

There's no fool like an old fool, Dottie thought.

"Ginger, if there's anything puzzling or doesn't figure about him, you must ask him about it. And if you don't, I will. Did you talk to Carl about him?"

"Yes."

"Well, that's good to hear. He can tell you stories that will make your hair curl. Florida is loaded with rich widows and the world of young men who prey on them. Why Palm Beach is lousy with walkers, young dandies get paid by rich widows to take them to balls and dinners. A lot of them move in. Very few marry, however, probably on the good advice of their lawyers. But they pay plenty. Talk to Carl. He could write a book about the gigolos of Palm Beach."

"Kevin is not some gigolo! Dottie, he's going to be my husband!"

"I'd like to know about his medical condition. Could be pancreatic cancer? And he's just looking for a place to die comfortably?"

"Dottie, you're horrible. But as a matter of fact, the other day, I was in the guest room checking the flowers, and I looked for his medications to write down and ask the pharmacy. So don't think I'm not curious myself."

"Good girl. And what did you find?

"I found two prescription bottles, but then I went to write them down and —"

"And what?"

"Oh, nothing, I . . ."

Throughout this conversation, Ginger was trying to hold up a barrier between her friend's concerns and her own. But Dottie's campaign of questions had worn her down.

Dottie knew her friend too well. Her clouded brow meant something.

"Ginger, what is it?"

"Well, I've told you everything, wait here, I'll be right back."

Ginger dashed downstairs to Kevin's room. She returned with the vials in hand and a newspaper clipping. She handed the clipping to Dottie and went to her desk to write down the prescription names. Dottie looked at the clipping.

"Oh my God, honey. He *is* a fortune hunter."

"I know how this looks, and it needs an explanation. Kevin is not a fortune hunter."

"Who saves obituaries? No one saves an obituary unless he knows the individual or has a plan: a plan to approach the widow, a widow who might have investments, insurance, and a life of luxury with a house, a club, all of it, and Ted's money."

"But I don't have Ted's money."

"Not yet. Has he asked you questions about the estate?"

"Not really. Hardly. Well, a little. I haven't gone into details, but Kevin is very concerned for me."

"Ginger, has it occurred to you that Kevin is very concerned for Kevin? Carl is going to work that out. It's the law, he knows the law, and the kids will get schooled in it, too. Have you thought about how Kevin waltzed into your life, heart, and home? Next it will be your bank accounts. He's clever and charming and in you, my dear, he's found a package!"

"I am absolutely certain that Kevin loves me, as certain as I've ever been about anything."

"As certain as you were with that Frank?"

The thought took the wind out of her. She had felt certain of Frank and his love and look what happened there. Oh, she wished she had told Dottie her secret, but she couldn't tell her now. It was too much. Yet she loved Kevin. So, what if she was a rich widow, a package? Kevin was a package, too. Young, fun, and suave. What if she was in denial about his motives. What if he was looking for a rich widow? What if she didn't care?

"Of course, we'll talk about it and the clipping. Well, so what if I am a package? Bert was a package, wasn't he? Ted was a package. I was going to mention it, but then I was in New York, and I haven't yet figured out how to explain why I was going through the nightstand in his room — "

"It's your house. And he's the one who needs to explain!"

"And he'll have a good explanation. Please, give him a chance. I swear you'll adore him. He's no gigolo or some fortune hunter! I know you have my best interest in mind and that's why I'm not angry about your suspicions . . ."

"They aren't only *my* suspicions. Clearly, you have some of your own. Believe me, I would love to eat my words. You deserve love in your life. But Ted worked too hard to build a business and make his money for you, his children, and grandchildren. And as selfish, and lazy as those kids might be they are his flesh and blood and more deserving than Mr. Kevin McCoy."

Ginger stood up, gathered the bottles and the clipping.

"I wrote down the prescriptions. I'll call my doctor tomorrow." She hurried downstairs. She wanted to put everything back before Kevin returned. When she returned Dottie was waiting for her. They were both tense.

"Look, Dottie, it's noon. Let's go to the beach cabana for lunch. I'm dying to hear everything that's going on in Atlanta. Then tonight you and Kevin and I are going to Diane and Bill's for dinner."

"Oh, that will be lovely, dear."

Dottie wondered just what Diane and Bill thought about Kevin McCoy. Maybe Dottie would have a minute to ask Diane. Maybe they knew more about him.

"Let's go. I'm starving. But I always am — and that's why I don't look like you!"

CHAPTER 31

"DIANE, HONEY, WHY you're still pretty as a picture. And Bill, you're just a hunk. There's no one like you in Atlanta, not since Bert died. I'm so glad to see you two."

Diane hugged Dottie.

"Oh, it's been too long, come sit. Bill will make you a drink. Hi, Ginger. I haven't seen you since you were hobnobbing with the countess of so and so — "

"Edington," Kevin said.

"I've been holed up, I'm afraid. And getting ready for Dottie's visit."

"Holed up — ?"

"In my studio."

"And what have you been doing with Ginger so occupied? Have you been practicing your putting? Since Bill has converted you to the game?"

Kevin threw his head back and laughed. Everyone greeted him warmly, especially the women, Ginger noted. The clothes she had bought him had arrived and he looked like a million bucks. *He was a package.* Of course, women were bound to be jealous. Even Dottie. Ginger would have to get used to that.

"Bill just got back from DC. I'm sure you two men will have a lot to discuss."

"Things are hopping there as always," Bill chimed in. "I was saying to a certain senator, one on my side of the aisle, we'd best watch out this year. Look at what a circus the last election cycle was!"

Kevin was about to start a round of questions, but Bill turned to Dottie.
"Martini?"

"How nice that you remembered," Dottie said, positively oozing with Southern charm.

"I never forget. Two olives, right?"

He winked at her. Dottie laughed, utterly delighted.

"Have you been able to get in some golf since we covered the course?" Bill asked Kevin, then he turned to Ginger. "Ginger, are you in a bourbon mood or wine?"

"I'd love wine, thanks."

"Come here Kevin, you can help. I think you know your way around my bar by now."

Kevin didn't take well to being bossed around like a servant, still he smiled amiably.

"Ginger, when are you going to regale us with tales of the countess?"

"I would, only I never met her. There was flooding in Devonshire, so she got on her private jet — "

"With Ginger's painting," Kevin added.

"With my painting, yes, and left New York." It was nice how proud of her Kevin was. She beamed at Dottie, with a touch of defiance.

"And so, you were stranded in New York, all by yourself? What did you do with yourself?"

Suddenly, everyone was looking at her, waiting for her reply.

"If a girl can't amuse herself in New York, she's hopeless!"

The quip bought her some time.

"Luckily, I was at The Plaza and right across from Bergdorf Goodman." Everyone laughed, and her panic passed. "You were worried about me, but I was worried about Kevin. Thanks for taking him under your wing while I was away."

But Bill seemed determined to pre-empt any attention Kevin might receive.

"Here," Bill said, passing glasses to Kevin. "Deliver this to the ladies, then help yourself."

Over dinner the topic of conversation alternated between Dottie in Atlanta and Bill in Washington. Kevin noticed that Ginger seemed quiet for much of the evening. Every time he looked at her or winked, she seemed not to see or just looked away. Was something bothering Ginger? Maybe all the old friends together without Ted stirred up memories. Eventually, it struck Kevin that Ginger was avoiding him. And when he resorted to squeezing her hand three times, she didn't respond. Had she already forgotten their secret language? As soon as dinner was over, she stood up.

"We should probably leave. I have some things to do before the party tomorrow, and I promised Dottie I'd take her to all the shops in town."

"Kevin, are you shopping with the ladies?"

The host hadn't talked to him all evening, and now he wanted to get in a finishing dig.

"No, I'll let the girls go. I'll think I'll visit my old school, Air Safety, and see what's going on."

That was a decent answer, Kevin thought. No one knows I'm out of a job and no one needs to know. But the truth was, Air Safety brought back bad memories. Kevin had applied to be a captain and been turned down. He had always flown in the third seat. No wonder. He'd had a few vodkas in Tokyo too close to flying time. They'd given him a warning, but then they found out he did it again in Hong Kong. Just my luck, he thought. Only Kevin had never had much luck. On the day he was born, he was given away. Those memories burned inside him. Sometimes his anger was so strong he felt capable of murder. He was getting desperate ever since Manalapan. Now Dottie was here for four more days, then he could get on with his plan.

Dottie was making a long-winded, Southern goodbye.

"Thanks y'all. A visit to 3-Oaks would not be complete without dinner at the Butler's. Diane, you're a hostess we all can learn from. And Bill, speaking of elections, why you ought to run. You know everything and everyone in Washington!"

Exactly what Bill thinks, Diane thought. Dottie knows just what to say, particularly to a man. Ginger was the same. Kevin McCoy was certainly attractive. She noticed how he kept glancing and gazing at Ginger all evening. When was the last time Bill looked at me that way . . . ? I wonder if he's looking at anyone in DC these days. Funny how, even after ten years, the trust never comes back completely. The anger fades though. Diane admitted she felt jealous of Ginger. It was only natural. She wondered if it would work. I wonder what Dottie thinks of him? She'd grab her at the party tomorrow.

"Goodbye, everyone, see you tomorrow."

Kevin jumped into the cart with Ted's initials and speeded along the path. He certainly is making the place his own, Dottie thought. Ginger had been quiet all evening, she noticed. At one point, when she looked across the table at Ginger, she wondered if she was going to cry. But it was hard to tell for sure in the candlelight.

The three walked into the house.

"Ready girls?" Kevin said.

"For what?" asked Dottie.

"For a nightcap by the pool?"

"The only thing I'm ready for is bed," Dottie yawned. "You can tell Diane grew up in the South. All Southern ladies know how to entertain, even with a hamburger!" Dottie laughed. "The flowers are another giveaway. Big bouquets are gauche and tacky. The simplest arrangements convey graciousness."

"Well, I love Southern belles and you two lead the pack."

"Thank you. Now good night, you two. I'm going upstairs."

"Me too," added Ginger, with a yawn that Kevin suspected was fake.

"No nightcap?"

"I don't think so. We've a busy day tomorrow. But help yourself. I know you will."

The ladies climbed the stairs together murmuring something or other.

As Kevin poured himself a drink, he wondered: Did he detect some sarcasm in her comment? No, Ginger didn't mean anything by it. He shouldn't be suspicious or jump to conclusions. It made him uneasy that he'd hardly been alone with her since she returned from New York. Dottie was the priority, and she'd warned him. Besides, nobody likes a threesome. Threesomes never work. He would have Ginger and everything else in just a couple of months.

CHAPTER 32

FRIDAY WAS BUSIER than Ginger had anticipated. Margale had to touch up the silver. The linens had not been used in years and were not fresh. The flowers arrived, but Dottie was not satisfied with the arrangements. The two friends had just finished redoing them when Tommy from the receiving room arrived with a FedEx. With her clippers in one hand, Ginger took the envelope and checked the return address. It was from Carl Phillips. Immediately, she pulled off her apron, put the clippers down and took the parcel upstairs. Hastily, she slipped it into her desk drawer, putting it, and its possible contents, out of her mind. Then, she quickly changed clothes for an outing with Dottie.

"Ginger? Ready to go?"

"Ready! Coming!"

I'll open it and read it first thing tomorrow, she thought.

Heading down the stairs, Ginger called to Kevin.

"I'm out here," he answered. She found him at his spot on the terrace, reading by the pool. He looked great in his new swimming trunks.

"Dottie and I are going to some shops. We'll probably grab lunch in town. You okay?"

She felt a little sorry for him. She tried not to make it seem like she was avoiding him.

"You gals have a great time."

"Guests are coming at 6:30. Jacket, no tie."

Dottie stepped out onto the terrace.

"I love the informality of 3-Oaks. Atlanta is all buttoned up," she said.

"I know," Kevin replied. "It's perfect here."

Two weeks ago, her life at 3-Oaks had seemed perfect. Now, there were doubts. Well, I'll know everything tomorrow. She prayed that, at last, her fears and her friends' suspicions would be put to rest.

LOUISE AND HENRY Baker were the first to arrive. They were *always* the first to arrive. Some people are just so predictable.

"Darling, oh, you're so beautiful. Love becomes you and so does turquoise. Those aquamarine earrings. Didn't Ted give you those? For your anniversary?" Louise said this loudly and pointedly, no doubt hoping Kevin would hear. "Of course, my daddy gave me so many gifts, jewels and horses, poor Henry is at a loss as to what to buy me. Isn't that right Henry?"

"That's right. I'm utterly lost," he said, grimly.

"Now where's that handsome young man? Are you having the time of your life?" Louise arched an eyebrow. "Oh, Dottie! Darling . . . It is too wonderful to have a visit from a true Southern aristocrat. You look adorable! *You never change.* My daddy used to say that about your mama. Ginger, you know my daddy knew Dottie's mama. Both our families raised thoroughbreds. Those were the days! Oh, and here's handsome Ken — yoo-hoo, Ken — !"

"Kevin," Ginger said.

"Yoo-hoo, Kevin. Come talk to me or better yet, get me a gin and tonic on the rocks and then let's talk."

Louise batted her eyelashes. Kevin played along.

"Right away, Princess."

Saved, Ginger thought. Louise is a one-woman show. Let Kevin entertain her. He was so good at flattering women. Watching their interaction reminded her of Dottie's warnings and her own unease. But then, did it matter? Did she care? They would be happy together. Who else would she spend her money on?

Other guests arrived, Diane and Bill, Sally, Jennifer, Alice, and Missy Warren. All her pals from 3-Oaks. Ginger watched Kevin closely as he greeted each woman. Charming and confident, mixing drinks, he truly stepped into the role of 'man of the house.' No one seemed to object. As women buzzed about him, he was at ease. Men shook his hand heartily and suggested golf, and maybe lunch before or a drink after. She usually enjoyed her own parties, going from guest to guest and talking to everyone. Tonight, was stressful though, as Ginger was not the only one watching Kevin. She could tell that Dottie was still skeptical, and so was Bill. But Ginger was sold. He radiated confidence and was so handsome in his new clothes. Ginger was determined to marry him.

The din and merriment increased until, by nine o'clock, there wasn't a cheese puff, a slider or a shrimp left. Just as she predicted, the 3-Oaks crowd made a meal out of the ample *hors d'oeuvres*. Just as she predicted, the Bakers were the last to leave. Henry was literally dragging Louise out the door.

"I loved everything," Louise slurred. "Absolutely everything, including your sweetie-pie."

Kevin rolled his eyes. Ginger smiled.

"Glad you did. Good night." She closed the door and sighed. "That's always a challenge. Well now, come. Let's sit and have some nibbles."

During her parties, she never ate. The caterers knew this and always set ample *hors d'oeuvres* aside for Ginger to enjoy afterwards. Ginger placed some cheese puffs and bacon wraps and other bites on a plate and settled into a chair. They were all basking in the afterglow of a successful gathering, especially Kevin.

"You really know how to throw a party. I felt right at home here and with your friends."

Dottie tried not to scowl.

"I'm so glad. Kevin, Dottie, eat up! This is the best part of a party. Help yourselves to a drink!"

Dottie poured herself a Diet Coke and sat with a plate of mini crab cakes. Kevin made himself a scotch. He's never one to turn down a drink, Dottie noted.

CHAPTER 33

"GOOD MORNING MARGALE." Ginger called downstairs from her bedroom. "Is Mrs. Morris up yet?"

"She's on the terrace with Mr. McCoy."

"Oh! Would you let them know I'll be down in half an hour? We can have breakfast then."

"Mr. McCoy is about to go fishing. Said he was going to add to his Thursday catch for dinner tonight."

"Yes, that was the plan. Is there enough, do you think?"

"Not yet. But Mr. McCoy assured Mrs. Morris he'd have plenty later today."

"Okay, well I'll come down and say goodbye."

Ginger laughed, she loved his confidence, his optimism. She glanced in the mirror. She looked a little tired. With the great success of the party, maybe even Dottie was finally under Kevin's spell. Certainly, Louise was his biggest fan. The FedEx envelope was waiting for her in her desk. She would look at it after breakfast. She wandered out onto the terrace where she found Dottie and Kevin, her past and her future.

"Another gorgeous day in Paradise, and here are my two beloveds."

"Morning, gorgeous."

"Kevin was just telling me about the fish he caught on Thursday and saying he hopes to bring home more this evening. I love a man who brings home dinner!"

"I want to give you two girls plenty of time. Ginger's so happy when you're here."

"Breakfast first?"

"Nope. I'm meeting Captain Bill at the diner at 10. You two are welcome to join. Dottie?"

"I wouldn't dream of 'rocking your boat.' But I look forward to dinner. There's nothing like a fish just plucked from the sea and set on a plate. Ginger may want to go. You and Ted used to love to fish in the Bahamas."

"Yes."

Dottie turned to Kevin.

"Too bad you never knew Ted. Or did I get that wrong?"

Ginger sighed. It was early for an inquisition.

"I never had the pleasure."

"Your loss. There wasn't a man in the world who didn't admire Ted."

What was the old bird getting at exactly? He had an idea and made a pivot.

"I know he was wonderful."

"So, you did have dealings with him?"

"No, but he had to be, to win a woman like Ginger."

So smooth, thought Dottie, and with irresistible physical wrapping, besides.

"I think we would have gotten along. We both loved to fly. We had a lot in common."

I am not so sure, Dottie thought to herself.

Ginger wanted to put an end to the questioning. "Yes, I enjoy fishing, but today I'm going to stay with Dottie. We'll see you for dinner. Dottie and I have plenty to do and talk about."

Probably too much, thought Kevin. He was grateful to make his escape. At the party he'd endured drunken women brazenly flirting with him. In the morning, there was old Dot looking at him sideways and making insinuations. So, the salt air and the comradery of men was exactly what he needed. Plus, there'd be plenty of beer on board. He had tried not to let anything get under his skin. He told himself that she was not avoiding him, and that the new normal would return as soon as Dottie hit the road. Only 48 more hours. Then, a few more old tunes, spins in the hallway, ice-cream cones, and he would close the deal. There would be a prenup, of course. But with no heirs, why should it not be generous? Then, with an unlimited allowance, a small plane of his own and a sportier car, he'd trade in that tank, Ted's Lexus, for something flashy. Maybe a Ferrari. Soon enough, the days of wine and roses would begin.

He crossed to Dottie, and she offered her hand. Once again, he kissed it and bowed. It was amazing how this courtly behavior came to him, thanks to a childhood in the South.

"I'm off, ladies. Wish me luck!"

Kevin left the room looking like a man out of a magazine, outfitted from head to toe in clothes Ginger had bought him for his birthday.

"He is Prince Charming, Ginger. Why he had me laughing! And I usually don't find my sense of humor before breakfast."

"All the women seem to be under his spell. And the men like him, too."

Dottie kept her chat with Bill by the bar to herself. Seems that on his day's long outing with Kevin, he was hard put to pin Kevin down on his true political position. This caused Bill to shake his head and reserve judgement.

"He may not be fourth generation Atlanta like you and Louise," Ginger said.

"Oh, come now, you know that I'm not like that! Mama was, but I am not. I am sure he's from a nice family. His father was a doctor and all. I just don't like the appearance of gold-digging, first generation, fourth, or any generation. Until he explains why he has a clipping about Ted — "

"Why is that so important?"

"It is clear he never knew Ted, so why did he have a clipping about his passing?"

"Regardless of why or why not, you saw how everyone loves him."

"Prince Charming is charming, no doubt. Can't say I blame you for falling for him."

"You seem to be the only one on the fence. But I've made up my mind — and I think truly it's the only mind that matters here — and his, too, of course. I am in love with him and planning to marry him."

Finally, she was straight with Dottie. Finally, she showed some backbone and had a say about the course of her own life. For three years she'd been alone. For three years she had been faithful and with Ted every day. She deserved joy. She thought of Charlie Taylor and hoped their time together had made him realize this, too. It was not easy being perfect to a spouse who had left in every way except physically.

"You know better than anyone what I lived through with Ted. Finally, I have a chance at happiness. Why shouldn't I take it? Maybe he thinks of me as his fairy godmother, I really don't mind."

"You mean, Sugar-mama."

"Dottie — "

"I'm sorry, Ginger. I want everything to work out. But please, have that conversation with him for your old friend's sake, and tell me what he says. And talk to your doctor, too."

"I will. I promise. But Kevin has brought so much love, and yes, romance into my life, why would I mind offering him financial security?"

"I just hope everything works out."

"It will. And Kevin and I want to share our happiness with you. That is, when you can get away from your tribe!"

The two friends had come to a truce.

"I've got a few things that need my attention. Then let's have lunch. Louise

Baker wants us to lunch, only who knows if she remembers."

"Louise speaks through the grape after five," said Dottie with a sigh. "You do what you need to do. I think I'll pick one of those delicious books you set out for me and read by the pool."

Once again, the two friends walked up the stairs.

"What would Ted have thought of him, I can't help but wonder . . ."

"Ted wanted your happiness above everything else."

"So why didn't he sign that second trust?"

"That is a mystery. Other people are always a mystery."

CHAPTER 34

WITH THE FEDEX from Carl in hand, Ginger looked around for a spot. The porch off her bedroom was inviting. She opened the French doors and was greeted by the fragrance of the greens and the sound of birds. The golf course was always beautiful, whatever the hour or weather. But on this Saturday, it was especially so. Dottie's appreciation for 3-Oaks made her even more alive to the beauty. And Dottie's constant talk about Ted made him seem present. Every Saturday morning, he was on the course with his golf buddies, like Bill. Of course, she knew that Bill would be the last to embrace Kevin. Jealousy took many forms. She had to give everyone time. Ted would have been with his foursome, right now, right there on the green. He would look up, bow to her, wave to her, or throw a kiss. For a moment, she watched a familiar pantomime. Golf carts rolled up and pairs, mostly of men but some women, too, piled out. They set up by the green, positioned themselves, gazed at the flag way off, then got into position. Concentrating on the small ball, they shifted, then swung. The balls arced skyward and into the distance. One by one, and without a word, they hit the ball and watched it fly. Ginger could never hear what the golfers said to one another; still, by their postures or gestures, it was clear how they felt about their drives. Then, they piled back in their carts and drove off. With Ted there had been smoothness, regularity, and predictability. The new chapter of her life was bound to have some bumps, surprises, and delights.

She sat on a chaise, pulled open the envelope and removed the contents. She felt calm. She had stood up to Dottie and shown her resolve. Regardless of what was inside, Kevin was the next chapter of her life.

Dear Ginger,

The attached information, which you requested in our meeting last week may cause you distress. I deeply regret that I must inform you of these facts. I have kept the report brief. When you are ready, contact me for further details gathered by my team in Jacksonville.

Sincerely,

CJP

There was no moment for thought. She turned the page and anxiously scanned the words. For an instant, they baffled her. Then, when the words and their meaning registered, they became a club that bludgeoned her senses.

"Oh my God. My God!" Ginger bolted up and the pages dropped around her. She staggered inside and collapsed on the rug. She was limp and could not make it to the bed. "No, no! No. No!" Then her words devolved into sobs and howls. Nausea roiled her. She crawled towards the bathroom. But the convulsions wracked her, and Ginger was sick on the rug. After, she made it into the bathroom and pulled herself up to the sink, leaned over and threw water on her face. She looked in the mirror and saw only a ghost. Was this a dream?

She heard pounding.

"Ginger! Ginger, what's wrong?"

The sound of Dottie's voice proved that this was no dream. Dottie rushed in.

"*What happened?* I was by the pool and heard you. Oh God, you've been sick! Let's get you to bed. What did you eat?"

Ginger was frantic. She could still only make sounds, not words.

"Heavens, Ginger, *talk to me!*"

Supporting her, Dottie got her on the bed. "You're shaking! You're cold as ice. Dr. Marcus. Margale must call him immediately. Is this food poisoning?"

Ginger curled herself into the fetal position and moaned more.

Dottie hit the intercom, but there was no answer. Had Margale gone out?

"Ginger, talk to me."

She answered Dottie by pointing out to the chaise.

Dottie looked around.

"What?"

Dottie noticed the papers and the FedEx envelope.

She went out and studied it.

"Why, this is from Carl. Is it news? About the trust?"

Ginger was making terrible noises. Frightened, Dottie gathered the pages and studied them as Ginger had done only moments before.

"You're a *mother?* You had a child that you *gave up? You had a child with Frank Pierce?* Is this true?"

Ginger nodded.

Dottie looked back at the pages and gasped. Then, she, too, was plunged into shock.

"Kevin McCoy is your *son?*"

Ginger's wails were proof enough.

Moments ago, Dottie had been by the pool, enjoying a book, with no idea of the scene unfolding. Now, Ginger's violent sobs reverberated in her own body. The room felt like a crime scene, or an accident, and she was the first responder. Luckily, Dottie was an old hand at mortal crises. At her bedside, Dottie gathered Ginger in her arms, held her and rocked her. It felt as if Ginger was releasing a storm of grief, a torrent of tears she had never allowed herself to share or shed. But

Ginger was not conscious of Dottie. She could only feel her pain.

"There, there," Dottie said. "Oh my God. There, there."

The more hysterical Ginger was the more Dottie steadied herself. She had no idea what would come next, but it was clear that the crisis had only just begun.

"Cry, Ginger. Cry as much as you like, for as long as you like . . ."

She cried unabated. Dottie felt Ginger would exhaust herself, but then another wave of anguish overtook her. At last, when the sobs grew slightly less frequent, Dottie glanced at the clock. She had to think for both. She got a cold cloth and washed Ginger's face. Then, she went to the study, dropped ice into a pair of crystal glasses and poured from Ted's stash of White Label. She sat down by Ginger.

"Here, drink this. We'll figure this out."

"I'm sorry, I'm sorry, I'm sorry! I never told you about my baby!"

"Nonsense. And never mind."

"I'm a terrible friend. I wanted to; it was so hard to keep this secret, but I was ashamed. I never told anyone about my baby. Not a day has gone by that I haven't thought of him. Then, this. *Oh, Dottie!*"

Ginger started to gag on her words.

"What?"

"*I almost . . . married my son!*" Ginger fell back against the pillows, trembling. "Dottie, please help me. I can't read anymore."

"You want me to?"

Ginger nodded feebly. Her eyes and her face were transfigured by crying.

As Dottie read, Ginger stared. She felt empty. She wished she were empty. If only she could be empty and prevent the nausea, the feelings, and the thoughts.

When Dottie finished, she took hold of Ginger's hand.

"Kevin McCoy has led a colorful life. He's many things that we suspected. He spent time in Southern Florida under the auspices of another woman. He lost his position as a pilot. He was grounded after multiple incidents of drinking close to flying time. And he's on unemployment. The last page is another letter from Carl saying a detailed report would follow. He knew the adoption information was so important that he needed to send this immediately, given the circumstances. Ginger, you must face all of this but not right now. What you need to do is to decide what to do. Carl also writes that Kevin's birth father — "

Ginger shuddered. "Frank."

"Frank Pierce was killed in a private plane crash five years ago. He was on a hunting trip, elk or something, in Colorado, and his plane went into the side of a mountain. The whole sad history is there."

"I can't read it. I don't want to know anymore. I just feel scared and lost, like a girl again. Ted knew this about me. He always protected me. Why did he have to go? None of this would have happened if Ted was alive!"

"Ginger, Ted did not think of you as a child. He knew you were smart and strong. Ted would not have had any other kind of woman by his side for all these years. He trusted you with everything, his estate and even his foundation. Why he made you co-trustee. That's a big job and not one you give to a child!"

"Maybe he wasn't taking care of me. In the end, he favored his children, and I don't even know why . . ."

"It was a clerical error, not intentional. You know what happened to his memory! Carl says the mediator and the state of Florida will have that settled in just a few months. But, Ginger, let's put that aside right now. We must deal with Kevin McCoy."

Her agitation returned and she started to ramble.

"This is not the son that came out of my womb, who has lived in my mind for 50 years. In my mind, my son looks like Frank, only with my red hair. He went to the best schools. He was strong and loved the woman whom he called mother. I imagined him working in a skyscraper in New York. In finance. He takes the train to Connecticut where he lives with his wife and his children, grandchildren I would never know. Oh, how that pained me to think of, even though it was a wonderful dream! He did good works. He was on the board of the Audubon Society. He was like Ted, a good citizen. Every year on his birthday I celebrated my son and grieved him all at the same time. This man is not my son! He can't be!"

"Ginger that is very lovely, but it's fiction. Made up fantasy. Mothers accept that their children rarely match their ideal. That's not real life. It's not my life and it's not yours. Bert Jr. just got out of rehab, again. And Katie's third, Ben, has Downs Syndrome, and we count our blessings every day he's with us."

"I have just imagined my son for so long, to see this fraud, this gold digger, a desperate cheat, and a liar! And to think, *to think!* No wonder I felt so comfortable with him, he was mine! *My blood!* I just shudder to think. Oh, Dottie! What if, what if I had let him follow me up these stairs!"

Ginger had been ready to do that. Then, the call from Avery and being diverted to New York by the countess. God, thank God for her art, for her gallery, for those sudden switches that kept her from returning home.

"But you didn't. That's all that matters. Now, Ginger, what are we going to do?"

"I don't want him to know. I don't want to think of him as my son. I want him out of this house, out of my life. I can't have that fantasy anymore, and I'm not ready for *this*."

"Then get rid of the nightmare and get back to your life."

"But I can't, I can't — "

"Can't what, child?"

"I can't get back, I'm so ashamed!"

"Ginger, no one needs to know anything. Stop this. You have a wonderful life and friends. Just look around you. You have no financial worries, and your health is good. You have so many blessings. I thank the Lord every day for giving me another day and for as long as He continues to give me more days! So, you must look to the Lord for strength and get through this."

"But what do I do?

"You just tell him to get out. It's your house. It's your decision, your life."

"What do I say?"

"You don't have to say *anything*."

"I can't do it."

"You can and you have to. Tonight."

"Tonight!? What do I tell him?"

"Tell him you need time to think about Ted, your grief. Ask him to leave. That's it. Ginger, when he gets back from fishing, you talk to him and stand firm. You can do this. For three years you've been strong. You've handled everything life tossed you, and never faltered. Let yourself get angry, it's OK. Be furious; it will give you strength. Kevin McCoy is just like his father who abandoned you!"

"How did I not know? Now I see it. The dancing and driving fast. The laugh, the way he threw his head back! I should have known!"

"Everything is clear when we look back."

"Oh, I just didn't imagine!"

"How could you have?"

"When he told me it was his birthday, I should have known then! I've always hated that day! But I didn't!"

"Of course, you didn't, what are the chances?"

"I knew I felt uncomfortable. I had the nightmares. But I just thought I'd have Carl investigate his past before, before I — "

"Before what?"

"Before I married him!"

"All right, all right. Now there will be time, Ginger, to feel all these feelings. That was a good instinct, and you told Carl your secret. You've lived alone with that secret long enough."

"I was afraid Ted wouldn't want me if he knew! My grandmother helped me through it, the adoption. No one else in my family ever said a word. It was like those months of my life never happened. They evaporated, and my baby disappeared. I grieved him. Maybe if I had kept him, he wouldn't have turned out like this. It's my fault."

"What about Frank. Did he take responsibility? What sort of man runs out on a pregnant woman? Especially back then. Then, men from a certain class were honorable. Ginger, you made the right decision. And you've got to be strong now and take your stand. He is not your baby. This is a grown man, who's taken advantage of a widow. A man who preys on others, an intruder, and a thief. Get rid of him."

"How can I do that?"

"I'm going to ask Margale to bring up a tray and some tea. Then, you rest. When Mr. McCoy arrives back from fishing, I'll knock on your door. It is vile behavior to use other people and to deceive them. Think about that. Focus on that. When he returns, I'll keep him occupied and you can get dressed, then come down and tell him to pack up and leave."

THEY WERE BOTH resolved. Dottie left her and Ginger fell into a deep sleep. Later in the afternoon, she heard the knocks on her door. Ginger had forgotten everything for a moment. Sleep was a wonderful escape. But now Dottie stood by her bed.

"Mr. McCoy just returned from fishing. It's four o'clock. Throw something on, honey, and let's get him out before nightfall. You don't want Margale smelling up this house, cooking the fish. We'll go to the club. Now let's just get going and get this over with."

Ginger got up. She had to do exactly what Dottie told her to do. How dare Kevin McCoy take advantage of her and lie to her. Ginger shuddered. She went to her closet, threw on jeans and a shirt, brushed her hair and walked downstairs. He was on the terrace with Dottie.

"Good afternoon, Kevin."

"Hi, beautiful. Oh, you should have been with Captain Jim and me. The water was perfect, like glass. I was just telling Dottie. We went 15 miles out. We watched dolphins dancing. Caught pompano and grouper, I bet Margale's grouper is even better than Eddie's."

It was her turn to speak. She looked helplessly at Dottie. She gave Ginger a stern nod and spoke. "I'm going upstairs. I'll be on my porch. Nice to meet you, Kevin."

And Dottie left.

"Is Dottie going? I thought she was here for a few more days —"

Ginger steeled herself to speak.

"Dottie's not leaving. You are."

Kevin swayed backwards a little.

"What'd you say?"

"I want you to leave. I've been thinking, and I need time, time alone. We have many wonderful memories, but it's over. Please collect your things —"

"What?!"

"And move out."

"Move out?"

"That's right."

"Move out? When?"

"Tonight."

"I just spent two days fishing to bring you dinner and I come back —"

"I've cancelled dinner —"

"And dinner's off and you tell me to move out? What's going on? Is this a joke? What did that old bat say?"

"This has nothing to do with Dottie."

"What brought this on?"

"Please, I don't want a scene."

"What do you call this? You ambush me and don't want a scene — ?! You say we're going to spend our lives together, say you love me and care about me, and now I walk in the door, and you tell me to move out? With no explanation? Are you out of your mind?"

"I'll ask Margale to help you."

"Let's keep her out of it."

"I'm sorry, but I've made up my mind."

"Is this a split personality? Or Alzheimer's, or what — ?"

"I'm completely of sound mind, and I will say it again. Get your things and get out."

"I hope all your rich, fancy friends see me walking to the gate with my suitcase and hitchhiking on Ocean Road. Who knows, maybe one of them will give me a ride. And I'll give them an earful about what a psycho bitch you are!"

It was too awful; she hadn't thought through the details. He'd turned in his car and it was too late to call the Hertz in town. But he'd been drinking, and she had to keep things from escalating.

"Take Ted's car. Take the Lexus. I don't care."

"That's for sure. With your type, everything's disposable — cars, people. You rich folks are all the same."

Kevin turned and started to walk away. The fight seemed to be over. But she couldn't take the blame. She was compelled to follow him. At the door of the guest room, he turned and glared at her. It was like she was looking at Frank. Rage surged through her, and she saw red.

212

"Kevin don't forget to take all your things. Your prescriptions and the clothes I bought you for your birthday. And be sure to take the clippings in the drawer by the bed. You wouldn't want all that research to go to waste."

She turned and walked upstairs. She picked up the phone.

"Margale, please let me know when Mr. McCoy leaves. He'll be taking the Lexus. Oh, and we won't be eating tonight after all. Pack up the fish, please."

"Yes, Mrs. Johnson."

What to do? What to do? She couldn't go to her room. She had too much energy. She had to stay alert until he left. She knew that Dottie also was listening, anxious for some sign of his exit. She went to her studio.

There on the easel, she came face to face with the painting of the back of the man on the beach. She saw clearly that when she thought she was drawing Kevin she was painting Frank. She took out her brushes and, with a surge of creativity and a surge of self-loathing, she painted. She lost track of time and place. She painted passionately, feverishly. In this zone she was free from the vice of reality, just as she had been as a girl. She was in the realm of her imagination where she could breathe freely and revel in creativity. She stayed this way for a long time. Then, the slam of the door and the sound of the car leaving brought her back to the present.

He was gone. Ginger collapsed on her chair and the sobbing began again.

CHAPTER 35

INCENSED, KEVIN HURLED clothing into the back of the Lexus. His camel cashmere jacket, piles of shirts and boxes of shoes. Heaps of fine clothes were thrown in the back like garbage.

Everything had been going according to plan until that snooty old bitch showed up. How dare they go through his things? How dare she tell me to leave? She'd be sorry. Ginger would never have anyone as much fun and as young as he. She had had 40-plus years with Mr. Boring Business and then three years with a breathing corpse. But now it was over. She'd regret it.

Damn! He pounded the steering wheel.

He'd thrown the clippings on the front seat. He'd have to look through the other obits tonight, wherever he settled. Back to the seedy motels, that is until he could find another rich widow.

He had enough money to last maybe a month. He'd gone through his severance. He was heading north but didn't know where.

The worst part was that he'd liked her. A lot. When she was in Palm Beach, and New York, he had looked forward to her return. He wasn't even faking it. He missed her. She was smart and kind. He truly believed she adored him. The old rage surged in his body. No, he'd never had any fucking luck with women.

The sky was dark. He heard thunder. Kevin floored the accelerator. The speed seemed to calm him. The pedal was to the floor.

A sudden Florida storm flooded the road.

The car skidded.

Kevin never saw the tree.

"OFFICER PORTELLO HERE. Crash on 95N, by the Bee Line. Send an ambulance. Whoever's in it is trapped in a crunched can. Close lane one, this is a fucker and could take a while. Have a chopper standing by and notify emergency at Orlando."

"Roger," said the voice on the other end.

Officer Portello pulled the hood over his head and pushed open the car door. It was dark and hard rain was dashing down from the sky, lit by the freeway lights. He'd been a Florida patrolman for 20 years and he'd seen a lot, but this was a particularly bad wreck. He rushed to the driver's side of the vehicle. The dark blue car had hit squarely, smack in the center of the tree. Portello peered in the window of the driver's side and saw the shoulder and the arm of the driver, a man. He yanked on the door. It was locked. He banged on the window.

"Hello? Hello?"

No answer.

"Can you hear me?"

The figure did not respond or move.

He dashed to the passenger side. It was empty. He pulled on the door, but it, too, was locked. He checked all the doors. The driver was alone and there was no getting at him.

Officer Portello pulled out his radio. The canopy of the tree shielded him from the pelting rain.

"Portello here. Just the driver in the vehicle. Can't get at him. He's nonresponsive. Get the jaws of life over here, and quick. Poor bastard."

Now the rain was coming down in sheets. Florida often had such sudden storms and flash floods. Lightning cut the sky, and, for an instant, lit the horrible scene. Waves of water blew across the highway, like it was now a shallow river. The helicopter would have a helluva time setting down. He knocked again fiercely at the window.

"Hello? Hello? Can you hear me? Make a move if you can hear me."

Again, no response. All Portello could do was wait. Soon, he heard the sirens of a fire engine, then he saw the swirling lights. The vehicle pulled up and the team jumped out.

"How long's he been there?" The emergency worker shouted through the rain and wind.

"Not sure. The driver's alone, but no way I can get to him. Helluva storm."

"It's worse further south. Flash flooding through Cocoa. I'm Sam and these here are Jones and Walter. We've got to get that branch cut back to get him out. Let's go boys."

In the distance, there were more sounds of sirens. Busy night for ambulances, Portello thought. Hopefully it would ease up as quickly as it came. He watched them work and said a prayer for the driver.

They worked quickly but the rain was a bitch.

The ambulance arrived.

"Ambulance? Better call the morgue," he muttered. No one could survive this. Not even the old tree.

Half an hour later, a body was gently extracted from the wreckage.

"A light pulse. Let's get him on the stretcher."

Miracle, thought Portello.

It was nearly another ten minutes before the chopper arrived. Waiting on the ground, they heard it before they saw it.

The pilot set it down nice and neat in the desolate road. The team leapt out and grabbed Kevin. Moments later the chopper lifted and reared towards Orlando.

The noise was deafening but Portillo, Sam and the others were used to it. They walked back to the wreck.

"Search the vehicle for ID. Then get it to Yard 44. We can't do a thing until we get an ID from the hospital. Good job guys, as always. Doesn't look like the poor fellow has much of a chance, but if he survives it's because of you. Good night."

In the chopper, a pair of paramedics huddled over Kevin, feeding him air, taking his vitals. They shared a look.

"Pulse is falling."

"Come on, buddy. Hang on."

"We're twelve minutes out."

They exchanged another glance.

"We gotta shock him."

They clamped him and shocked him. His body convulsed back to life.

"Atta boy."

The chopper set down on the roof of Orlando Emergency. Orderlies were standing by.

The door opened.

"We just shocked him. His pulse is back but barely."

The stretcher with Kevin was lifted and then lowered. A guard stood by holding open the elevator.

"We got him," said the lead guy. "Dr. Jamal is waiting."

Kevin was in the OR for a marathon procedure. After, Dr. Jamal gave him a 50/50 chance, which, he admitted to himself, was probably optimistic.

CHAPTER 36

THE TIME WAITING for Kevin to make his exit from Ginger's house was one of the most unbearable intervals of Dottie's life. Dottie had listened to the argument from her room upstairs. The tangle of voices, both shrill and low, followed by inexplicable silences. It reminded her of being in the hospital waiting room while her daughter gave birth or while her grandson underwent another surgery. Mortal agony. She could only imagine what it was like for Ginger.

At last, Dottie followed the distinct noises of Kevin, dragging his suitcase out of the house and his muffled voice, clearly cursing. With the finality of the slamming door, Dottie breathed again, and exhaled a sigh of relief. The house was quiet, but she stayed in her chair, listening. Not until the sound of the car roaring out the driveway, did she spring up to find Ginger. But Ginger was not in her bedroom.

She went downstairs. Margale was nowhere to be seen, either. The guestroom was empty.

"Ginger?"

"Out here," a listless voice answered.

Ginger was on the terrace on a chaise, staring straight ahead.

"There you are honey. Are you okay?"

"Did you hear?"

"Yes. I heard. You did the right thing. You've had a shock. You need nourishment."

"I can't go anywhere. I can't face anyone."

"Is Margale still here?"

"Yes, but I don't want that fish."

"I think we could both use a liquid refreshment, first. I'll make us a cocktail. Stay put. Then Margale and I will have an ice box review. That's what our cook used to call Sunday suppers."

"I'll just drink, thanks."

"Well, you can do that for sure, missy, but you're running on empty. I'll bet there's soup or sandwiches or something."

"Okay," Ginger answered, robotically.

Anybody could have told her what to do and she would have done it. The best idea, however, was doing nothing at all. She was immobilized. If Dottie hadn't been there, she would have collapsed and remained catatonic. The last few weeks had been about death. First there was Ted's death, that finality. And now the death of her relationship with Kevin, another finality. Then there was the death of her hopes and dreams. All her exhilaration, all her certainty, all her expectations had been delusions. He had deceived her, and she had believed that she was lovable. Anger, disappointment, and humiliation roiled inside. Added to this was the sickening horror: Kevin was her son. This truth leveled any hope of resilience or recovery. Which emotion should she deal with first? And how on Earth could she face it all alone?

Dottie brought in drinks. A scotch on the rocks for each. She went through the menu of the emergency supper Margale already had underway. Ginger drank her drink but clearly heard nothing.

"Dottie? Don't leave me."

"I planned to go on Monday, but I certainly can't leave you like this."

Dottie took the glasses and refilled them. Margale brought in trays with warm consommé, toast with butter, creamed spinach, and scrambled eggs. Ginger left her plate untouched, but she finished the second scotch.

Both women were quiet. Ginger was clearly numb, and Dottie trembled for her. After a while, Ginger made a move to go upstairs. It was hardly after eight. But Dottie went up with her and helped her into bed.

"I'm right next door. Wake me anytime. You'll feel better tomorrow, I promise."

Sunday was worse. Everything that had been vague now was vividly real. Kevin had almost been her lover, her husband. It was all exceptionally sordid. The nausea returned again and again. The little food she'd consumed, she wretched up and then slept more. When consciousness returned, along with it the facts, she wretched again and returned to bed, delirious with her own thoughts. Sometimes things like this happened in books, only not in the books she read. All her life she had been thinking of the baby she gave away and the kind of man he would become. Kevin, her son, turns out, was a cheat and a liar. A man who was rotten to the core. How could this be her child? Preying on older women for their money? He was half of his father. Ginger rolled over and drifted off into a drugged sleep again.

Sometime later a knock awakened her.

"Ginger . . ." Dottie called. "Are you okay?"

"I was asleep."

"It's 3:00 in the afternoon, honey." Dottie waited on the other side of the door. "Do you want a little something?"

There was another pause.

"I want to sleep more."

"Margale is making vegetable soup." No answer. "You sleep. I'll be back in an hour when it's ready."

Later, Dottie did not wait to be invited in. With all the authority of a matriarch, she burst into the room with a tray and set it down on the table by the bed. Then she marched over to the French doors and pulled the curtains open. In the two days sequestered in her bed in her room, Ginger had not seen the Florida sun and she winced. Dottie pulled the chair over to the bed and sat down.

"Now, honey, Margale made the soup just for you."

Ginger looked at her helplessly.

"Starvation is not going to ease the pain, child."

Ginger stirred herself and tried to sit up. Dottie arranged the tray and Ginger took a sip of the steaming broth.

"Let's watch a little TV. Take your mind off things," She switched on the news and adjusted her chair towards the big screen TV.

"My, my, just look. There's so much going on in the world. These poor people! Can you imagine? One day you're having dinner with your family and the very next your home is destroyed; half your family is missing and you're looking for them in the rubble? Now how do you contend with that?"

Dottie was caught up in the aftershocks of an earthquake half a world away. Ginger was suffering the aftershocks of the truth and waking up in the ruins of her dreams. She felt like a child again. She remembered how when she came home from school it was always to an empty apartment. If the girls had picked on her, or if her teacher had criticized her, she would race home forgetting that no one would be there. Both of her parents worked. They both had to work to afford Miss Hall's and the trappings that went with it. No one was ever at home to comfort her. That was when her art started to mean so much to her. Drawing was her way of forgetting the hurt. Living in her imagination, she forgot what the girls had said to her and the hurt of being excluded. Losing herself in a picture or canvas, Ginger forgot that nobody was home. Now Dottie was there and Margale was there, but it would be so much worse when Dottie was gone.

Dottie, however, was still fixated on the news.

"Goodness! All this conniving in Washington. Whenever the news switches to something on Capitol Hill, I always search the screen looking for Bill. He's always in the thick of it!"

Ginger didn't answer. She was still thinking about the earthquake. She remembered how she used to imagine her son helping people somewhere in the world after such a disaster. She had pictured him saying goodbye to his wife and children in Connecticut and going around the globe to volunteer, leading rescue efforts with compassion and skill. He'd donate his own money to help because he wanted to give back. So, it stung her afresh to remember who her son was: a liar who took whatever he could from whomever he could. Now it was blindingly clear to her that from the beginning Kevin was like Frank. The gestures, his love of speed and dancing. Most of all, his character was Frank's.

"Ginger? Did you hear what I just said? I was talking but you were a million miles away. I said, let's go to the village tomorrow. I've got to get something for the grandchildren. You know, never come home empty handed! It'll be good for you."

But the prospect of leaving her bed was impossible. How could she go out and into town? What if she saw Diane or Louise, or any of the women who had flocked and swarmed around Kevin just a few nights ago? What if one of those men asked after Kevin, hoping for a golf game? One look at her would tell them everything they needed to know.

They watched *60 Minutes*. Or Dottie did. Ginger couldn't wait for it to be over. She loved her friend, but she had no room for anything besides her own reality. She was relieved when Dottie gathered up the tray and left her alone again.

CHAPTER 37

ONDAY WAS THE same. Ginger only took some sips of soup and water and, at the end of the day, scotch. Dottie could see that she was losing weight. She was already thinner, and her cheekbones were more pronounced. Still, Ginger refused to go to town. Dottie and Margale were worried. Was it time to call the doctor? They debated this endlessly. Finally, Dottie threatened her friend.

"Ginger, if you don't get up, I'm calling Dr. Marcus and going to ask him to come to the house."

"Don't, please. I'm just tired."

"Ginger enough is enough. You lost your heart, and you lost your head. So what? All you've really lost is a month or so of your life. You can't let some fortune hunting cad get you down."

"You mean, my son!"

"Nobody belongs to anybody, honey. You never had the chance to nurture him and raise him right. I doubt that his adopted parents are responsible for the way Kevin turned out either. Things happen that can't be explained. The good Lord made everyone different, didn't he? Why, look at my Laura. My little debutante daughter, didn't get those civil rights genes from her father, or me. Laura just developed that way. She became who she is, that's all. Laura Morris, my little debutante, one of the organizers of the Atlanta March for Civil Rights. We have never been so surprised or proud. Now, missy, I'm going to turn on the shower for you. If you're not showered and downstairs in 30 minutes, I'm going to pick up that phone and interrupt Dr. Marcus's golf game."

A half hour later, Ginger came downstairs.

"That's better. Margale is making you some stew. You've got to get your strength back. Your jeans are already hanging!"

Margale brought dinner to the terrace. Ginger took some sips and Dottie talked.

"I felt very alone once, right after my Mama died. Oh, I was married, and I had children, but my Mama was my strength and my best friend. I remember thinking, I'll never be safe again. Then, her butler, Wilbur, died. Two weeks after Mama. He had been with Mama for 50 years. He couldn't live without her. When Mama rang, Wilbur followed. I guess she rang for him from heaven, and he decided it was best to go on up and see what she needed."

Ginger smiled. She remembered Dottie's mother and Wilbur, too.

"Now tomorrow we're going to town for the grandkids, without fail. You know I plan to leave on Friday. You'll be fine . . . in time. Now, you've got to know that Carl phoned and asked about you. I told him you were adjusting to the situation. I told him you did the right thing, and that Kevin McCoy was gone. Oh, and he had some news about the trust and the kids."

"What news?"

"Jim Donnelly told him that the kids want to settle, and the negotiations are coming along. He made the point that Ted took very good care of you. We agreed on that."

"Did Carl say anything else about Kevin?"

"Only that he had more information, and that he'd send it along. I told him no hurry. You knew all you needed to know."

"Heavens, how much more is there . . . ?"

"You'll read everything when it comes in. Knowledge is power."

"If it doesn't kill you."

"But wait until you're strong. That's what matters now. You hardly touched your dinner. Ginger. You have got to cooperate. I can't leave you scrawny, weak, and bedridden!"

"What will I do when you leave?"

"I'm only a phone call away or an hour by plane. I just love this King Air that brought me here and is picking me up. You can hop over to Atlanta any time. So don't you worry. Plus, I know the real Ginger and more about her now. The Ginger who had the courage to give her baby to a couple who could provide for him. Let that Ginger come forward."

Coaxed by Dottie, Ginger ate more of her dinner. Dottie talked about Ted and Bert and didn't seem to notice that Ginger wasn't listening. She was just glad that she wasn't alone.

CHAPTER 38

I T WAS DAYS before Kevin made a sound. "Mr. McCoy? Can you hear me?"

There was no answer.

Kevin had heard a voice, but just barely. He could not make out the words. Nor could he open his eyes. He drifted downward into a dark pit, and for another day he stayed there.

On the third day Kevin opened his eyes. A shadow crossed his vision, and he could make out a blurry moving figure.

"Where am I?"

He didn't recognize his own voice. It was raspy, like a needle scratching on an old vinyl record. It hurt to speak. Breathing hurt, too. And he had no clue how to move.

"Easy now, Mr. McCoy. You're in the hospital in Orlando. You've been out for three days. You had an accident but you're one lucky fellow. The tree you hit didn't survive, I hear."

"Who are you?"

"Dr. Jamal. We operated on you for seven hours. The whole floor has been waiting for you to wake up."

Kevin had no memory of an accident. He was deathly tired. He drifted off again and slept some more.

Two days later he was able to open his eyes and keep them open. He looked at the end of the bed and saw his leg heavily bandaged, inert in a leather sling. His left arm was bandaged and strapped to his side.

Dr. Jamal approached his bed.

"Well Mr. McCoy, today should be a little bit better. You seem to have stabilized. Good work."

"I need water. Please, I'm thirsty."

"I'll have the nurse bring you ice chips. We'll keep an eye on you the rest of the day, maybe even get you out of the ICU."

"What happened to me?"

"There was a bad storm Friday and driving on the 95 N near the Bee Line, you had a crash."

"I hit someone?"

"Luckily, no. You hit a tree. You broke your shoulder, fractured your femur and hip. There was some organ damage, but we were able to put you back together. Now it's just a matter of time, rest, and eventually, therapy. Recovery may take several months Mr. McCoy, maybe a year. But, as in everything in life, so much depends on you. Once you start physical therapy, we'll get a better idea. But for today, we're grateful you're among the living, Mr. McCoy. The car is wrecked and the tree you hit had to be removed. But you are going to be okay."

The car . . . Ted's Lexus. It was only then that Kevin remembered Ginger, and everything else. He didn't feel physical pain, he was too numb for that, but now the psychic pain was excruciating.

"What happened to the car?"

"I don't know. That's a problem for another day, Mr. McCoy. For now, I want you very still."

"I need water, please."

"Gail will be here in a little while. She'll take care of you. I'll check in on you later and see how you're doing. You're a lucky man."

Kevin closed his eyes. He didn't feel lucky. The only thing he could feel was the wetness on his cheeks. Tears were rushing down his face. He was so parched, he wished he could drink them.

He heard a woman's voice.

"Hello, Mr. McCoy, welcome back to the living. I'm Gail, and I've been monitoring you since your arrival."

"Thanks."

"You're welcome. Open your mouth."

He did so. First, he felt a weight on his tongue and then the shock of cold. His mind formed a remote thought: *Ice chips.* He sucked fiercely. Nothing had ever tasted so good.

"Now hold on there. Not so fast. Let them lay on your tongue and dissolve. They'll last longer. Otherwise, I'll have to bring an ice machine in here."

He slowed down, but only a little.

"You've been through it, the accident, and the operation, too. And we've given you all sorts of medications to keep you comfortable. Just lie back, that's all you need to do for a while."

Kevin concentrated and spoke.

"The car . . . ?"

"The fate of the car has not been my primary focus as of late. But I'll see what I can find out. Maybe tonight we'll try some broth. But we'll have you on an IV for the next few days. Mercy, this one's almost empty."

Kevin wanted more ice chips and tried to ask, but Gail pre-empted him.

"You need to rest."

CHAPTER 39

WEDNESDAY MORNING, MARGALE knocked on her door. "Mrs. Johnson? You have a call from an Officer Portello. He wanted to talk to Mr. Johnson. I told him how Mr. Johnson passed about a month ago, but that you were here."

"I'll take it up here." Ginger reached for the phone. "Hello?"

"Mrs. Johnson?"

"Yes? Hello."

"Officer Portello, Orlando police here."

In a flash, Ginger knew that this was about Kevin. She sat up in bed.

"Yes, what is it officer?"

"My condolences Mrs. Johnson."

"What do you mean?"

"I understood from your housekeeper — "

"Margale — "

"That Mr. Johnson passed recently. My sincere condolences."

"Thank you. What may I do for you?"

"Saturday night, just before the Bee Line Expressway there was an accident. Navy blue Lexus. The man driving was a Mr. Kevin McCoy, but the registration was in the name of Theodore Johnson."

Ginger couldn't think. She felt cold all over, yet perspiration ran down her back.

"Is he alright? What happened?"

"Was the vehicle stolen, Mrs. Johnson?"

"No, Mr. McCoy is an acquaintance, a friend of mine. Is he alright?"

"That I can't tell you. I can tell you it was an awful bad wreck and took three men and some time to get him out."

"Where is he!?"

"A chopper took him to Orlando Emergency. It took days to get the ID from the hospital. You'd have to contact Orlando to find out what happened to Kevin McCoy. But, in general, they only give that information to family."

Ginger hesitated. "Can you just tell me please what happened? What time was this?"

"About six pm, at the height of that storm that came up sudden. He skidded and ran smack into a tree. Car crumbled like foil. It appeared he was driving at a very high speed."

Her voice faltered as she spoke. "What do you need from me, please?"

"We'll mail the registration to your residence. I guess the rest you'll take up with insurance. Again, I'm sorry Mrs. Johnson."

"Mr. McCoy is just an acquaintance."

"I mean, my condolences about Mr. Johnson."

"Of course. Goodbye."

Ginger put the phone down and stared at it. She felt like she was watching someone else. She could not breathe. Pain gripped her chest. *Was this a heart attack?* Hands trembling, she poured water from the carafe on her table. But she could not lift the glass to her lips . . .

WHEN GINGER OPENED her eyes, she was back in bed, Dr. Marcus was sitting nearby, and Dottie was hovering about.

Bewildered, she looked from one to the other.

"What happened?"

"It appears that you fainted, Ginger. Luckily, Dottie came in to check on you — "

"I came in and you were lying on the floor! I called Margale and she paged Dr. Marcus."

"Luckily I was nearby on the golf course," he said with a smile. "And I wasn't having too good a day out there."

This explained his golf attire.

"Ginger, I thought you'd had a heart attack, or a stroke!"

"You gave us a scare."

"What happened to me?"

"You fainted. No heart attack, no stroke. Your blood pressure dropped and then so did you. You've had a tough time, I know. Losing Ted. Your friend Dottie is a regular professional. I'm on campus, so just phone if you need me. Going to the seafood buffet tonight, but always available. Maybe you should come, too. The women tell me you haven't been eating much. A buffet would do you good."

The doctor said goodbye and Margale walked him out.

"Ginger, what happened?"

"I thought I was having a heart attack after I hung up with Officer Portello."

"What did he want?"

"Kevin's been in an accident. Ted's car. Friday night. He was airlifted to Orlando emergency. Dottie, my son could be dead."

In the next instant, all the repulsion, disappointment and anger she had felt for Kevin McCoy vacated her. It was replaced by a blank space, at first. Then, her heart was overtaken with yearning and love. She had abandoned him once.

Now he might leave the world without knowing who she was and a mother's love. Ginger reached for the phone, then Dottie took it from her. "Dottie! I have to find out if he's alive! The officer said he was barely alive!"

"Then let me find out. Tomorrow. Ginger, he's a grown man facing the consequences of his own faults. Let him be."

"He's my son."

Dottie handed over the phone and Ginger dialed.

"Orlando Emergency? Uh, patient information, please."

Ginger and Dottie shared a look while they waited.

"Oh, hello. I'm calling to find out about a patient...? Kevin McCoy. Is he registered as a patient there?"

There was another pause. Both women were hanging on the answer.

"Not Kendra, Kevin. K-E-V-I-N. McCoy." There was another pause, which lasted mere seconds but seemed interminable.

"I see. When was that? Okay. No, no. That's all I need. Thank you."

Ginger hung up the phone. "He's there. He's been moved to a private room. He's out of the ICU."

"Well, good. That's great news and a relief. Now, I want you to rest."

"I'm going to Orlando."

"Ginger, I do not advise that!"

"He has to know the truth."

"No, he does not. Ginger, you just collapsed. You've had an awful disappointment and a shock."

Ginger threw off the blankets and stood. "He might not see me, but I have to try. He has to know the truth — "

"Ginger, what would the doctor say? You're not thinking clearly."

"Kevin has to know who I am. I need to tell him before it's too late."

"I do not advise this. You must put this phase of folly behind you and get on with your life. Ginger, fifty years ago you did a difficult and brave thing. You gave your baby up for adoption. I read what Carl sent. Your baby went to a good home. Kevin is *their* son. You've had no connection for 50 years. You have a whole new chapter of your life waiting for you. Don't give it to this man. He's made his own bed and now he's got to lie in it. Better to live with the son you've imagined. It's too late."

"It's not too late. It's never too late for anything, especially honesty. I have never been honest about my past. Not even with you. Secrets keep you isolated from the people you love. I can't live this way anymore. If I tell Kevin, it might help him. I owe him that."

"I seriously advise you to reconsider. I am not sure you are in a state of mind to make such a decision. By telling Kevin, you are telling the whole world about your past, and about everything else."

"What do you mean?"

"I mean that you were *living* with your son."

"I have nothing to hide. He lived in my guest room."

"I believe you and your friends will, too. But what about others?"

"What of it. Let them gossip."

"That's a bold position, Ginger. Kevin McCoy might not want the truth. Have you thought of that?"

"Dottie, I am doing this for him but it's selfish too. If I don't try and make this up to him, it will kill me."

"I don't advise this. Your life is perfect. You have everything. Let him go. I know Dr. Marcus wouldn't advise this right now either. I certainly don't think Ted ever would."

"Ted is dead, Dottie. How many women who have given up a child get such a chance?"

Dottie pondered her friend. "I see there's no stopping you. But please, wait until tomorrow."

Ginger nodded. Then she leaned into Dottie and sobbed in her arms.

CHAPTER 40

DOTTIE MADE THE arrangements for Ginger's trip. She packed for Ginger, found a hotel, and made her reservation. She instructed Margale to put together a quick lunch and then pack one of her famous picnics so Ginger would have home-cooked food during her stay.

The following day, and after an hour and a half drive, Ginger checked into the Sea Drift Motel. Glancing around as she walked to her room, she smiled. Leave it to Dottie to find such a charming spot. But Ginger only stayed there a minute. She set her things down in the room, turned around and drove straight to Orlando Emergency. Infused with a new purpose, Ginger had left her shaken and bedridden self behind.

"LET ME SEE. Kevin McCoy, I know he was just moved..." The woman at the front desk at the hospital scanned her computer screen. "There he is. He's in Room 406." She looked at Ginger.

"Is he expecting you?"

"No." Ginger's heart started pounding. Would they let her through? Did she need his approval to visit?

"You're family, right?"

Ginger took a deep breath.

"Yes."

"I figured. I totally see the resemblance. I'm glad you're here. Mr. McCoy hasn't had any visitors. We've all kind of adopted him."

Ginger managed a tense smile.

"Room 406 is three doors past the nurse's station, on the right."

Ginger headed down the hall. Afraid that the woman might remember that Kevin had to approve her visit and call her back, she propelled herself forward. The door to Room 406, was slightly ajar and she crossed the threshold without knocking.

The sight of him stunned her. He lay utterly still. One leg was in a contraption and elevated. One arm was strapped to his side. His head was bandaged, and his eyes were closed. Standing in the shadows by the foot of his bed, she wanted to turn and run. Dottie's words came back to Ginger. She was right. *What was she doing here?* How could she take on this broken man, his wayward life, and problems? Who was he to her anyway? If she left, he would never know anything or any more about her. No one would. But if she spoke, everything would come to light. Her friends at 3-Oaks would know her secret. They would learn the true motives of the man she'd flaunted before them. They'd know she was a fool. They'd know that she had fallen in love with her own son. She would bring shame on herself and on Ted, as Dottie had said. These thoughts and emotions raced through her, yet Ginger was immovable. Her heart pounded so loudly she felt he might hear it. And maybe he did because he spoke first.

"Who's there?"

"It's me, Ginger."

Ginger moved into the light. There was a moment when she thought he couldn't comprehend or hear. He said nothing. Then, he groaned.

"What are you doing here?"

"A police officer called me. They found me because of the car. And Ted's registration."

Even in this weakened condition, his limbs strung up in a hospital bed, his cynicism stirred in him. "Of course. The car. You're concerned about the car. I'll pay for it."

"Kevin, I only found out yesterday that you were in the hospital. I came as soon as I could."

"I don't want to talk to you. I'd appreciate it if you'd go."

His head throbbed. It was bad enough being in this condition, but her presence made everything so much worse. He'd made a shocking and terrifying discovery that night driving in the rain: he cared about this woman. And, it was because of her, and the way she had disposed of him, that he was lying wrecked in a hospital bed. All he wanted to do was forget her. But she had to show up and see him like this.

"I'm here because of you and me."

"There is no 'you and me.' You ended that. I came back and handed Margale fish to make for dinner. Your friend said, 'nice to meet you, Kevin,' and I was like, *What?* Then you come in and tell me to pack up and leave, with no explanation. Now, I get to throw *you* out —"

"I owe you an explanation."

"Not interested. Now go. Get out of here!"

"There is something you need to know. *Please.*"

Kevin tried to shut her out. He didn't have the strength to move, let alone fight. It was humiliating to be seen like this.

"I'll say what I have to say and go. I promise. Then I'll come back so we can talk further. After that, you can decide if you want to see me anymore."

She regrets her decision, he thought. Curiosity got the better of him. Half-hopeful, half full of hatred, he lay still.

Ginger began. "When I found the clippings in the drawer, I was stunned.

I couldn't figure out why they were there. I asked my lawyer to investigate you and look into your background — "

He burned with humiliation. "You spied on me? Get out!"

"No, wait. Give me a chance. I asked him to investigate something else, too. Let me tell you a story. The story of a young girl who fell in love with a handsome young man."

"I'm not interested in any fairy tale, Ginger — "

"Hear me out. Please. This is hard. The young man told her he loved her and that he wanted to spend the rest of his life with her. But she was of a middle-class background. He was from a prominent family. His mother told him that if he married the girl, he would be disinherited. He chose the inheritance. The man's name was Frank Pierce. I was 19 years old."

"So, the girl's you? That's the point?"

"Yes, it's my story — "

"You were rejected and want sympathy?"

"My parents were devastated and ashamed. They sent me away to live with my grandmother. I was heartbroken over Frank, but my grandmother took care of me. She always did the right thing. She carefully researched and found an adoption agency. I couldn't raise my baby, so I just accepted the idea of giving my child away. Until . . . until — "

Kevin kept listening with his eyes shut. Without looking at her, he sensed her mood had changed. Curious, he opened his eyes. Ginger was crying.

"Until what — ?" he said with all the cynicism he could summon.

"Until you were born. Until I held you."

Vertigo jolted him. Involuntarily, with his unbound hand, he grabbed the metal bar of the hospital bed and held on. The room literally swerved.

Ginger spoke quickly.

"When I saw Carl and asked him to learn everything about you, I also shared documents my grandmother had saved about giving up my baby for adoption."

"What are you saying?"

"I learned all this while you were on the boat fishing. The report from Carl arrived before the party, but I didn't read it until you were out that day."

"Shut up! Get out!"

He reached for the phone but knocked it off the bedside table causing a bad clatter. Ginger did not even move to pick it up.

"It's true. Teresa and Timothy McCoy adopted my child."

Kevin wailed loudly and other noises quickly followed.

"He's lying! He's in with your kids. They want to keep you from me by telling a disgusting lie!"

The door flung open, and faces stood in the doorway, looking from her to him. A nurse rushed to his side, took his pulse and glared at her.

"Get out!" he said in a tone that gave her chills. "Get her out!"

"I'm sorry," Gail said. "You'd better leave."

Ginger turned and left the room.

In the hallway, a nurse was rushing towards her. "Is Mr. McCoy alright — ? The monitor shows his blood pressure spiking — "

Before she could respond, another orderly pushed past her and towards Room 406.

Ginger quickened her walk out of the hospital. Outside, the harsh noon sun stabbed her eyes. Blinded, fumbling in her pocketbook, she dropped it and everything in her bag spilled onto the tarmac. On her knees, tears streamed down her cheeks.

Suddenly, a young woman and her son were beside her.

"Mikey! Help the lady."

The boy knelt by Ginger, collecting the spray of coins from her purse.

"Looks like we came by at just the right time."

"I was visiting my son. He was in an accident."

"Oh, dear," said the woman. "Is he okay?"

"The doctor says he's improved."

"I bet he was happy to see you."

Ginger paused.

"He's lucky. We're both lucky."

The beguiling boy held out his hand.

"Here's your money, ma'am. 53 cents."

"Thank you."

"Need help finding your car?"

Ginger wasn't sure where her car was. She assured them she was alright, yet she wasn't convinced of that either. She wandered through the lot. It was as if the woman who had parked the car was different from who she was now. Before she was a child, attempting to circumvent the truth and its consequences. Now she was a mother, a woman who owned her life. If he didn't believe her, or if he didn't want to hear more, there was nothing to be done. He would put it together enough to know that it made sense. He might find some peace, even if it meant he finally had a target for his hate.

Finally, Ginger found her car, got in and closed the door. In her car, she felt safe from his fury. Over the years, she had imagined meeting her son. In her imagination, she'd played out all sorts of scenarios but never had she imagined this one. She prayed he'd recover from the shock of the news. She was sure that he would recoil at certain memories. She thanked God for her instincts, not allowing him to follow her up the stairs. Her diversion to New York was a blessing, and then the arrival of Dottie. She gasped at the thought of just how close she had come to bedding her own son. But her angels had been with her the whole time. Kevin had his angels, too.

She drove away. She only wished she'd thought to leave her name and number at the nurses' station. If her son got worse, Ginger had to know.

BY THE TIME she arrived back at the Sea Drift, Ginger had decided to stay in Orlando longer. She checked with the desk and made the arrangements. She was exhausted, but Dottie was waiting to hear from her. She called home.

"Johnson residence."

"Margale?"

"Mrs. Johnson, how's your trip going? Have you had a chance to eat the food I packed?"

"Not yet, Margale."

"You've got fried chicken, potato salad. And peach cobbler."

"Thank you, Margale. I will eat as soon as I talk to Dottie. Is she there?"

She didn't have to wait for an answer. Dottie picked up the line.

"I've got it, Margale."

Margale clicked off.

"Well? Have you seen him?"

"Yes. He didn't want to see me. He was hostile, understandably so."

"Did you tell him? Gosh, child, I've been on pins and needles. Tell me everything."

"He's in bad shape. One leg's in traction. He's got a bandage wrapped around his head. It was terrible to see him. But he's out of intensive care. He was not happy to see me —"

"Okay, but did you tell him?"

"I told him briefly what I had come to say. He didn't want to listen —"

"That was brave. What was it like?"

"So many times, over the years, I've imagined meeting my son, but I never imagined this!"

"How'd he respond?"

"He shouted and told me to leave a dozen times."

"You are courageous!"

"It was chilling. He was so cold. I had no idea how he would react. I told him about being young and in love, and Frank Pierce, and being sent away, about my grandmother who took care of everything. I have no idea when he understood. But when he did, things got worse."

"Poor baby, what did he say?"

"He said it was all lies. Carl and the kids invented it, to keep him away from me. It couldn't be true. He screamed for me to leave."

"Okay, well, that's that. When will you be home? Margale is cooking up a storm."

"I'm not coming today."

"Good idea. Wait till the morning, set out when you're fresh."

"No, I mean, I want to stay. I have to give him time to think. I need time to think."

"You are quite the heroine! Well, I can stay until the end of the week."

"No, Dottie. Thank you, but I want you to go home. You've been such a good friend. More than a good friend, a mother really. Go home to your grandchildren."

There was a pause on the line.

"Tommy has a recital tomorrow afternoon. If I leave Treasure Beach in the morning, I'll be in the front row after school."

"I will never be able to repay you Dottie."

"Nonsense. I'll phone you when I get home. There's no right or wrong here. Emily Post never wrote about how to handle a situation like this. So, follow your heart."

"Thank you, Dottie."

They hung up.

Ginger opened her picnic packed by Margale. At a small table in the lanai of her room, Ginger ate the fried chicken, the potato salad, and the cobbler. She was famished. She couldn't remember when she last ate a meal. Then, watching the sunset, she noticed the rows of clouds — pink, red and practically violet. She wanted to capture them in paint. She thought through the last fifty years of her life. They'd been good for the most part. She knew that she was lucky. She'd give Kevin tomorrow and then on Friday she'd try to see him. Then, she would go back to 3-Oaks and back to her normal life. Whatever normal was.

CHAPTER 41

FRIDAY MORNING, GINGER stepped into the hospital elevator. Pushing the number four, her hand trembled. She worried that the hospital staff would remember her and try to prevent her from seeing Kevin. She headed straight to Room 406 and was alarmed to find the bed empty. She went to the nurse's station. A young man was at the desk. Luckily, he did not recognize her.

"I'm here to see a patient."

"Name?"

"Kevin McCoy. I looked in room 406, but he's not there."

"Oh. Mr. McCoy's in the courtyard downstairs. I just wheeled him out. He asked if he could sit outside for a few minutes and his doctor said it would be good for him."

"Who's his doctor?"

"Are you family?"

Ginger nodded.

"Dr. Jamal. He's the best. It's good to see Mr. McCoy out of that room. For a few days, we weren't sure he would make it. Take the elevator back down to the ground floor. Walk straight ahead and through the double doors."

Ginger turned and walked to the elevator. As it descended, she steadied herself with some deep breaths. The doors opened and she could see the courtyard garden. The doors to the outside opened with a *whoosh*. At once she saw Kevin. He was in a wheelchair with his back towards her. The bandage had been removed from his head. That was a relief. She walked around to face him.

"Hello."

He looked at her blankly.

"You look better today."

He said nothing.

"I've come to tell you more, if you'll hear me out."

He did not shout her away. Was this remoteness due to his medication? She sat on a bench and waited quietly. She noticed there were tears running down his face. She wanted to take his hand or embrace him, only she didn't dare. She started to cry, too. They sat silently. Neither dared to look at one another, but they cried side by side.

Finally, Kevin spoke, and in a voice she'd never heard before.

"I'm your son, only not one you recognized. When you found the clippings, you learned the truth about me. You know what I am and who I am. I'm not a captain for Northwest. I was always in the third seat, but you probably know that too."

"None of it matters to me."

"What happened to Frank Pierce?"

"I never knew, until I got that report. He died five years ago. He was in a small plane in the Rockies. His one passenger, a man, also perished in the crash."

"He was a pilot?"

"Yes, and a sportsman. He was in Colorado hunting elk; I think. On the way home, there was bad weather. The plane hit a mountain face."

"The bastard got what he deserved."

"He was not . . . that. He was young, and weak. He did what was expected of him. He was in the family business."

"What was that?"

"They had stores. They don't exist anymore. From what I read, he seemed to have trouble finding what he wanted. Particularly in wives."

"Like father, like son. Did he have other kids?"

"He had several wives. With his first, he had a girl. The second wife went to rehab, and the marriage didn't last. His third wife, the one he was married to when he died, they had a little girl. She was about 12 years old then. So, you have some half-sisters.

"I'm no better than my old man."

"He made some bad choices. We all do Kevin. You were abandoned at birth, then you chose to leave your parents. You thought you were taking control of your life by running away, and then the drinking caught up with you."

"You know my whole history from your spies," he spit this out at her.

"I'm sorry. Maybe it's too early to talk like this."

"It's a little late for mother-son time. You want a son at this late date? *I was almost your husband.* How can you sit there so calmly? Rich people make no sense to me. I can't wait to hear what the 3-Oaks set makes of this."

"I am not calm, Kevin. I've been completely distraught. When I left here the other day, I was sobbing in the parking lot. Ever since you drove off and left 3-Oaks, I've been reviewing my entire life. Everything changed for me when I heard about the accident. I knew it was my duty to help you. I want to try to be a mother."

"That ship has sailed. Sorry."

"I don't know what it's like not to know where you came from, or who your real parents are. But I know the pain of not belonging. That's very familiar to me. Maybe someday you'll let me say more. I just wanted you to know where you came from, and what happened. I pray you can try to understand."

"You want my compassion. It's not right to ask this of me."

"I'm sorry."

"I came out here to rest."

She stood.

"Let me wheel you back to your room. May I?"

Gail came out, glanced at her, then crossed to Kevin.

"Just go," he said.

Without a word, Ginger left the courtyard. She was about to exit the main doors when inspiration hit her. She turned around and went to the reception desk and asked to leave a message for Dr. Jamal.

Back at the Sea Drift a certain peace settled over her. At last, she had done the right thing by her son. The mystery of his birth was solved for him. Whatever came next was up to him. Maybe now Kevin would make the right choices. She hoped to help him. However, if he hated her and refused her help, she would have to live with that.

THE FOLLOWING MORNING, she called the hospital and asked to be put through to his room. She was surprised when he answered.

"Hello?"

For a moment, she was befuddled, wondering what she should call herself with Kevin. "It's me. I'm going back to 3-Oaks today. I wonder if I could stop by first and see you."

There was a pause.

"Are you there?"

"I'm here. You can stop by. I'm not going anywhere."

"Thank you. I'll be over within the hour."

Ginger felt a surge of hope. She had been up half the night hatching a plan. All she needed was a chance to present it to Kevin.

WHEN SHE ENTERED Room 406, he was sitting up in a chair and his color was better.

"I just 'walked' a little in the hall. Dr. Jamal said I'd get used to pushing that thing on wheels."

He pointed to a walker by the door.

"I thought I'd be using one of those before you," she said. He smiled. Her hopes soared and this gave her confidence.

"Thanks for allowing Dr. Jamal to speak with me. I thanked him for taking such great care of you and assured him that all your bills would be taken care of. He told me you'd be ready to leave and go to the rehab center next week. There's a very good center here, he said. But I told him there's also one in Treasure Beach. The doctor said either facility is fine. He said that you'd be there for a month, maybe less, depending on your progress. After that, you'd be an outpatient for about six months. Sounds like a long haul, I know. But eventually, you'll be back to normal. He said you were very strong and there should be few residual problems. If any."

Kevin was remote again. She noticed that he wasn't looking at her. He was gazing out the window, his thoughts seemed caught up in the blue sky. She continued.

"I'd like you to come to Treasure Beach. I would be near you and could help. Then, I'd like you to come and live with me while you finish your therapy. I know it's a little late to start being a mother but it's the best I can do. It would give you time to heal and think about things. You'd have no worries. You could concentrate on getting well."

He offered no response to her plan. Had he even heard what she said?

"Think about it, okay? You don't have to decide now. Dr. Jamal said that you'd be discharged at the end of next week."

Finally, Kevin turned and looked squarely at Ginger. He took in her beautiful face. Her long, reddish hair was in a ponytail. He looked into blue eyes, remarkably like his own. She looked relaxed, like he'd never seen her. Her expression was warm, and she glowed.

"Please, think about my offer seriously. We will have time to talk. But right now, the most important thing is for you to get well." Ginger's eyes were moist.

"I'll think about it," he said and looked back out the window.

Ginger had the impulse to put her hand on his shoulder, but she couldn't bring herself to touch him. She left the room.

The whole drive home she felt numb. She didn't know what would happen. She'd have to wait and see. She needed time, too.

Chapter 42

G INGER SPENT THE following days feverishly sorting through her house. She had to get things in order. With Margale working at her side, she started upstairs and went through Ted's clothes and belongings. She called the 3-Oaks Thrift Shop and arranged for pick-ups. The Thrift Shop's proceeds would go to the 3-Oaks Foundation which generously contributed to community charities. Ted would approve. Also, Ginger selected a few special things of Ted's — gold trophies, plaques for distinguished service, photos of him on the golf course hosting politicians, celebrities, and prominent businessmen – and set these aside for his children. Ted had kept elaborate scrap books of his times and trips with his grandchildren. She set these aside as well. While Ginger was determined not to carry a grudge, neither did she want to appear to be appeasing anyone with mementos of their father, as if hoping to influence the outcome of their legal issues. She would wait. There was a time for everything.

Waiting. This was an activity, and an art. Ginger was doing her best to be good at it. Sifting through the closets and drawers in her home, she was attempting to clean out not just old things, but also old ways of being and thoughts. Her tireless activity distracted her while waiting to hear from Kevin. When would he call? What would he say? What if she never heard from him again?

Within a week, Ginger and Margale had finished the upstairs. Expending energy, she found she had more reserves of it. This was something Ginger had meant to do for years, ever since Ted moved to The Memory Unit. But she could never bring herself to part with his golf clothes and tweeds. She had always felt that she was waiting for something. For what? For Ted to return?

The sound of the phone jarred her. She answered with excitement but was immediately disappointed.

"Oh, hi. Hello Diane."

Sequestered in her house, occupied with the contents of closets and drawers, Ginger had managed to avoid all social interaction. She knew this would not last. It was only a matter of time before her friends called and the questions began. It was fitting that Diane, her best friend at 3-Oaks, was the first.

"I've been worried about you! I haven't seen or heard from you in a whole week. Is Dottie still here? You girls probably got into a whole heck of trouble! I haven't meant to neglect you. But the boys were here and with their wives. You know how time-consuming children are!"

Ginger had rightly relied on everyone being too caught up in their own lives to be wondering about hers.

"Dottie left and I got inspired to clean house. I've sorted all of Ted's clothes and a lot of his personal things — "

"Time to make way for the new, after all — "

"Things for the foundation and things for the kids, that is if I even speak to them again."

They laughed ruefully.

"Any news?"

"No. Nothing definite. But Margale and I have been working like trojans!"

"What's Mr. Handsome doing?"

Ginger took a breath. Here we go, she thought.

"Kevin's gone."

"Back in the pilot's seat? I thought he was on leave for months?"

"He's not in the air. He's just *gone*."

"What do you mean? You mean, *for good?*"

"I'm not sure. But honestly, for the moment Diane, trust me, it's a long and complicated situation. And it's all for the good. Let me explain later. The thrift shop truck is about to arrive, and I'm worried they'll take the wrong boxes."

It still hurt. A lot. But Ginger had to be brave. Her busyness could not hide the fact that she hoped she'd need space for her son. This is what she wished for more than anything. Would he give her the chance to be a mother?

"Okay. Well, when you're ready to tell me, Ginger, I'm ready to listen. Look, Bill comes in tonight and we're going to the club tomorrow. Why don't you join us for dinner. *Just us.* You know, Bill. He needs an extra pair of ears to listen to *All Things Considered*, DC edition."

Ginger wasn't brave enough to wade in those waters. Not yet. She'd have to tell everyone at 3-Oaks eventually. Diane was certainly the best person to speak to first. This was the problem with how public she'd been, openly broadcasting her amorous feelings for Kevin. Everything would be easier though if there was some resolution. Or, slightly easier anyway. But day after day there was no call, no word from him. Deep down she suspected the awful possibility that she might never hear from him again. It was a thought she dared not dwell on. It made her frantic.

"Ginger?"

Ginger had forgotten that Diane was still on the line.

"I said, it will be an *early dinner*. Bill is always exhausted after his week, and he has an early tee-time in the morning. Come on, you need a break. Clearly, you've been through something. It'll be good for you."

"Margale could sure use some time off."

It was a smart strategy and a good idea to begin with her best friend. After all, when Bill strayed, and took his lady friend to Le Cirque de Soleil in Las

Vegas, it was Ginger who'd held Diane's hand. Diane probably felt it was time to return the favor.

"Okay. Tomorrow night."

"Good! 6:00. The Grill. Casual, easy, early!"

"6:00. Thanks, Diane. Bye."

THE GRILL AND Kevin. All those dinners at The Grill with Kevin. It upset her stomach to remember the romantic and tumultuous feelings she'd had for him. Of course, in hindsight, it made sense. She'd projected on Kevin her unresolved feelings for Frank, feelings which she'd suppressed ever since he'd left her and throughout her marriage with Ted. Now that she knew all, she understood all. The romantic feelings had vanished. Again, Ginger thanked her angels that they were spared a terrible consummation, one that would have been impossible to live with. Sometimes at night she woke in a panic. What if they'd not been spared? On those nights she reached for the Ambien on her bedside table.

During the day, she had feelings, but they were wholesome, the feelings of a mother for a son. These feelings had also been thwarted and suppressed, since the hour she gave her baby to another mother and father. It stunned her the way they asserted themselves now. This was the pure maternal love of a mother for a child. Was it too late for this? She was certain that Kevin, too, had to adjust. Could he overcome his long-term resentment of his imagined birth mother who had abandoned him? She had good reason to suspect, at least, that he had never felt romantic love for her. The clippings killed that illusion. But they both needed to adjust. In the meantime, Ginger had to carry on. She could not hide any longer.

CHAPTER 43

THE NEXT NIGHT, Ginger was soothed by performing her usual rituals of getting ready to go out. She selected her clothes carefully. She made a point of not wearing clothes she'd worn with Kevin. She needed armor, new attire to face the new phase of her life: A widow, a woman alone and, she hoped, a mother.

Just before 6:00, she got into her golf cart. Her golf cart, not Ted's. Maybe she'd donate Ted's to the clubhouse or the garden center. In the driver's seat, she drove along the greens towards The Grill. The air was soft and warm. It felt like a kindness or a caress. She parked and looked up at the sky. The evening star had just become visible. Ginger made a wish. Maybe by leaving the house, she was giving Kevin the space to call.

With her head held up, Ginger entered The Grill. She looked around for Diane and Bill. She knew Diane would not bring up Kevin. Diane would not push or pry. She could certainly rely on Bill not to bring up Kevin; Bill thought and talked mainly about Bill. They'd have a meal, an early evening, and then Ginger would return to the sanctuary of home.

The Grill was packed. As luck would *not* have it, Louise was the very first person she encountered. Clearly Louise was looped.

"Ginger, darling. Dottie gone? Haven't seen you girls since that divine party."

Louise loomed overly close. Ginger could smell the gin on her breath. "Where is everyone? Where have you been?"

"Dottie had to go home. We had a wonderful time."

"The aristocrat has left us. How's the Countess of Somewhere? And where is Ken? Your stallion?"

Ginger didn't bother to correct her.

"Oh, I see Bill and Diane. Meeting them for dinner. So good to see you —"

Ginger broke away. I will *not* see you later, she thought, even if I have to leave through the kitchen!

Diane gestured to Ginger. Studying her friend, Diane knew that Ginger had been through it. Just what *it* was she didn't know, but dinner at The Grill was not the time and place to find out. She kissed her friend.

"Sit here. Sit between us."

Ginger needed to be buffered from the eyes at other tables. One of the drawbacks of living behind the gates was this: People ignored you when you were there but noticed when you were absent.

"Hi kids. Louise is already popped. It's going to be a long dinner or maybe a short one for poor Henry and whomever else is doomed to be in her company."

"She must have had a few after bridge," Bill said.

"Or maybe a couple of dressing drinks," Diane said. "How does she face her mornings, I don't know!"

"Nights are tough for Henry," Bill said. "But mornings must be hell for Louise."

Ginger flashed on nights with Kevin. Many evenings she'd imbibed more wine than usual, and she blushed at the memories.

The waiter appeared.

"Hello Joe. Speaking of drinking. Ginger. What would you like, my dear?"

"Bourbon on the rocks, with a twist."

"Diane, honey?"

"A little vodka on ice, and an orange peel, thank you."

"I'll have the same," Bill said.

"I'll leave the menus," Joe said, smiled and left.

Wasting no time, Bill launched into his DC report. "Congress is a mess. Nothing's getting passed. One side of the aisle will never pass anything that increases taxes. The other side of the aisle only wants to raise taxes on the rich. That's it. A stalemate. A broken record."

Ginger had to wonder if Bill reveled in the conflict. But she was hungry. Diane must have read her mind. When Joe returned, and she said, "Bill, let's order. The kitchen's going to get crowded, and you said you wanted an early night."

"Sure honey. Joe, bring us another round and we'll give you our order."

So much for an early evening, Ginger thought. But it was good to be out. Bill was on a roll and Ginger felt safe bookended by her dear friends.

During dinner, a couple of friends stopped by. They visited their table, saw Ginger, and said, "How's Kevin?" Or "Where's Kevin?" Diane, an adept defensive player in the social game, fended them off. Ginger knew she would have to repay Diane by sharing the whole story, and soon. After coffee, they left The Grill and, under the dark sky, headed to their carts and said their goodbyes.

"Thanks for getting me out. Bill, I love being filled in on the news from the capital."

Bill kissed her on both cheeks and got into his cart. Diane hung back by Ginger.

"Let's take a ride and lunch. There's lots to catch up on."

"Oh, God, I miss Star so much. I haven't ridden in ages."

"How's Monday or Tuesday?"

"Let's do Tuesday. Thanks, Diane, for *everything*."

Driving the ribbon of road through the golf course, Ginger's thoughts returned to Kevin. Had he phoned the house? Would he ever call? Deep inside she knew the answer. *It was too late*. She had to make a new life for herself: a life without a husband and without a son. Her house was in order. It was time she faced the Johnson children and the estate issues. Ginger had to talk to Carl. She bristled at the thought. Their conversation would surely begin with the subject of Kevin and that would be awkward.

CHAPTER 44

MONDAY MORNING SEEMED like a good time to make the call. It was only a moment after she said hello to his secretary that Carl jumped on the line.

"Ginger, it's good to hear from you. Lily, I've got the line — "

He waited for Lily to click off.

"How are you? I've been concerned about you Ginger."

"Hi Carl. Thanks. It's good to hear your voice. I thought it was time I checked in."

"Well, good. Dottie called me after she got back to Atlanta. She's filled me in on a few particulars. I'm glad to know you've landed on your feet."

"Thanks to you, and your people in Jacksonville. It was a shock, that's for sure."

"Funny how life is, the twists and turns. It makes life interesting, and difficult. How is he doing? Are you in touch, or no?"

"He's recovering, but I don't know much more. And adjusting. I've been sorting through things. And now, I've got the house pretty much done. Seems like a good time to get other matters settled. I mean, Ted's estate."

"Good. I had a phone call with Jim Donnelly. Everyone's agreed to mediation. We have asked for depositions to be taken and he wants you deposed, as well.

You think you could make it down to Palm Beach?"

"Sure. When?"

"Friday? I can schedule the deposition for Friday."

"Okay, I'm not sure how these things go, though."

"Not to worry. I'll send an email with pointers on what to expect and how to prepare. You'll be fine."

"That would be helpful."

"By the way, is it true you sold a painting to a princess? I had no idea you were a famous artist. Dottie didn't let on at all."

Carl had a gift for diffusing tension. Ginger laughed.

"She's not a princess, just a countess. And I never met her. But someday I'll get to England, meet the countess, and see my painting. I've had so many surprises, and shocks, lately! I can't wait till everything settles and I can return to my studio. But tell me, should I fear the children?"

"I don't think so. At the end of the day, the Johnson kids understand they could lose money if they go to court. Plus, there are the court costs. I think they want to settle. I know Jim Donnelly wants this settled. I think they're wearing him down. So, this is my gut instinct, after 50 years of professional experience. By the way, did you look at the second packet?"

"Yes. It's very helpful reading things in black and white, especially when life gets so gray. I'm lucky to be in such good hands. Thank you, Carl."

"Just doing my job. I'll have Lily call you with times for Friday."

It would be strange to do that drive again. But good. Ginger needed time and space to think about her past, about Frank and Kevin, and to remember her long married life. Mostly Ginger needed to give thought to her future. She had Dottie and Diane, Margale, Berdetta, her homes and her art. Just then, she heard another truck in the driveway. She was glad she had so much to give to the 3-Oaks Foundation.

CHAPTER 45

T UESDAY MORNING, GINGER and Diane trotted, cantered, and galloped across the fields adjacent to 3-Oaks. After, breathless and exhilarated, they dismounted Star and Hunter, and turned over the reins to Robert. They were both winded, happy, and famished.

As they walked to the club for lunch, Ginger nervously eyed the terrace. "Let's sit on the end, shall we? There's a breeze there."

Also, it was the least crowded space; there would be no ears nearby to listen in on their conversation. They sat, ordered Cobb salads and Arnold Palmers. Ginger suspected the question would come quickly, and it did.

"So, where's Kevin?"

Ginger had told it once, so she was prepared to tell it again. The best way to recount the whole story was to tell her 'fairytale,' as Kevin had cynically called it: the young woman, the handsome man she fell in love with, the scandalized parents, the kind grandmother who harbored her, researched and arranged for an adoption, her secret, stored in a safe, finally shared with Carl in Palm Beach, and passed on to his team in Jacksonville. Once again, Ginger took pains to be calm, and clear. It was easier the second time. Diane listened, enrapt. More than once, she gasped, but she did not interrupt. When Ginger conveyed the current situation with Kevin, including his accident and hostile response when she visited him at the hospital, it was clear that she was finished. Diane had tears in her eyes.

"Oh my God, Ginger. What you've been through!"

"I'm sorry I never told you my secret. But I never told anyone, not even Ted knew, or Dottie. My parents never brought it up. My grandmother never did either. It was as if my pregnancy, the birth of my child and the adoption had never happened. It seemed better to keep it that way, I guess. It was only real for me."

The waiter seemed to have forgotten them; the service was strangely slow. But neither Ginger nor Diane cared. Ginger had laid out the secret story of her life and neither of them were thinking about food. Diane seemed dazed and Ginger felt relief.

"This is so hard, and so incredible. To give a baby away and never to see him at all!"

"I thought of him every day of my life. I knew it wouldn't be right to look for him. He had a family. A mother, a father, brothers, and sisters, too, probably. Sometimes I thought I would go mad trying to picture him. Or I'd look for him in a crowd of strangers, like in some city. I'd think: *Maybe he's here. Maybe my son is near me right now.* Whenever I saw a boy with red hair and about the right age, I thought: Could he be my son? I always thought he'd be a redhead which is ironic because Kevin isn't. One time, I followed a man down a street thinking maybe he was my son. But Kevin isn't even a red head, though he does have my blue eyes."

"You know, despite the age difference, we all felt comfortable with him and now I know why. He's your son! Does he look like his father?"

"He doesn't, no. His build is similar. It's like he was sort of an echo of Frank, but a very faint one. There was always something familiar about him. I thought it was because we were spending so much time together and that we were, like, soul mates . . ."

Truly it was all incredible. The friends gazed off, in the direction of the greens and the ponds.

"But it was also fate," Diane finally said. "I mean, he happens to wander into an open house at 3-Oaks. I mean, it's like a situation out of a movie."

There were parts of the story that Ginger did not share. Like the part about Ted's obituary in the drawer and Kevin's hunt for a rich widow. There was no need to smear him. She prayed that his future would be different, that he would be different.

"What happens next?"

"I'm giving him time. He's in physical therapy. I offered to let him stay in the guest room — by the way, *he always slept in the guestroom.*"

Obviously, Diane and everyone else would be curious and focused on this point. Speaking openly was the best policy. It helped immensely that this was the truth, despite the lurid fantasies her friends and neighbors were having about Ginger's relationship with her 'young stallion.'

"I want to help. I just don't know if he's going to let me."

She also kept it to herself how he was fired, and other details of Kevin's lifestyle she'd read about in Carl's report. She only had an obligation to tell her story. She would share it with some key, well-chosen people at 3-Oaks. Maybe her book club, maybe she'd even tell Louise. Telling Louise would certainly get the story out quickly. More quickly than publishing it in the local paper, she thought.

"I'm going to tell people the truth. I guess I was a foolish old woman, thinking the way I did, but the way things have turned out, I wouldn't change anything. Because I found Kevin. No one owns anyone. I'm sure the parents who adopted him nurtured and loved him. Still, it was terribly hurtful when he learned that he'd been given up at birth."

Ginger told Diane about Kevin overhearing his parents' conversation and the despair that it had inflicted. She stopped there. Again, she thought, that's all anyone needs to know. Maybe at 3-Oaks there were even people who'd been adopted who'd appreciate his story.

"But why tell people? I mean, do you have to?"

Diane felt worried for her friend. When this story got out, there would be a scandal, with a capital S.

"I'm tired of carrying the secret of having had a baby and giving him up. I planned to go to my grave with it, but now, under the circumstances, I want people to know. People can comment or judge me, think, or say whatever they like. I don't care. My story reunited me with my son, and being a mother is now the best thing in my life. Why would I hide that, Diane?"

Diane was amazed. Ginger was usually so timid.

"I guess you're going to have to tell people. Especially if Kevin comes back to 3-Oaks. You know, he really is a nice man. And I see the resemblance, the blue eyes . . ."

Their food finally arrived and for a while they ate in silence. Diane was marveling at Ginger's story, and how it changed everything.

"What do you want me to do? I'll do anything I can to help you."

"I wonder if maybe I could rely on you to fill in certain details, if necessary."

"There's going to be gossip, you know."

"Yes, but my story will be yesterday's news soon enough. I'm not going to be the hot topic for long — that is, I hope not. But whatever happens, I have you and Dottie and other pals who will be supportive. They might be shocked. I am sure you are. Let them think sordid details, but I thank my angels, and his, that nothing sexual happened. I believe that God, or the angels, has a hand in everything. Having my son, however strangely he returned to me, well that's the best thing of all. I know that's how you feel about the twins."

"My boys have always been the greatest part of my life. Though it's different when they're in their 30s, about to be 40! My God! And have families of their own. You were always so good with them. When they used to get mad at me, they'd say, 'Why can't Ginger be our mom!?'"

Ginger laughed. She had known the twins since they were ten. Through them, she'd imagined her son, watching them go through school, then graduation and on to college. She had always been a part of their lives.

"Well, I hope he comes back. It would give me a chance to know your son."

Diane would do her best to help Ginger. A lot of people might not believe the truth. She did. Ginger may have been foolish, but who hasn't done foolish things? At least this fairytale had a happy ending.

"You must have carried a great deal of pain around with you all these years. Even though you knew you did the right thing . . . Was the guilt difficult?"

"I'm not sure I felt guilt. I was so young, and my grandmother assured me I was doing the right thing. But I felt shame. With my parents, every waking moment was working to maintain the appearance of decency. Miss Hall's school set a high bar. I'm sure there were a lot of shotgun weddings back then, but they were undoubtedly arranged by families from the same background and social position. Frank's family didn't approve of me, so I did the right thing, under the circumstances. None of us even considered an abortion. All Frank cared about was to protect his inheritance, that was the prime objective for Frank."

"Where is he now, do you know?"

"He died five years ago. He had three wives and two children. He died in a plane crash. He was flying the plane — "

"He was a pilot?"

"Yes, isn't that incredible?"

"Did you tell Kevin?"

"Of course. I told him as much as I could before he screamed at me and told me to leave."

"It's a lot to take in. For me! I can't imagine what it's like for Kevin! Maybe it's good that he's stuck there. It'll give him time to think."

Diane ate her salad. Ginger was lost in thought.

"Diane? Was it selfish of me? To tell him everything, I mean?"

Diane set down her fork.

"No, it would have been selfish to withhold the truth."

"I'm not sure I would have told him at all except for the accident. I mean, Diane, he could have died! I had to tell him his story. I wanted to tell him more, but he made me leave."

"The most important thing now is his recovery. I think everything's going to work out. I just have a good feeling about it. I mean, it's *complicated*."

"It is only going to get more complicated when it becomes public."

"Yes. But Ginger, remember other people's opinions really don't matter. When Bill strayed and we separated, I got unsolicited advice from all sides. *Leave him! Stay! Tough it out! Throw him out!*"

Ginger remembered the flurry of opinions around 3-Oaks.

"But I kept my own counsel. I went to therapy and when I decided that Bill was what I wanted, I didn't care about the 3-Oaks gossip mill. Sure, you hate to have everybody yapping and just want to be left alone. And those people that said terrible things about Bill to me, like Louise, I never felt the same about them again. Bill and I got through it. We kept our family together. You know, I'm relieved he's in Washington during the week, I'd probably hang myself if I had to listen to him every day. But then, on the weekend, I enjoy it. He really cares about our country and the government, and he's involved. He's not teeing off every morning at seven like so many men around here. I admire him for that."

"That's so true, Diane. And, by the way, he's an incredible father to the boys —"

"That's right. Taught them sports and instilled in them a strong work ethic. Bill's role as a father was a big factor in the equation of why I stayed. He's strong and firm and consistent, and a wonderful role model — until Las Vegas —"

"Yes, they're wonderful boys and it's in large part due to your mothering —"

"They had two mothers. Mom, and Ginger! We both have a lot to be proud of."

Ginger smiled, but then she sighed.

"It's just funny. I have so much history with the twins and I'm only just meeting my own son, at the age of 68. You know it's strange. But I bet Ted would have been just fine with all this."

Diane wondered to herself if this were true. But she didn't want to contradict her friend.

"Speaking of Ted, how's it going with the whole estate issue? Or maybe you've been a little pre-occupied — ?"

"I'm going to Palm Beach on Friday. Apparently, the kids want to mediate which is a good sign. Still, it's a little nerve-wracking."

"I bet. But then you'll come home — "

"And face the gossip mill — "

"You'll have the summer to relax and go to the beach. You'll ride Star — "

The friends shared a smile.

"Margale and I worked all week cleaning out Ted's things. That felt good. The house is emptier, but there's more space, too. I guess it's time to get used to being alone."

"You'll have more time to spend with your best friend. I could use a pal during the week!" Diane checked the time. "It's almost three. I've got to run. I'm going to the hairdresser. I am so proud of you, Ginger. You're going to be just fine. Remember, we have each other."

Diane left Ginger alone at the table. Glancing back at her, Ginger seemed so small. It is going to be crazy when everybody finds out, Diane thought.

Hendrick came by and removed the plates. "Anything else for you today, Mrs. Johnson?"

She ordered a cup of tea.

Sipping it, she looked out over the greens. For a second she imagined she saw Ted walking about, searching for a missing ball.

CHAPTER 46

GINGER DROVE TO Palm Beach on Friday. So much had changed since the last time she drove this road. Then, she had been uneasy about Kevin after finding the clippings, but she'd resolved to trust Carl and ask him to find out what he could. She had even brought the envelope that had rested in the safe for decades. Somehow, with Ted gone, she felt free to revisit her own past. But she had never imagined how her concerns about Kevin and her curiosity about her long-lost child were connected. Truly it was still a shock. She imagined that Kevin was still in shock. Maybe this accounted for his complete silence? Driving along she pondered an unsolvable puzzle: Was Kevin thinking as much about her as she was thinking about him? Or was he not thinking about her at all?

Lily greeted her warmly and led her into Carl's office at once.

"Ginger wonderful to see you."

A small man stood.

"This is Lawrence Sloane, from Jim Donnelly's office."

"How do you do, Mr. Sloane."

Carl was all business. He directed her to a chair. Mr. Sloane sat opposite.

"Ginger, would you like some water?"

"No thanks, I'm fine."

"Then, shall we begin?"

Ginger nodded. In an email, Carl had offered her this direction: Answer simply. Do not embellish. And offer no unsolicited information.

"Your full name?"

"Virginia Bennet Johnson."

"Where and when were you born?

"Atlanta, Georgia. 1956."

Lawrence Sloane, this stranger, questioned Ginger on all the facts of her life, and then the questions became more pertinent. And personal.

"Did Theodore Johnson, your husband, ever discuss his will with you."

"Yes, he did."

"Did he ever show you his will."

"No, he did not."

"Did he discuss the trust?"

"Yes."

"What did he discuss with you?"

"About the will or about the trust?"

"Both."

"Ted told me I would continue to live in the lifestyle that I was accustomed to. He made up a new trust to guarantee this. The first trust was drawn up before we were married, that trust had his children as beneficiaries of the income. The second trust he had written after we were married. It was the same as the first, except that in the second trust, I was the beneficiary of the income throughout my lifetime. He had discussed this in detail with me and with Jim Donnelly, his lawyer."

The questions continued. The attorney asked the same questions in different ways. When he had exhausted the different ways, it was over.

"Thank you, Mrs. Johnson. We'll be in touch."

The deposition was over, now she was alone with Carl.

"Not so bad, was it?"

"No, still, it was stressful."

"Well, you did an excellent job. He can present the facts so the mediator will be able to facilitate a resolution. We should have the depositions from the children next week. Then Jim and I will sit down and talk things through."

"I can't tell you how happy I'll be to get this over and resolved."

"It's been an unsettling time for you, to say the least."

"So much has happened. Driving down I was just in shock by everything that's gone on. Funny how one incident, a death, triggers so many other things. Kevin! My God, I still can't believe how that happened. I know that you've written the book on strange circumstances — "

"I've seen a lot of unusual situations, but you and Kevin pretty much top them all. How did you even think to give me the adoption papers? Did you suspect that Kevin was your son?"

"I can't say that I did. I mean, not consciously. Maybe, on some level, I sensed something. The clipping I found made me realize I had to find out more about him. There were similarities with Frank Pierce, but those were vague. Everything falls into place, in hindsight, of course. I shudder thinking of the way things could have progressed."

"Luckily, my people in Jacksonville found out, and quite quickly, what you needed to know."

"I think Ted's death gave me the opportunity, the space, to think about my child. I mean, Ted never knew about the baby. Right after it happened, right after I gave my baby away, I was trained to act like it never happened. But somehow, with Ted gone, my concern and my curiosity rose again. And Dottie had such faith in you. I never connected the two. On impulse I gave you the envelope. It was a relief to finally tell someone my secret. And thank God, it was you! I never would have told Kevin, had he not had a near death experience."

Like the best lawyers, doctors or priests, Carl was a good listener. Only after a pause did he speak.

"And how did he take the news?"

"Not well."

"Are you going see him again?"

"I hope so, but I've left that up to him. He's had enough pain. He's also inflicted pain. He needs time. I hope I'll hear from him."

"Time is the best physician. For everything."

"Yes, I guess. I hope. Thank you, Carl."

Ginger had a lot to think about on the drive home.

CHAPTER 47

T HE WEEKEND LOOMED ahead. No Ted to visit, no Dottie and no Kevin. This was the beginning of the last chapter of her life. There were so many widows and now she joined their ranks. They all must go through this. A feeling of disconnection, the lack of an anchor. She was one of the lucky ones, of course. She didn't have to worry about money. If the trust situation was not settled in her favor, she might have to tighten up some. But her life would go on at 3-Oaks. She had her home, health, hobbies, and her good friends. Also, she had a son.

But then, did she? It had been nearly a month. She could not count on Kevin.

Ginger would throw herself into her art. She had always lost herself in her painting, but now she would approach it as business. Hadn't she sold a painting to a countess? Maybe she should ask Avery to contact her, say how she regretted not meeting her in New York, and it happened that she was going to be in England, perhaps they could meet in person, at last? She would call her galleries and make it clear she had new work to show. She could even invite Charlie Taylor to an opening. She wondered how he was, and about his wife. It was always good to have a plan and a goal. She felt a little better. She picked up the phone and called Diane.

"Diane, how are you?"

"Ginger? How'd it go in Palm Beach with Carl?"

"The lawyer from Atlanta took a deposition."

"That's nerve-wracking. It's amazing how many ways a lawyer can ask you the same question."

There was a pause on the line. Diane knew why Ginger had called.

"Any word from you-know-who?"

"No. I think if I was going to hear from him, I would have heard by now. You know, I encouraged him to do his rehab at Treasure Beach but, well . . ."

"Ginger, look at it this way. You now know who your son is and where he is. This is a major development. You haven't known a thing about him for 50 years."

This was true. But could she admit that the fantasy of her son was, in some ways, preferable to the reality? And how knowing who he was and where he was yet having no access to him created fresh misery for Ginger.

"That's all true."

However, did she really know Kevin? No, no one ever really knows who someone else is, what's in their heart, their soul or what secrets they've stashed in a safe somewhere.

"Bill's home, seafood buffet at the club tonight. Want to join?"

"Thanks but I think I'll skip that."

"Oh, come on. We're sitting with Sally and Earl, so lots of real estate talk. And the Pembrokes. Emily and Tad just got back from Normandy. Tad is a great authority on World War II, you know. So, between him and Bill there won't be a lack of distracting conversation, that's for sure."

Ginger stayed quiet.

"When are we going riding next week?"

"Whenever you want. I'm as free as a bird," Ginger said.

"OK, let's talk on Monday. But the invitation for tonight stands. It's easy to make a six-top a seven-top."

They hung up. This is my life now, Ginger thought. Waiting to be asked

273

to dinner, to be the seventh at a table meant for six.

Suddenly, Ginger was flooded with the old feeling, the panic she used to experience as a girl at Miss Hall's School. Did all the girls know how her parents worked five jobs between them to send her to the elite school? Did they sneer about the apartment house where she lived? The snarl of insecurities made a knot in her stomach. When Ted was there, even in his latter days, she had felt protected from these feelings. But now they returned in full force.

All her bravado at lunch with Diane, her frankness, claiming not to care what other people thought. It was all a facade. She did care what people thought. The idea of revealing her secrets, her shame, and the truth about Kevin to the entire community made her tremble. Who was she kidding? She wanted to hide, to sell her house, move away and never return. Those feelings of being in control, of setting goals and making plans, the dream of her career as an artist, all evaporated in an instant. Ginger began to cry.

The phone rang, but it wasn't Kevin. It was Dottie.

"Ginger? Do you have a cold? I came down with a doozy last week, a gift from my grandchild. I don't know why a mother sends a sick child to school. When I was young my mama made me stay home an extra 24 hours after I had anything so much as a sneeze."

"No, I don't have a cold," Ginger managed to say, suppressing sobs.

"Honey, are you having a little cry?"

"Dottie, one minute I've talked myself up and the next minute I come crashing down. I had lunch with Diane, I told her everything only I couldn't bring myself to tell her about — "

"About what?"

"About the clippings and Kevin's lifestyle for the past year or so."

"Well, it's not necessary to tell such details to anyone. You and I will keep some things to ourselves. And what you feel is natural. All the commotion about

Kevin distracted you from grieving Ted. That's front and center now. There's no way around it, Ginger. When Bert died, even with all this family, I felt lost. *Lost!* There's a vast emptiness. No matter how active you are, the projects, charity work or travel. Every widow does these things to distract herself from the void. But time heals. I promise. The yearning for companionship lingers on. And it means that we were blessed to have had such a relationship. That's what it means."

"I felt so brave at first. I think I was just on a high or a rush. There was all this drama, finding my son, Kevin's life, the accident, and now that everything's settled down, I don't know what to do with myself."

"You get to live your life, a day at a time. That's what you are going to do. And about Kevin, you don't have to make any public announcement or take out an ad in the newspaper, for goodness's sake. Let it seep out."

"What do you mean?"

"Why not ask Diane to tell a couple of women. Let it get around that way. And then go out and keep your chin up. Then if Kevin comes to visit, everyone will know. Anyway, the most important thing is that you have found Kevin. And that he is going to be all right after that terrible accident."

"But do I really want everyone gossiping?"

"How do you propose to prevent that, my dear? Listen, give the gossipers the whole truth. Go to a club event, get it over with."

"Oh Dottie, I just don't know if I can."

"Well, I know you and I know that you can. In the long run people will admire you, and those who don't, well, to hell with them!"

"Diane asked me to the seafood buffet tonight."

"Perfect."

"I said no."

"Call her back and say yes. And tell her to call a gal or two, put your story out there. There isn't a single person at 3-Oaks who doesn't have a skeleton in their closet. I've lived long enough to know that."

"OK, I'll do it."

"Absolutely. Have a dressing drink and then go. I expect a full report tomorrow."

Ginger hung up the phone and called Diane back before her nerve left her.

"Diane? I'd love to join you tonight."

"Wonderful. I'll call the club right now."

"I want to ask you a favor."

"Sure. What?"

"Would you tell Sally about Kevin?"

"Tell Sally about Kevin? About him being your son? Why on earth would I do that?"

"I want it to be out. There's no better way than to have someone like Sally, who's in real estate and who talks to everyone. Better Sally than Louise!"

"I see your point. All right, if you're sure."

"Agree before I lose my nerve."

"Okay, I'll phone her now. I have to let her know the time we're meeting for drinks. How's 6:30?"

Ginger drew a deep breath.

"Okay. See you then."

"Do you want us to pick you up? Human shields?"

"No, I'll take my cart."

"You are one brave lady, Ginger."

They hung up.

DOTTIE'S IDEA WAS bold, but it made sense: Get it over with. She had nothing to hide. There was no shame in the truth, and everyone would know she had a son. Following Dottie's directions to the letter, she poured herself a dressing drink. Her hand was trembling so, at her dressing table, she alternately applied her makeup and had a sip of white wine. She now understood how this might become a habit. A lovely Chablis and me, she thought to herself. By the time she added the finishing flourish of blush, her glass was empty. Ginger stood and studied herself in the mirror. She had selected a white linen tunic, white pants, and gold sandals. White was the right choice. The shoes had a small heel, just enough. She'd fastened her hair up with a tortoise clamp.

Downstairs by the door, Ginger grabbed a pink wrap and threw it over her shoulder. This added panache and made her feel bold. She was ready. She boarded her cart and drove down the path to the clubhouse. The night air was refreshing. She felt ready for whatever came next.

Outside the clubhouse, as anticipated, the lawn was cluttered with carts parked every which way. The seafood buffet was hugely popular. Strategically, she arrived a little late. She could count on Diane to carry out her assigned task: To share her story with Sally. Being late gave the gossipers time to buzz and circulate the shocking facts of her life. Where her courage came from, she had no idea. Maybe it was derived from her friends and allies, Dottie, Diane, and Carl. Maybe it had something to do with all she had been through. Maybe it was because she was no longer a child or a wife. She was a mother now and everyone would know.

Let it be packed, she thought. And it was.

Harry stood by the door.

"Good evening, Mrs. Johnson."

"Harry, have the Butlers arrived?"

"Yes. Follow me, Mrs. Johnson."

He weaved his way through the tables, and she followed. The room was crowded with diners and there was a din.

"Hello, Ginger."

"Hi, Ginger."

She heard these greetings and smiled, but she didn't dare stop. It was like she was walking through a gauntlet. She kept her eyes ahead, remembering Dottie's words: *Keep your chin up.* Clearly Harry had heard her story. Never had he before escorted her through the dining room. Never had she needed an ally so badly. At the archway to the terrace, Harry scanned the crowd.

"There they are, over to the right, with the Bakers."

They shared a glance. It was obvious to Ginger and Harry that this was not ideal. Oh, well. There's no going back now. Ginger made a beeline to Diane. All heads turned in her direction. If there had been a spotlight trained on her, she could not have felt more conspicuous.

"Oh, there you are. Bill, Ginger's here," Diane said. He was talking to Henry.

"Hello, Ginger," said Bill and leaned in to give her a kiss.

"Hello, Ginger," said Henry as he leaned in to give her a kiss.

All eyes were on her. Ginger smiled, helplessly.

"Hi, darling." Diane leaned in and kissed her.

"Good evening, all."

"What can I get you?" Bill asked.

"A vodka tonic?"

"Pete, a vodka tonic for Mrs. Johnson."

Diane eyed the space between Louise and Ginger.

"Well, well, you're looking lovely . . ." Louise drawled. "I declare you look like a little old Southern belle with your hair all up on top of your head . . ."

"I am very Southern, indeed, so thank you."

"Your ears must be burning. Why everyone is buzzing about the new addition to your family. And *such an attractive addition —* "

"Louise, just shut up," Henry snapped.

"Why, Henry. You've never talked to me like that, in 40 years of marriage.

Must be the redhead in white. You know, she's back on the market!" Louise batted her eyelashes.

"Excuse us," Henry said, and he grasped his drunken wife's elbow and steered her away.

"Poor Louise," said Diane.

Ginger was trembling. Bill handed her a drink. She took a gulp.

"Let's find our table," Diane said. "We should get started before the line gets too long."

"Another drink, Ginger?"

"Yes. And right away."

Everyone laughed. Diane set out to find their table, Ginger followed. It was a baptism by fire, but Ginger felt only slightly singed.

CHAPTER 48

"GOOD MORNING, MARGALE. Can you believe it's July 4th. Why don't you take the day off? I'm going to the beach party with the Butlers later on."

"Thank you, Mrs. Johnson, but I have nowhere to go."

"Well, then relax. Do whatever you want."

"Thank you, Mrs. Johnson. Maybe I'll bake something special."

Ginger went into her studio. She was working on a new canvas, and it was hard to stay away. There were three figures, facing out. She sketched their bodies. Three women, it seemed. She worked feverishly and for a long time. Finally, she checked her watch and began to clean her brushes. The longest stretches she went without a thought of Kevin were in her studio with a brush in hand. Bill and Diane would be by to pick her up in a little over an hour. She had just enough time for a bath.

The Fourth of July party meant wearing either red, white, or blue. She chose blue and added red and white touches. I guess I'm in my blue period, she thought to herself. Kevin had not contacted her. She'd harbored a fantasy that they would be re-united by now and that she would bring him to the party. Even if he was convalescing, he could have enjoyed it. By this time, everyone had heard the story of Ginger and Kevin. She'd kept a low profile since the seafood buffet. The people she ran into were mostly discreet; it was easiest to avoid the subject entirely. It made things simpler, by far, that Kevin was nowhere in sight. Still his absence pained her. Ginger had not seen Louise again, either. Her luck was about to run out.

AT 3-OAKS, the Fourth of July was a major event; the staff spent days setting up the party. The beach had long tables skirted in red and white checked cloths. There were small American flags down the center. Blue bachelor buttons and red poppies in a row of white vases were set between the flags. When Diane, Bill and Ginger arrived, the grills were already blazing. There were lobsters, steaks, and chicken ready to be cooked, and a pyramid of husked corn on the cob. A long bar was next to the dune. A dance floor had been built near the dune crossover. A steel band was playing, making the mood especially festive and loud.

They found their table and put their wraps on the chairs.

"A perfect night. Bill, look! There's a full moon!" Diane said.

Ginger looked up and sighed. "It's so lovely. Look how the moon throws sparkles on the ocean all the way to the horizon."

Ginger recalled all the afternoons and evenings sitting on the beach or the boardwalk with Kevin. Talking and laughing, eating ice-cream cones. She remembered feeling both carefree and uneasy at the same time. Now, she had to settle for knowing who Kevin was and where he was. Several times she had the impulse to call Dr. Jamal. She'd picked up the phone, only to set it down again. Her son was a grown man; he could take care of himself and make his own decisions. She had so hoped to be part of his life, but she had to accept that he had made a different choice.

"Ginger? Earth to Ginger...? I said, what would you like to drink?"

"I was thinking about how much Kevin would love this."

Diane knew that Ginger was brokenhearted. At least his absence silenced the gossip mill, and that was a good thing.

"I'll have a vodka tonic, thanks. And Bill, for heaven's sake, put it on my tab. Just because you're the only man doesn't mean that I'm always your guest."

"Don't be silly. I love having two women in my life."

Diane gave him a look. *Open mouth, insert foot,* she thought to herself. She almost said it aloud but caught herself.

Ginger simply smiled. At that moment, Louise descended on their table.

"Hello, girls, how are y'all?"

"We're all fine," Diane said.

"Ginger! You look so pretty. Why, any young man would take a fancy to you, given a chance. Just keep — "

"Louise, why don't you just run along and find poor Henry."

"Poor Henry? What do you mean *poor Henry*? He was poor, until he married me. As poor as a church mouse!"

"You know you and gin are not good companions," Ginger said and turned, heading to their table. Diane and Bill exchanged a glance and followed. Ginger had never-ever stood up to Louise Baker.

AS SOON AS they sat, fireworks started flaring up into the sky and the crowd cheered.

Ginger, Diane, and Bill gazed up at the colorful explosions.

"Sure beats the chasers and snails we had when I was a boy. The fireworks were never like this. And of course, there was no ocean in Nashville."

"They're spectacular!" Ginger added.

"You know," said Bill. "I arrange the permits every year."

"We know," Ginger and Diane said in unison, sharing a glance.

"It's my favorite night at 3-Oaks and the food is fabulous."

"I think I've tried every single salad."

"Save some room for the apple crisp."

"I haven't saved room. But I'll make room. The Fourth of July feast at 3-Oaks is the devil's very temptation," Diane said, and Bill laughed. It was impossible not to be in good spirits.

"Anybody for a little nightcap?" Bill shouted over the bangs of the fireworks and the cheers of the rowdy crowd.

"I still have some wine, thanks."

"You want another, honey?"

"No. Are you sure you want another, Bill?"

"I don't have to navigate Ocean Drive and the police tonight. Just going across the street in the old golf cart. I'll just grab me a roadie."

An hour later, Diane was driving the cart and Bill was bellowing into the night.

"*God Bless America, land that I love —*"

The women laughed uproariously.

"He really means it," said Diane.

"No one's more patriotic than Bill," said Ginger.

"Too bad he wasn't around for the American Revolution. He'd have led the charge."

CHAPTER 49

A FTER THE FOURTH, things quieted down at 3-Oaks. A lot of members had houses in the Hamptons, on Nantucket or the Cape. Ginger could have gone to Nantucket, the Johnson children only went in August, but she wanted to be home in case Kevin called. Yet as July turned into August, her hopes waned. Was it possible she might never see Kevin again? Her son had been lost and then found and now he was lost again. She prayed he didn't feel as lonely as she did.

Ginger had her art. Her dream of committing to the business of art was becoming a reality. She had three shows on her calendar: the first was in Treasure Beach, an opening in the fall. The picture of three women was almost finished. The women did not have faces, but their bodies suggested three different ages. She had given each one a hint of red hair: the first vibrant, the second lighter and the red of the third, the eldest, was streaked slightly with grey. She had never attempted a self-portrait, but she recognized herself. Painting the figures had been a time of contemplation. Each era had been distinct, full, and interesting. The middle with Ted had been the best, but who knows? Maybe the very best was yet to come.

One day, Margale brought the mail. On the top was a large envelope from Carl Phillips. Ginger felt trepidation. She flashed on the last time she'd received an envelope from his office. But at least this one would not contain any revelations about Kevin. Still, it might be momentous, just the same. She took the parcel to her desk and opened it.

> Dear Ginger,
>
> Enclosed, is the resolution of the contested will and trust of your husband, Theodore Willard Johnson. The mediation of Johnsons v. Johnson has been settled by Dean Cochran, State of Florida, Office of Mediation.
>
> In short, the second trust by the deceased stands as written, without signature. The contesting parties, Jack Johnson, Bill Johnson, and Emily Moore agreed that their father's intention stand as stated in the second trust. Therefore, they have accepted the terms of the second trust. These papers validate this agreement.
>
> Carl Jr. and I are delighted to share this outcome with you, Ginger.
>
> At your earliest convenience, please sign and date where your signature is indicated and return the documents to my office in the express envelope provided. I will forward these to Jim Donnelly. We will have all monies transferred to you in a couple of weeks. At that time, I would like to discuss the trusteeship with you.
>
> Thank you for allowing us to help you in this matter. We look forward to assisting you with any further matters in the future.
>
> All my best,
>
> Carl

Tears filled her eyes. Ginger put the papers down.

"Thank you, dear Ted. Thank you. I wish you were here with me. I will be a good custodian of the fortune you worked so hard for, I promise," she said aloud.

Ginger fully intended to keep this promise. She had plenty of income, more than enough. Ted had taken care of her after all. She jumped up and out of the room. Suddenly, Ginger was ravenous.

"Margale, I'll have a tray in Mr. Johnson's study. Just cold chicken and grilled vegetables, please."

She wanted to be with Ted. She felt close to him in his room, among his pictures and trophies. He had loved it here. Ted's study was the first place he would go when he came home. She sat in her chair and ate lunch on her tray, gazing outside at the greens he'd loved so much.

After lunch, Ginger noticed the rest of the mail. She had not finished going through it and rifled through assorted bills. The bills can wait. She took the catalogs and opened the one from Bergdorf's. A long white envelope dropped out. It was addressed to her in an unfamiliar hand, rather scratchy. Curious, she turned it over. Her heart stopped when she read the name on the flap: Kevin McCoy. The address read: Cocoa Beach, Florida. Her heart was racing. Ginger studied the envelope. She'd never seen his handwriting before. She went to her desk and got her letter opener, slid the blade to the seam and got herself comfortable on her bed.

Dear Ginger,

Forgive me for taking so long to get in touch with you. I appreciate your offer to have me in Treasure Beach for physical therapy and then at your lovely house. Your forgiving spirit and generosity have touched me to my very core. The trauma of the accident and long rehabilitation has actually been a blessing. Because I am grounded, so to speak, I have been forced to think about what my life has been and what my future might be.

Now, let me fill you in on what's been going on.

I moved to Orlando Emergency Physical Therapy Facility a week or so after you left. Dr. Jamal recommended I remain close so he could keep an eye on me. He went over my physical condition and said that I was healing nicely. He mentioned again how lucky I was and especially because, when I crashed, my blood alcohol level had been four times the amount it should have been to be driving. He asked me about my alcohol consumption. I admitted that I had lost my seat at Northwest due to my alcohol consumption. He asked if I might consider talking to a counselor from the Drug and Alcohol Rehab Unit at Orlando. By some good fortune, not the Kevin you know, I said yes, I'm willing. I like to think I was channeling your good sense.

Tears started to fall again. Ginger settled back into her pillows. Curious and enthralled, she read on:

The counselor said there was a good chance I had a drinking problem. He said that as I was going to start physical therapy in a week, I could also start an outpatient rehab program at the same time. What the hell, I thought, heal body and soul. So, I did both. The physical therapy was grueling, the leg and especially the shoulder. But the most challenging therapy was in rehab for alcohol.

I'm not sure how much you know about these programs, but this is it, in a nutshell. Most rehabs are modeled after the Hazleton program, the mother of all rehabs, in Minnesota. The model uses the 12-step program from Alcoholics Anonymous to help a person break old habits and start over, to live a sober, productive life. It sounds easy, but I can tell you, it's the hardest thing I've ever done. It makes flying a plane seem like riding a bike! Since I am officially middle aged, I have a lot more years of denial invested in my alcoholism, a lot more things to figure out than some-one younger. I feel confident that having surrendered as completely as I can at this time and, relying on a Higher Power (whom I chose to call God), I will become healthy and whole one day.

But we can't just quit the bottle. We must do 'The Steps.'

Step 8 says: Made a list of all persons we have harmed and became willing to make amends to them all.

Step 9: Made direct amends to such people wherever possible except when to do so would injure them or others.

At the top of my list was my mother and my father, my adoptive family, that is. After a great deal of counseling and support from the other 'inmates,' as we sometimes affectionately refer to one another, I phoned my Dad. It had been eons since we communicated, about 25 years. He sounded older, but pretty much the same. He has retired from medicine, and lives in the same house. But more about Dad later! I asked to speak to Mom, and he said she had died four years ago of cancer. He said he had no idea where I was or how to get in touch with me. My mother had very much wanted to see me. He said my leaving had left a hole in her heart, but she never thought lesser of me for it. He said she seemed to understand my restlessness and yearning to find myself. I now realize that I had cut myself off from myself by denying them. My Dad was wonderful, no reprimands. Zero. He even came to visit. He's the same guy, though he seems kind of lost without my mother and he's retired. He put his arms around me and said, "Son, I'm glad you're back. Please don't ever leave again. Forgive me for anything I ever did to hurt you or to drive you away." Quite a scene. A pair of grown men boo-hooing like kids. I can't put into words what his visit meant to me. He also told me that when my mother died, she had left me some money. I had no idea that my mother had money of her own, but apparently her father, my grandfather, had set up a trust at his death and it was to be divided between John, my younger brother, and me. Another gift. The money has enabled me to get a small apartment on Ocean Drive in Cocoa Beach, a car (not a convertible) and to continue with my therapy. I go to three AA meetings a week and will continue, I hope, for the rest of my life. The AA slogan, "One day at a time," is my motto, but I'm thinking about what I might do when I physically recover.

The next person on my list to make amends to is you. I would like to do that in person. As you know, Cocoa Beach is only about 40 minutes north of Treasure Beach. I was hoping you would like to come up Labor Day weekend. You could come up Sunday early and go to church with me or lunch in the afternoon together to talk. You could spend Sunday night here. I have a very small guest room. Monday, I'm having friends over for a BBQ. I have a nice deck and grill and I'm not half bad at burgers and hot dogs.

Don't feel obligated if you're busy or would prefer not to come. Either way, I understand. However, I would like to see you, at a time of your choosing. Please keep me in your thoughts and prayers. You are in mine.

Kevin

When Ginger finished reading the tears running down her cheeks splashed onto the page. Ginger set the letter on her bedside table, pulled a tissue out from the box there, and dropped her head into her hands. The relief was overwhelming.

Kevin was alive. He was out of the hospital. He had settled not too far away, in under an hour's drive. He wanted a relationship with her. His tone was so different. He was an alcoholic. She had heard about rehabs, and the Twelve Steps. She knew that some very successful people belonged to such groups. But this frightened her. She looked at the typed page he had included. She'd assumed it was directions to his place in Cocoa Beach, but it wasn't. It was titled *The Twelve Steps of Alcoholics Anonymous*. She read through them. The words swarmed in her blurry eyes: admitted we were powerless over alcohol . . . our lives were unmanageable . . . a higher power could restore us to sanity . . . a searching and fearless moral inventory . . . admitted . . . the exact nature of our wrongs . . . were entirely ready to have God remove all these defects of character . . . made a list of all people we had harmed . . . and became willing to make amends to them all. She thought of Theresa McCoy and the pain she'd suffered, missing Kevin at her death. This was almost too great, Theresa's pain compounding her own decades of pain. How did women bear this? Exhausted, Ginger flicked out the light. Sleep rescued her from all her feelings.

CHAPTER 50

IN THE MORNING, Ginger called for coffee and juice in her room and reread the letter. Then, she picked up the phone.

"Dottie? Are you busy?"

"Ginger! Hi honey. Not terribly. Just arranging flowers with Dessie. I swear we could go into business, we're that good. Isn't that right, Dessie?"

"Yes, Mrs. Morris. We certainly could."

"D & D Floral Arrangement, what do you think?"

Ginger had to smile. "I love it," she said, settling herself on her bed and taking another sip of coffee. "What sort of flowers?"

"Well, we've got some rose varieties – Gertrude Jekyll and Cha Ching —"

"My favorite pink and I love the yellow!"

"Some calla lilies, what else —"

"Hydrangeas," Dessie said in the background.

"The hydrangeas are *enormous* this year. Like footballs only blue."

"Is it hot in Atlanta?"

"Atlanta is the devil's own playground in the summer, you know that. Now, Dessie, take these stems into the kitchen and put them in cold water, otherwise they'll wilt in this heat. I'm going to talk to Mrs. Johnson for a minute."

There was a pause on the line while Dottie waited. Then she said, "All right, what's happening? I know you didn't call me to get the weather report."

"I heard from Kevin."

"He called?"

"He wrote a letter."

"Yes, and . . . ?"

"Dottie, Kevin's an alcoholic!"

"Oh dear. Now, tell me everything."

"May I read it to you?"

"I'm all ears."

Sharing his letter made Ginger feel slightly calmer.

"Well, that's quite a missive from Kevin McCoy."

"He also included his home phone number. And a typed copy of *The Twelve Steps of Alcoholics Anonymous*. They're quite intense."

"Did you know he was an alcoholic?"

"I really had no idea. We both drank a lot during his stay, but I was always able to stop and go upstairs to bed. I know he stayed up nights, having a nightcap by the pool. And of course, I never knew what else he had, I mean after or before. The bar in Ted's library was right next to his room."

"Anyway, it sounds like that's in the past. He's faced his problem. That's admirable."

"I guess it's dogged him for years. I never really knew why he was on such a long leave of absence from the airline. I didn't dream it was *permanent*. I guess it had nothing to do with his stomach."

"Apparently not. Are you going to go see him over Labor Day?"

"I was thinking I'd go up for church Sunday and lunch. Then drive home and go back on Monday. I'd love to meet his friends, but — "

"It's good to have an escape hatch."

"That was my thinking."

"If something comes up that's uncomfortable — "

"I can drive home."

"Gracefully."

"Exactly. I hope it's okay with him."

"The most important thing is that he wants '. . . to make amends.'"

"I have more trepidation about that than anything."

"You will help him a great deal by just listening."

"That's not going to be the easiest thing," Ginger said, meekly.

"For you or for him?"

"I'm not sure I can stand hearing more of the details of his life. And now this!"

"But, Ginger, that's what your son needs you to do. He's trying to heal. All he asks is that you listen."

"Okay."

"And not judge. Do you think you can do that?"

"It's just hard taking on one more crisis. Ted, then everything with Kevin, then the accident, then everyone at 3-Oaks knowing all my secrets, and now this!"

"Crises come in clusters. But good things do, too."

"Which reminds me. Yesterday, the very same day I heard from Kevin, I got a package from Carl. Everything will be just as Ted wanted."

"According to the second trust, the unsigned one?"

"The mediator concluded, and the kids agreed."

"Well, well. If I felt any happier, I'd drop my harp plumb through a cloud. Carl is a great lawyer, and the children are not conspiring against you."

"They've always been a little lost, even when Ted was alive. Secretly, I feel sorry for them. Especially the boys. They don't *do* anything. It's hard if a man doesn't have a job and feel fulfilled, even I know that. Ted had tremendous self-esteem which he got from working and being responsible and successful. I just pray

Kevin can find a path for himself. Self-esteem drives a hard bargain, you have to get it all by yourself."

"Spoken like a true philosopher. Have you called him?"

"No," Ginger said timidly.

"Don't put it off."

Why was it suddenly so hard to call him?

"How can I ever thank you, Dottie? You've helped me through *everything*."

"No, you're the strong one! I've got to run and finish the flower arranging before the blooms or I expire from this heat! I'm meeting the girls for lunch. Keep me in the loop!"

"Honestly I can't believe how everything's working out."

"I'm tickled pink. Now, hang up and call your son."

"Okay. Bye, Dottie. I will.

Ginger hung up. Then, she took a deep breath and picked up the phone again and dialed.

"Kevin?"

"Hello. I was hoping you might call." It had been months since she heard his voice, and the sound made her tremble. Just like the tone in his letter seemed different to her, she instantly noticed a shift in his voice. She kept talking.

"Thank you for your letter. It arrived yesterday."

"That was fast. I only mailed it the day before — "

"You've made a lot of progress, I mean physically, mentally, well, in every way."

"I have made progress, physically, mentally, and in every way."

It seemed like Kevin felt as awkward as she did.

"Thank you for the invitation for Labor Day — "

"I don't want to put you to any trouble — "

"I'd love to come."

"Oh, that's terrific. As I said, my place is small. The guest room is very small."

"No, I thought I'd come both days. If you don't mind my coming and going, it's just easy for me to drive home, and then drive back Monday, for your gathering."

"Whatever you'd like."

"I'm not the best houseguest. It's a beautiful drive, by the ocean and I love to drive — "

She stopped herself. Was the topic of driving painful for him? She remembered how the dressing drink had calmed her and longed for a glass of Chablis. He sounded like a different person. Maybe that was the point: *Maybe he was a different person.*

"Terrific," he said again. "We can go to church, have lunch and spend some time talking."

"What time is church?"

"10:30. Is that too early?"

"Not at all."

"It's Episcopal, is that alright?"

They were taking turns being nervous. Was it possible that Kevin was having as much difficulty adjusting to being her son as she was to being his mother? Keeping her answers short helped maintain her composure. Or, at least, it helped her appear composed.

"Yes. Lovely."

"You have my address, 1006 Ocean Drive. It's the fifth light when you enter Cocoa Beach."

"The fifth light . . . when you enter Cocoa Beach . . ." she said, jotting it down. "May I bring something on Monday? Margale makes a wonderful potato salad and baked beans."

The mention of Margale brought back memories for them both. How could she avoid referring to their prior time together? And its ramifications? Would they ever have a new set of experiences to replace the awkwardness of their past?

She remembered him waiting at the foot of the stairs with a globe-like glass for her. She remembered dancing in his arms. All her dreams and hopes. Ginger felt a shiver of embarrassment down to her bones. Could each of them become a new and different person?

"Did you hear me…? Ginger? Are you still there?"

Ginger shook herself and refocused her attention. "I'm here. What did you say?"

"I said I'm sure Margale's cooking would be better than anything from the supermarket."

"How many people on Monday?"

"Maybe eight — ? I can handle the hot dogs and hamburgers. I've got those covered."

As much as she'd longed to hear his voice and as long as she had waited to speak with him, she wanted to end the call.

"Well, I'm looking forward to seeing you on Sunday."

"Not this Sunday though, the one after that." They kept trading places. Now it was Kevin who was the more composed. "Ginger, thank you. I'm glad you're coming."

"Me, too. Goodbye." She said and hung up.

Ginger stayed sitting in the chair. She stared out for a long time. Then, as if Ted were right there in the room, she spoke to him out loud.

"Ted, I have a son!"

CHAPTER 51

FLORIDA IS THE best kept secret in the summer. It's like Hawaii. The ocean is a beautiful, Caribbean blue. Most of the locals leave. The streets are empty, and the towns are quiet. Ginger soaked up the vacant spaces of summer. She needed to think, to be and to paint. While her neighbors vacationed in Nantucket or on The Vineyard or in the teeming capitals of Europe, Ginger stayed home, allowing herself time to catch up with the events of her life. She was grieving Ted and grieving the loss of the role of wife. After the tumultuous relationship with Kevin, she was regaining her equilibrium, returning to herself, centering her life on being a painter. The opening of her show in Treasure Beach was approaching. The latter half of August, Ginger worked feverishly in her studio and painted night after night. She woke early and painted more. Margale delivered most of her meals to the studio. Then, on the Sunday before Labor Day, Ginger got in her car to drive to Cocoa Beach.

CHAPTER 52

I T WAS A LOVELY morning and early. No one was on the road. The ocean alongside the highway was as flat as glass. Ginger put the top down. The beauty filled her with positivity. Setting out, she felt ready for whatever the day brought.

But the drive was short. Approaching the Cocoa Beach exit, her anxiety increased. How would he treat her? What would he look like? How strange that he wanted to go to church. Was this the transformation that AA leaders demanded? She wasn't looking forward to hearing Kevin's stories. At least she was prepared. Ginger knew all sorts of thing about him already. She'd read through Carl's two reports; they did not paint a pretty picture of Kevin McCoy. But she reminded herself of Dottie's words. To heal, Kevin needed to talk and so she needed to listen. This was her job as his mother.

Ginger saw a sign, *Entering Cocoa Beach*, flipped on her blinker and turned off the highway. As she did, butterflies fluttered in her stomach. She drove slowly along the main street, counting the five lights and grateful every time she got a red. At the fifth, on the corner, on the ocean side of the boulevard, stood a small, five story building. She pulled into the parking area and took a spot facing the beach. She entered a glass door, searched the directory of names, and saw K. McCoy. She pushed the buzzer and straightened her summer shift. Even though she was waiting to hear his voice, she was startled when she did.

"Hello?"

"Hi, it's me. Ginger. I'm here."

She felt foolish. Of course, he knew who she was and where.

"Hi. Uh, wait there. I'll come down. We'll go straight to church."

For a second, she thought he might call her *mom* and bristled at the thought. That would be too uncomfortable. She stepped back outside and waited, gazing at the ocean. Now a wind was stirring, and there were waves. Ginger wished she was somewhere else. What amends would he make to her? What had she been thinking to tell the truth to him and everyone else? She could have kept her secret and Carl's report hidden in Ted's safe forever.

Kevin walked out into the sun. He was tan, smiling. He was using a cane, which was unexpected. She avoided eye contact. All of this was excruciating. She wished to be alone in her studio, with a brush in hand, protected from all the feelings that flooded her upon seeing Kevin, her handsome son, approach her. She wanted to laugh, she wanted to cry, she was proud, she was ashamed. The conflicting emotions wreaked havoc on her composure. So, she fixed her eyes downward and on the dark wooden cane he was using.

"I forgot to warn you," he said, referring to the cane.

With a slight hobble, he neared her, put a hand on her shoulder and kissed her cheek. Looking briefly into his blue eyes caused more confusion. It was like looking into her own. In a flash she felt that he had the same jolt of recognition, an unassailable confirmation of their mother and son bond. They both looked away. Luckily there was the vast ocean for them to escape to and pretend to contemplate.

"I told you it was right on the ocean. It's not 3-Oaks, but it's mine . . . Thanks to my mother. I mean, Theresa — "

"I know."

"How lucky can a fellow be? Two mothers? And one of them, standing right here. Thank you for coming. It means a lot."

She dared a smile up at him. But they both turned away again and looked back to the ocean. The waves crashed noisily onto the beach.

"I wanted to show you my apartment and the view from there. But we can do that after church."

"Would you like me to drive?"

"That would be great. I can drive, but it's not the easiest. And my car is not exactly a convertible."

This minor reference to their early days was uncomfortable. They turned away from each other and walked to her car.

"It's just a short way," he said.

In the car, their physical proximity was charged. And at church, in the wooden pew, Ginger kept the space between them unnaturally wide. The church was charming. The pews were more vacant than not.

Before the start of the service, Kevin nodded to some of the other parishioners. During the service, Ginger mostly gazed at the stained-glass windows. Her eyes studied the figures of Jesus, his apostles, and followers, just as she had distracted herself during chapel week after week for years at Miss Hall's. The only part of the service she engaged in was standing and singing hymns. When Ted's favorite came up, *The Old Rugged Cross*, Ginger sang with gusto and Kevin smiled. But they each held their own hymnal and made a point of not sharing.

After the service, they joined the receiving line. When it was their turn to thank the minister, she realized she had no recollection of the homily.

"Good morning, Kevin," the minister said.

"Reverend, I'd like you to meet my mother, Ginger Johnson. Ginger lives in Treasure Beach. She's visiting for the weekend.

"Nice to meet you, Mrs. Johnson."

"Call me Ginger — everyone does."

The minister smiled and said, "Thank you, Ginger. We love having Kevin here. He hasn't missed a Sunday since he moved to Cocoa Beach. When he first came, he was in a wheelchair — "

"For my first three weeks. Then I was on crutches. Then came the cane. Now, I'm with my mother. That's what I call progress!"

Everyone laughed.

"I'm very grateful for his recovery."

"So are we at St. Mary's. Peace be with you both."

"Peace be with you, Reverend."

"Come back and see us, Ginger. We're here every Sunday."

In silence, they walked to the car. Finally, Kevin spoke. "I guess I rambled a little. I'm not used to introducing my mother. I hope to get better at it."

"I'm flattered to be introduced like that, Kevin. Even if I didn't have anything to do with your upbringing. I wish I had gotten to meet Theresa McCoy. I would have liked to have thanked her."

"She was wonderful. I just didn't realize it until it was too late. How many sons get that?"

"Get what?"

"Two mothers and a second chance at being a son."

Ginger blushed. She didn't know what to say.

On the drive back, Kevin pointed out a favorite diner and a couple of spots where he attended AA meetings. At his building, Ginger parked in the same spot. They both stared out. The ocean was a safe place for their attention, they were still struggling to look one another in the eye. Ginger glanced at him sideways. He looked like Kevin, but he was changed from the man he was before. The change was both subtle and obvious. He felt more like a stranger, even though she now knew that this was her son.

"Are you hungry?"

"Church always makes me hungry," she confessed.

"Me, too! We could just eat here. Make sandwiches and take them to the beach. Or maybe you'd prefer a restaurant?"

Ginger hesitated, remembering how they had chased each other down to the waves, danced and frolicked in the ocean. Before she could make up her mind, he spoke again.

"We're here. Let me show you my place, then we'll decide."

Kevin's apartment was tidy and nice. There was an open living room with a dining area at one end. By it, was a small kitchen. Kevin indicated that the two bedrooms and the bath were down the hallway. A balcony ran the full length, with an amazing view of the water. The tour of Kevin's apartment only took a minute or two.

"It's small, but what more do I need?"

"It seems just right."

"Thanks. I like it. But I'm not sure how long I'll be here. I haven't made any real plans yet. The program, I mean, AA, likes us to live one day at a time. My primary purpose is to stay sober one day at a time."

"Let's not go anywhere or to the beach. Let's just stay here and talk."

"Great! I've got cold cuts: ham, turkey, Swiss. Let me get the deck ready. The table might need a wipe down," Kevin moved slowly and looked serious. He was nervous too.

"I could make the sandwiches."

"That'd be great. Everything's in the fridge."

He grabbed a sponge and stepped outside.

Alone in his kitchen, Ginger froze. It had been a long time since she'd been in charge of a meal, even one as simple as sandwiches. She had to brush aside her nerves and get command of herself. Pulling open cabinets, she found glasses. She drew open drawers and found a humble collection of silverware and grabbed a knife. The cold cuts were in the fridge along with mustard and mayonnaise, but the bread was nowhere in sight. *Where did he keep his bread?* She was just about to ask when she found it hidden in an old-fashioned bread drawer. She laughed with surprise. Ginger hadn't seen one of those since her parents' apartment.

"Kevin, one or two sandwiches?"

But he was out of earshot. Never mind. It's better to have a few. Ginger could hardly believe what was happening in her life. She was in an apartment in Cocoa Beach and making sandwiches for her son.

They sat at a circular, wrought iron table on the terrace, facing out. The sandwiches were pretty good. Gazing at the now rough sea filled the silences as they ate. They watched pelicans diving for fish. The seagulls looked on, hoping for a dropped fish. It was hard to know where to begin talking. She wanted to let him take the lead.

"The wildlife here is special to me. There are so many varieties. It makes me happy to see things flying."

"What are your plans, Kevin?"

"I want to find something to do here. My mother left me a good inheritance, but I can't live off it forever, and I don't want to. I want to make my own way. I'm used to that. Though I admit, I haven't earned a paycheck for a while."

They fell silent and went back to watching the swooping birds.

"They're beautiful," Ginger finally said. "I love the white ones. At 3-Oaks, late in the spring, there are hundreds of white pelicans. They just land and sit on the lake for hours. It's like a bird convention."

Kevin threw his head back and laughed. The way he did, the way Frank had. Why did she think this would be easy?

"A bird convention. That must be some sight."

"That's what Ted used to call it." Everything seemed awkward. "Ted's work was an integral part of his life. My art is a big part of my life. Especially now."

"How's your painting going?"

"It's going very well. I'm just about to have some shows."

"That's wonderful."

"The first one is in Treasure Beach."

"When's that?"

"October."

"Can anyone come?"

"I was hoping you would come."

"I'd love to."

"You'll find something you want to do, Kevin. When you're well and ready. But first things first."

"I know. I have faith. God certainly works in mysterious ways. I mean, look at us."

They both smiled shyly. Ginger could almost hear Dottie's voice. It said: *Don't force anything. Just listen.*

"I want to do something around planes. I love flying, I really messed that up. The booze creeps up on you. You know, there's a rule: No drinks 24 hours before flying. I thought I could cheat that. Just a little bit, like 18 hours before. But 18 became 12, and then ten and then eight and then one day it was only three hours before take-off. I got caught and was given a stern warning. The second time was it: *Out.* I didn't know I had a problem. That's what we call *denial.* I mean, in the program. I used to chat-up women on the flights. Usually, they were older. Not always, but usually. I would walk down the aisle of first class in my uniform. They'd be alone and heading to Japan, Hong Kong, or Bangkok. Usually Hong Kong, for shopping. They'd ask me if I was staying in Hong Kong, and for how long. Typically, I had a three or four-day layover. They almost always asked to meet for drinks. Which led to dinner and . . ."

Ginger looked out over the water remembering Dottie's words.

"It was after a couple of these incidents that I got caught. One of the women, Priscilla, had given me her card. She lived in Manalapan and said that if ever I was in South Florida to look her up."

Ginger didn't let on that she already knew all about Priscilla. Listening to Kevin disclose these relationships was excruciating, but more than anything she wanted him to heal.

"I had no intention of looking her up. Zero. But then Northwest fired me, that's when I went to Manalapan. It was two years of boredom and humiliation. It was selfish of me. I'm aware of that. One night, at a big charity ball, Priscilla referred to me as her *boy toy*, and everyone roared with laughter. That was the last straw. The next morning, when she went to her masseuse, I packed my things and left. I got a cab to Thrifty car rental, chose the fanciest, fastest car on the lot, and just started driving. Treasure Beach was the only place I knew. I was furious and desperate. What was I going to do? Call my old man? It had been decades. I had no place to go home to. So, I hatched a plan to find a rich widow. You'd think my experience with Priscilla would have been enough, but no, I was looking for an easy way out. In Palm Beach, I stopped and bought some papers and then drove to Treasure. I was at the Sands Motel, and I admit it, Ginger. Yes, I studied the obituaries. I found three names, and Theodore Johnson was one. But because I knew Treasure Beach and was in Treasure Beach, I decided to try for Mrs. Johnson."

Kevin was reliving his nightmare, and she was reliving hers.

"But how did you find me?"

"Simple. I got the address and phone number. I called the real estate office at 3-Oaks, said I was in the market for a place, and found out about the open house. They left my name at the gate."

"You walked right up to me."

"I told one of the servers I was meeting Mrs. Johnson. She looked around. You were in the living room, sitting on the sofa. That was it. But I made sure to have had a couple of drinks before I arrived. You know the rest."

Bitterly, Ginger reproached herself for thinking that a dashing younger man might fall for her. She *was* an old fool, just as the gossipers had said.

"I know you think I'm hopeless and immoral. And I am, I mean, I was. I planned it and executed it. I have to live with that forever. I'm sorry, Ginger. I don't know how to atone for my actions. I hope I can somehow. But you had to know the full story."

They didn't say anything. Finally, Ginger spoke.

"You were looking for the easy way. But I was too. Because of you, I didn't have to face my feelings about Ted. And, obviously, you were a much younger man —"

"I have to ask. Did you ever think of him? I mean, of Frank. My biological father?"

It was a fair question, but she blushed. Then, she answered quietly and deliberately.

"Did I think of him? No. I didn't. But on some level, I knew something. It came out in dreams. I had nightmares. Now I guess it was a warning. It came out in the figures on the canvas. I didn't think of him, but I was uneasy. Then I felt so comfortable with you, like I knew you."

"When you were gone, I missed you in a way I couldn't account for. I mean when you were in Palm Beach and then New York. And that night, when I came in and you told me it was over, told me to go, it broke me —"

"We both felt things, sensed something but we weren't aware of why —"

"That's it. I mean, I can't compare my connection with you with my connection with anybody else. Ever. Now, obviously, I understand."

She was so touched. He had loved her, but not like Priscilla or the others.

"I just hope you can forgive me," he said.

Kevin was the one with courage.

"I thought because Ted had been unwell for so long that my mourning was over, but in fact it was extremely difficult coming back to my house alone. So, when I met you at the Warrens, and felt comfortable with you, I made a major misjudgment. So, I want to apologize to you. I am just so glad that you are part of my life. And . . . I hope to be a part of yours."

"You are a part of my life. But I wish — "

Sobs broke up his words. "Tell me, Kevin, how can I help?"

"Why can't I be a son you can be proud of — ?! I want you to be proud of me. I wish I was better — "

She took his hands, and he gripped hers. For the first time they looked at one another deeply.

"You are better, Kevin, because you're real. I want you to know that, even though you were my secret, I never forgot about you. I dreamed of you; I tried to conjure an image of you. Your father made his choice, and I had to accept that and let him go. But I never gave up the hope, or the prayer that I would find you and see you again."

Now sobs came out of her. And awkwardly, with the tabletop between them, they held each other with their arms, their heads leaning forward, and tears falling onto their empty plates.

"I hope you can forgive me!"

"For what?"

"For giving you away . . ."

"It's okay, Ginger, it's okay," he said and instinctively, he gently patted her on the back. The comfort she took from this was immeasurable.

The beach was darkening. Ginger wiped her eyes.

"Look at us? How 'bout I get some Kleenex?"

She laughed.

"That would be good."

Kevin stood and, limping slightly, he went into the apartment. Ginger looked out over the water. The sea was free of birds now and the beach had emptied. Ginger said a prayer of thanks, for her whole life. 50 years of anguish had vanished with that kindness from her son.

It was time to make the drive back.

They were both standing, wiping their eyes.

"See you tomorrow? What time?"

"I've asked everyone for 12:00. Drinks; in my case fresh coconut juice, my new health obsession; start grilling at around 1:30, so come whenever you want. Let me take you down."

"No need. I'll see you tomorrow at noon."

They shared a brief embrace, and he opened the door for her. Ginger rode the elevator alone. In her car, she put the top back down and drove home to 3-Oaks. She felt exhilarated, exhausted. It had been a day of difficult emotions, and it was a day she'd cherish forever. A day she had always dreamed of. A day with her son. She now had two things more precious to her than anything else in her life. Ginger had her son *and* his forgiveness for what she had done.

CHAPTER 53

W HEN GINGER OPENED her eyes the following morning, after a dreamless sleep, she lay in bed for a long time. She felt wonderfully alive and full of energy, elated by all the possibilities. She wanted to rush to her studio and finish paintings; she wanted to call Dottie and thank her for insisting she be fearless and honest. She wanted to phone Diane and tell her that Kevin seemed restored to his best self. She wanted to call Robert the stablemaster and ask him saddle up Star for a morning gallop. These impulses on the first day of the rest of her life presented themselves to her. She lay in bed in a sort of euphoria watching light flit and dance on her egg-shell blue ceiling. All these impulses were bound together by a single idea: gratitude. Ginger said a prayer out loud.

"Thank you. Thank you Ted, for the rest of my life."

Ted had supplied the frame, this freedom, but Ginger's life was now her own canvas on which to create. She knew exactly what to do next. She picked up the phone by her bed and called Margale.

"Good morning, Mrs. Johnson."

"Good morning, Margale, I'll be down at ten."

"Your breakfast will be waiting for you."

"I leave for Kevin's barbeque at 11-ish."

"Everything will be ready to go."

Ginger indulged herself in a special bath. She added her lemon verbena oil and soaked for a long time. After, she pampered herself with her finest lotions and her most precious powders. In her dressing room she looked for clothes suitable not for a date, but for her new role as a mother. She was delighted when she found in a drawer something that she had bought years ago at Bergdorf's but had never worn. It was a silk tunic of vibrant colors in an abstract pattern and still wrapped in its tissue. It was perfect. She chose lilac trousers to match and a flat sandal. She sat at her table and did her makeup and put her hair up in a French twist. She was ready for the day and ready to speak to Margale.

Ginger ate breakfast on the terrace. When Margale finished her work in the kitchen preparing food for the barbeque, she came outside.

"Good morning, Mrs. J. The buns are in the small thermal bag by themselves since they're hot, and the potato salad is in the other."

"Margale, there's something I need to talk to you about."

Margale shook her head back and forth.

"Now, if it's the secret of my cobbler or any of my baked goods, you know no one gets the recipes." This was one of Margale's favorite rants, Ginger laughed and let her go on uninterrupted. "Not while I'm alive. I have told you, many times, I will leave these recipes in my will. I've made those arrangements, but until then —"

"It isn't about your recipes. There's something I've kept from you. Something serious."

Margale eyed her. "Something about Mr. McCoy?"

"Yes."

"Oh, I know about that."

"What do you know?"

"I know that young man is family."

Ginger was taken aback.

"How do you know that?"

"I figured he was some blood relation. A cousin or a son. Something. I knew it from the eyes. His eyes are a perfect match to yours. I suspected, then put it to the test."

"What do mean test?"

"Remember that day you were away? I made toast from Mr. J's banana bread loaves left in the freezer. From my mother's recipe."

"You still have those in the freezer?"

"Uh-huh, and I gave some to Mr. McCoy. Guess what?

"What?"

"Mr. McCoy didn't touch the banana bread. Only thing that man ever left on a plate that I saw. That told me everything."

"Kevin is allergic to bananas?"

"Yes, he is. Just like you are. And that's no coincidence. That be genetics!"

"Margale, Kevin is my son."

"No news to me. Like I said, I knew he was family. That night when I heard you two going at it, I was dancing in my room. When he drove off, I was on my knees, thanking the Lord. I expect now that you know your true relation, he'll be around again and in the right way."

"Yes," Ginger, marveling at Margale, brushed aside a tear.

"I packed those homemade sweet pickles, too. You just tell him Margale sent them. You hurry on, Mrs. J. If you go now those buns will still be warm when you get to Cocoa."

CHAPTER 54

ON OCEAN DRIVE, Ginger drove along quickly and the freeway was a breeze. But the business section of Cocoa Beach was busy, and traffic slowed. This time, she felt no dread, only a lightness and happiness. She pulled into the parking area. There were more cars in the lot. Ginger never thought to ask Kevin who was coming, probably some of his new friends from AA.

She rang the buzzer, and was immediately buzzed in. Upstairs, she pressed the doorbell, and a woman opened the door.

"You must be Ginger. I'm Jenny Anderson, a friend of Kevin's. I live upstairs. Kevin has told me all about you. Here, let me take those bags, I'll put them in the kitchen. I'm just finishing the deviled eggs. Everyone's on the porch. Go right on out. That's a beautiful tunic. It looks like a painting. Oh, and I see the resemblance. You two have the same blue eyes."

"Thank you," Ginger said and walked towards the terrace. The glass sliders were open. Kevin was at one end of the porch with a woman and two men. Two little girls sat at the table playing Scrabble. They hardly looked up from the board.

"There you are," Kevin called to her. "Ginger, let me introduce you to everyone." He gestured towards the man and woman.

"Ginger, I want you to meet my brother John, and my sister-in-law, Liz. This is Ginger, my mother."

"So happy to meet you," Liz said, giving her a hug. "Kevin has done nothing but talk about you." Liz had the kindest eyes Ginger had ever seen.

"So great to meet you, Ginger," John said, and he surprised her by embracing her warmly, as if, at long last, they were meeting. When he released her, Kevin was speaking. She turned next to the older man.

"Ginger, I'd like you to meet Timothy McCoy. My dad."

She loved him at first sight. Timothy offered his hand and she took it.

"Welcome to our family, Ginger," he said with a smile.

END

ACKNOWLEDGEMENTS:

I WOULD LIKE to thank my daughter, Aubrey Thorne Carey, a brilliant writer in her own right, astrologist, and life coach, for listening and encouraging me. In Los Angeles, years ago, Aubrey encouraged me to take a writing course which unlocked my creativity.

Also, I'd like to thank Dr. David Hellman for his support. He, along with Dr. Julie, made it possible for me to finish the book.

My thanks to Elizabeth and Chad at the Vero Beach Book Center. They guaranteed my book its own display in their lovely bookstore, giving me the necessary incentive to complete the manuscript.

I wish to thank my granddaughter Avery Carey, for her insightful comments; Virginia Best, artist and editor of the Pansy Picture books series for listening and reading through passages, her brilliant mind is always helpful; my good friend, Barbara Baldwin, her interest motivated me to keep going. Most of all, I'd like to thank Devon O'Brien, my writing coach, for her great editorial ideas and for inspiring me to become a novelist.

Previously Published Books by Cynthia Bardes

Children's Picture Books by Cynthia Bardes
The Pansy the Poodle Mystery Series:

> *Pansy at the Palace*
> *Pansy in Paris*
> *Pansy in Venice*
> *Pansy in New York*
> *Pansy in Rome*
> *Pansy in London*
> *Pansy in Africa*
> *Pansy in Alaska*

Children's Early Chapter Book by Cynthia Bardes

> *Pansy's Rainbow*

For more information visit:
www.pansythepoodle.com
nbnbooks.com